IN A LIFETIME

WENDY SMITH

Edited by
LAUREN CLARKE

Cover Design by
BOOKISH GRAPHICS

BOOK ONE OF THE LIFETIME SERIES

❀ Created with Vellum

ACKNOWLEDGMENTS

A huge thank you to my usual suspects. Lauren, for editing my words and making them readable. Sarah for her beautiful cover. And Christine for spreading the word. You ladies rock!

Thank you too to everyone who has posted, tweeted and shared a teaser or a post. I am so grateful for all your support.

When I was writing In a Lifetime, I am Giant released a song called 'Kiss from a Ghost' which I played about a million times. I don't know the origin of the lyrics, but I really felt them. They seemed in sync with Matt seeing Ella first, but in trying to do the right thing for someone else, losing her to Sam.

I wanted to use a couple of lines from the song for the book and asked I Am Giant for permission to quote them. All credit and huge thanks for use of those lyrics to I Am Giant. These guys were gracious enough to let me quote them, and that really helped my vision take shape.

Check them out. iamgiant.com

This book is set in New Zealand and is written in New Zealand English.

PART I

You stopped the world

CHAPTER 1

MATT

It was one of *those* nights. A house full of people at various stages of intoxication. Some had coupled up, some chatted up others, some danced, and some sang karaoke.

Speaking of which, for the love of all things holy, didn't anyone know all the words to *The Final Countdown*?

My best friend, Sam, and I, had a party at the end of every semester, and every semester it ended up more work than the time before as the crowd grew. Outwardly, this was something cool and exciting we did to let off steam. Inwardly, I couldn't wait to see the back of the noise.

However, this was our last student party, so for one final time I decided to grin and bear it. I had to admit that despite knowing what the clean up would be like in the morning, this was fun.

Even if it was my turn to stay sober.

Our first party had ended in near disaster, with a drunken student curling up in our garden, despite the cold weather, and falling asleep. When she ended up in hospital, Sam and I had decided that we'd take turns staying sober, watching over our guests to make sure that nothing bad happened to anyone.

It sucked to be the sober one, but on the upside, no one had hurt his or herself since.

People packed our living room. Most I knew to various degrees, and some I didn't. There were always people who tagged along.

Sam sat on the couch, his arm around some lovely little brunette, his tongue so far down her throat he must've been searching for something. It never took Sam long to find someone to make out with. Me? I've always taken my time.

And then I saw her, sitting in the corner, all alone. Her dark hair hung in big curls, framing her heart-shaped face. She had impossibly blue eyes with long eyelashes, and rosebud lips stained a brilliant shade of red, the colour standing out against her alabaster skin. She looked like a porcelain doll.

In her hands she cradled a bottle of pre-mixed vodka and lemonade, sipping it through a straw she held between her thumb and index finger, her nails painted to match her lipstick.

I don't know why I hadn't noticed her earlier. In a room full of T-shirt-and-jeans-wearing students, she wore a dress that would have been at home in the 50s, a little tight with the curve of her breasts pushed up over her neckline.

I died and went to heaven.

Taking a deep breath, I took a step toward her. To my right, on the edge of my peripheral vision, I caught a glimpse of another girl, her hand over her mouth as if she was about to hurl.

Damn it. As the responsible, sober one, I'd have to take care of this before getting to anything else I wanted.

From the table to my left, I grabbed a bucket. It had been full of ice for beer bottles to sit in, but now the beer was gone, and the ice was a giant slushy.

Dumping the contents into a nearly empty potato chip bowl, I thrust the bucket in front of the girl.

Not on my carpet, you don't.

Either I could put this drunken girl to bed in one of our rooms, which could prove inconvenient if something happened with my dream woman, or, I could drive drunken girl home and risk never seeing dream woman again. That was probably the right thing to do, no matter what my penis tried to tell me.

"Honey, where do you live?" I asked, casting my eye across the room and trying to remember every detail of mystery girl's appearance. Hopefully, if I could get this woman home quickly, I'd be back in time to talk to the girl in the corner.

"Waiuku." She groaned.

Shit. That was at least three-quarters of an hour drive each way. Too expensive to put her in a taxi. And I would guarantee she had no money.

Her lips were downturned, and any life that might have been there had disappeared from her eyes. She looked dull, over it.

"Can you take me?" She pleaded.

I didn't have a choice. That was our party code—take care of anyone too far gone. I'd be gone for at least an hour and a half.

"Grab your things; we'll get out of here. Sooner I get you home, sooner I can be back." Hopefully no one else would need taking home. I swept the room, checking for any others who might be in trouble.

Rolling my eyes, I approached the back of the sofa, tapping Sam on the shoulder. He continued to devour the girl he was kissing, ignoring me as I sighed.

"Sam." I shoved his shoulder—hard.

He broke away from the girl, who gave him a lazy smile, and looked back over his shoulder at me, frowning. "What?"

"I've got to take someone home. We've got a sick one."

"Whatever," he said, turning away.

"The girl in the corner. Make sure she doesn't leave."

He grunted agreement, glancing up and then returning to his lip-lock with the girl who didn't even look at me.

One last glance at the woman who had caught my eye, and I left.

She'd better still be there when I got back.

~

"Pull over, pull over."

I slapped the steering wheel. "Again?"

The girl's face was white as marble, and her hand was on the door handle, despite the bucket she cradled.

"Fine." I flicked on the indicator and pulled over to the side of the road. She flung the door open, tripping as she fell out of the car, stumbling away from the vehicle as she vomited. The night air was chilly, and the temperature plummeted in the car, making me shiver.

"Best night out ever," I mumbled, my mind wandering to the girl back at home.

"It's not my fault. You're driving so fast, the streetlights going past make me feel sick." She pouted as she crawled back into the car, buckling up her seatbelt and grabbing hold of the bucket again.

"I'm doing the speed limit. We're on the motorway. If I get caught pulling over like this, I'll be in the crap." I indicated and pulled out. Thankfully there weren't many on the road at this time of night.

I so want to be home.

The GPS read out instructions as we drove, and we weaved through the rural roads once we left the motorway. I was beginning to think we were never going to get there when the machine told me in stilted English that we'd arrived at our destination.

The girl, whose name I still didn't know, smiled. Her face stayed drained of colour, and I got the feeling that she'd be seeing a lot of the toilet bowl tonight.

"Do you want to come in?" she asked. She was cute. Any other time I might have considered it, but she'd just spent the last hour vomiting every fifteen minutes.

Are you insane?

"No, I should get going. I need to make sure no one else needs help."

"Oh." She pouted.

I rolled my eyes. "Go on inside. I hope you feel better in the morning."

She slowly nodded, holding the bucket out for me to take.

I held up my hand, shaking my head. "No. You keep it."

"Thanks." She opened the door, the cold night air rushing in and reversing the effects of the heater again. At least it'd be a warm, uninterrupted ride home.

"No problem. Take care."

As I flicked the indicator and pulled out and into the street, I pondered the girl at home. Would she still be there? Had I missed my chance? Even if she was gone, maybe I could track her down. But then again, I didn't know who a lot of the people were at the party.

What a waste of a night.

The drive home was at least shorter than the drive there, with no stopping along the way. The motorway was quiet, and cars were few and far between.

I pressed buttons on the radio, trying to find something to keep me company. Anything to fill the lonely drive back.

I'm such an idiot.

I should have splashed out for a taxi for the drunken guest, even if it meant not eating for the next week. It'd be after two when I got home, and most people would be long gone. All I could do was hope that the one person I wanted to be there had stayed.

The closer I drew to the city, the more comfort I drew from my surroundings. Mount Eden had been home for the past few years while Sam and I had attended the nearby university. We'd been lucky that we'd found a rundown old villa to live in for lower than market rates. While property prices and rents went up around us, our landlord was happy he'd found responsible long-term tenants. Well, responsible most of the time.

The house was quiet, deserted when I got home. As I pulled into the driveway, I grimaced at the thought of the mess to clean up. No doubt Sam would be lazing in bed tomorrow, leaving me to tidy. That was what I would have done to him, if our roles were reversed.

I slid my key in the lock, turning the old brass door handle and pushing. The wooden door creaked as it opened, and I took a step inside.

I walked straight into the living room. In the centre of the floor were two people going at it like bunnies. At least I wouldn't have trouble tracking mystery girl down.

Naked, she was even more beautiful, her full breasts peaking into rosy nipples, her curvy hips grinding as she rode my best friend. Her long dark hair spilled down her back in curls, curls that Sam tugged at, making her moan.

I couldn't move, transfixed by the sight, the excitement at seeing her naked tempered with the knowledge that Sam was inside her.

"Close the door, man." Sam grinned up at me.

The woman's eyes flickered open, and she gasped, crossing her arms to cover her breasts as I turned my head. I kicked the door closed behind me and began the uncomfortable walk past them to my bedroom.

"Sorry," I said, as the light faded behind me.

When I closed my eyes, I could still see her—that creamy skin, her mouth formed into a perfect red *O* as she threw all her concentration into screwing my best friend.

I'd never wanted anything so badly in all my life.

She was his.

CHAPTER 2

SAM

Sam closed the door.

Now for the clean up—always the fun part of these parties. He wasn't even sure why they did this anymore—it was tradition for him and Matt to have these gatherings. It wasn't as much fun as it had been at the start.

These days they got more people they didn't know, and it had become less of a celebration between friends and classmates, and more of a random gathering that had no real meaning.

Not to mention that as they grew older, the women seemed so much younger than they'd been when the two of them had started. They weren't really; that was just the way Sam processed the giggling, flirting nature that he'd been dealing with all night. Cute, but not what Sam was looking for. Although, not even Sam knew what that was.

He'd spent half the evening on the couch making out with a girl who had then gone for another drink and hadn't come back. What a waste of time that was, putting all the effort in and not even getting laid.

He sighed as he turned back to look at the now deserted room, meeting the eye of a girl he hadn't spotted earlier. She sat in the corner, sucking her bottled drink through a straw, her bright red lips forming a perfect circle as she raised an eyebrow at him. One perfectly shaped eyebrow that sent a burning through his veins as their gazes locked.

"Hey," he said. "Sorry. I thought everyone was gone."

She slid the straw out from between those lips so slowly; he dropped his hand self-consciously to swing over his lap. Those red lips parted, and she ran her tongue across them. "I'm not."

"I can see that." Sam moved closer, his curiosity piqued by her flirting.

She tilted her head and smiled. "I'm Ella."

"Sam."

"I know."

Now she stood, walking toward him, a sway in her hips that made the ache in his groin even worse. She wore a black vintage swing dress, tight around her waist, boosting her breasts.

Ella stood in front of him, running a manicured fingernail, the same colour as her lipstick, down his chest.

"And how do you know me?" Sam asked.

"I've been in your mathematics class all year."

He grinned, shaking his head. "I don't think so; I'd remember you."

"I usually sit right at the back. I've seen you."

She was close now; he could smell her perfume, like the scent of honey. Thoughts of summer and sunshine ran through his head, and the urge to grab her, rub his face in her hair, breathe her in, was overwhelming.

Her skirt brushed against his hand, and he flattened his palm, trying desperately to hide his growing hardness.

His feet glued to the spot, he raised his eyes to meet hers. He was sure his heart beat faster than it had ever done before. This girl was gorgeous.

From the way her breasts heaved, she was feeling the same way he was.

Perhaps the night wasn't about to end so badly after all.

~

ELLA

ELLA OPENED HER EYES, millimetre by millimetre. Blinded by the bright light blaring through the windows, she slammed them shut again, sighing at the effort.

Warm arms wrapped around her, and she rolled over to check out the man with whom she'd spent the night.

The blue eyes she remembered were closed. She'd raked her fingers through the closely cropped brown hair. He was as good looking as she'd thought with light stubble on his strong chin. The urge to run her tongue over it was overwhelming.

Instead, she ran her hand across his smooth chest.

She'd made her move as soon as everyone else had left, skulking in the corner until the opportunity arose. She sat in the same maths lectures as he did without him noticing her. When she'd stood in front of him, squeezed into that dress that made her breasts pop, he'd paid attention.

In a tangle of lips and limbs, they'd ended up on the living room floor. She'd pinned him to the ground, astride his hips, and rocked his world. At least, that was how it seemed. They'd ended up in his bed, curled around each other and going for seconds. If she remembered correctly, even thirds.

The dull ache between her legs reminded her of the thirds. No one had ever done that with her before, got so carried away that they both wanted to go all night. It had been the small hours of the morning when the two of them had finally collapsed, exhausted, ready to sleep.

Sam stirred beside her, lifting his hand to cover hers on his chest, squeezing her fingers gently as he turned his head toward her. Those gorgeous blue eyes of his, full of sleep and mischief made her shiver, the ache turning from a sore pain to a longing one. Right here and now, Ella couldn't get enough of this man who seemed to like her as much.

"Hey," he whispered.

"Good morning," she said, sucking in her bottom lip, her cheeks blazing hot.

"That it is." He grinned, leaning over to kiss her, his lips warm and soft with a hint of beer.

She smiled as he broke contact, her heart thumping hard at the touch of his gentle hands.

"Do you want breakfast?" His eyes bore into hers with so much intensity she dropped her gaze.

"Are you offering to make it?"

He nodded. "I'd be happy to. As long as you're okay with toast and coffee; that's about as much as I can cook."

"I think I can cope with that." She surrendered to another kiss, this time one long and lingering as Sam pulled her closer.

"Round four?" he whispered.

Ella laughed. "I think I can cope with that."

~

SAM

MATT SAT at the kitchen table, eyeing Sam as he crossed the room.

"Good night?" He took another bite of toast, his expression devoid of any real interest in the answer.

"Amazing. Seem to remember you being witness to some of it." It was vague, but the memory of Matt opening the door as Ella rocked on Sam's groin was vivid. The night-time breeze had been cool, causing Sam to shiver and Ella to cover those luscious breasts of hers.

"Yeah. Sorry about that." Matt seemed quiet, subdued, and not his usual happy self.

"What's up your butt? Didn't find a girl to spend the night, I noticed."

Matt rolled his eyes. "I spent half the night driving to Waiuku and back for some girl who drank too much. She asked me if I wanted to stay, but she'd spent the trip puking on the side of the road, so I can't say I was that interested."

Sam laughed. "Sorry, man. It should have been a better night for you. At least one of us got laid. Multiple times, too." He grinned at a disinterested Matt. The other man buried his nose in his coffee, and Sam turned toward the counter. Steam rose from the kettle. At least he wouldn't have to wait to make coffee. After his marathon sex session with Ella, coffee was top of the list.

Shit.

He hadn't asked Ella how she took her coffee. Picking up two slices of bread, he dropped them in the toaster. Black. He'd make black coffee with no sugar, and she could do what she wanted with it. Like she'd done what she wanted with him. His lips twisted into a smile at the thought of her—those beautiful breasts, the curvy hips, the sweet smell of her skin. He'd never been with anyone like her.

And she'd kept up. He'd partied with girls all night only for them to fall asleep after having sex. Ella wanted more, wanted him. They'd both been exhausted when they'd fallen asleep, and yet when they woke, he still couldn't get enough.

"Is that coffee ready?" Her soft voice came from behind him, and he turned to see her, back in that dress he'd wanted to tear off her last night. She'd been made up immaculately; now her brown hair fell naturally in soft curls around her shoulders. She'd transformed from a vamp to the kind of girl you want to take home to Mum and Dad, sweet and sexy.

"Sure is. Take a seat, and I'll bring it all to the table. Oh. Ella, this is Matt. Matt, this is Ella."

Matt grunted, opening his laptop, blocking them both out. He must have still been pissed not to score while Sam had the delectable Ella. She sat opposite Matt, flicking glances between him and Sam, smiling nervously.

She was perfect.

All he knew was that he didn't want her to leave.

CHAPTER 3

MATT

A week later, we were parked in front of the television, getting ready to watch a game of rugby. Ella had stayed overnight every night since the party. Sam and I had the whole day with only the two of us. It'd be good to have a boys' night.

Sam grinned, stretching his legs out and reaching for the popcorn bowl. He picked up the remote control, flicking through the channels until he found the rugby game he was after and sighed contentedly.

"I'm gonna marry that girl," he said.

I rolled my eyes. I'd heard that before, but something told me this time it was different. "Dude, it's been a week."

"I'm serious. Ella is the most amazing woman I've ever met. She's beautiful and intelligent, and she screws like no one's business. I mean it; she's insatiable."

Yeah, I want to hear that.

"We can find one for you next. Someone with big tits who likes to ride the Matty train."

I buried my face in my hands. No matter how close we were, I could never bring myself to be that crude. At least, not out loud.

"So you *have* to talk like that?" My hands muffled the words, and Sam laughed loudly.

"Sorry, man. I am so happy that this girl not only adores me, she wants to spend every available second hanging off my cock. How perfect is that?"

It'd be even more perfect if you'd shut the hell up.

"I know we're friends, but I don't need to know about your sex life. Or anything else to do with your cock." I reached into the popcorn bowl, but the conversation had put me off touching anything Sam had, and I dropped my hand to my side, focusing on the game instead.

Let's watch this in peace and have a quiet evening.

No sooner had the game kicked off than there was a tap at the door.

"That'll be Ella. I told her to come around if she wanted to."

I groaned as Sam rose to answer the knock, the sound hidden by the crowd roaring onscreen. Somewhere deep inside, I had hoped that this would fizzle out, that Sam would forget about Ella and move onto the next thing.

No such luck.

She sat in the centre of the couch beside me, Sam sitting beside her. She smelled like honey, and I placed my hand on my lap in case *someone* had ideas of misbehaving.

"Hey, Matt," she said, as sweet as her aroma.

"Ella." I knew my tone was short, clipped. Anything more and I would have said something I regretted. *I love you, Ella.* Urgh, what am I thinking?

"You're right on time, babe. The game started a minute ago. Want some popcorn?" Sam picked up the bowl, offering it to her, and she reached into the white Tupperware container with those perfectly manicured red nails.

"Thank you for inviting me," she said, snuggling up to Sam, nibbling at the popcorn while Sam shoved entire handfuls in his mouth.

"You never need an invitation," he murmured, nuzzling her cheek before returning to the food.

She met my eyes with a frown. "I didn't want to interrupt your TV viewing."

I turned back to the television, blanking her.

"Don't worry about that. You're welcome here anytime. Isn't she, Matt?"

"Sure." My gaze fell back on Ella. She pleaded with her eyes, and it took everything in my power not to smile and tell her everything was alright. Because it wasn't. I wanted my best friend's girl. And nothing was making that go away.

I forced a smile and went back to watching the screen.

Don't look at her. Don't look at her.

Out of the corner of my eye, I saw her bury her face in Sam's neck. Concentrating on the television was difficult with the smell of her honey perfume so near. All I wanted to do was to close my eyes and breathe in that scent.

Something hit my leg. A stiletto had fallen by my feet, and I cocked an eyebrow, tilting my head slightly toward Ella to see what on earth she was doing without making it obvious.

I needn't have bothered. Sam had her pinned to the back of the couch, his tongue pretty far down her throat from the looks of things. Her legs were tucked up under her, and she'd kicked off her shoes as she curled up with him. Neither of them noticed me looking.

It was creepy. I didn't want to share the couch with them while they were making out, but this was the best vantage point for the television. I could excuse myself and head off to my room, but this was my house, too. Besides, the television in the lounge was bigger than the one in my room.

My decision was made easier about five seconds later, when Sam stood, pulling Ella to her feet. She giggled as he led her toward his bedroom, disappearing without a backward glance. I had the television, the game, the popcorn, and myself to spend the evening with. *So much for boys' night.*

I lay down on the couch, resting my head on one arm, extending my legs. I picked up the popcorn and leaned over to put it on the table before lying back down. At least I could watch the TV in peace.

As the game went on, my eyes grew heavy, and I woke being

nudged to move. Ella stood over me, smiling as I pulled myself into a seated position, and sat beside me.

I licked my lips, unsure of how long I'd been asleep.

Last thing I remember ... oh, forget it.

"You two are as bad as one another." Dimples appeared at the corners of her mouth as she grinned.

I shook my head, yawning, still trying to wake up. "What?"

"Sam fell asleep on me. I mean, not literally *on* me, but we were cuddled up and next minute, he started snoring. I came out here to get away from the noise to find you fast asleep."

"Was I snoring?" I scratched my head, yawning again.

"No. Maybe I should have stayed out here with you." She laughed. "I'm going to get a drink and watch the rest of the game. Do you want one, too?"

"Sounds good. The popcorn's cold, but if you want it, go for it."

As she walked away, I couldn't take my eyes off her. The way those jeans fitted around her hips ...

Stop it.

She returned with two beers, holding one out for me. "I'm sorry if I interrupted your boys' night. Sam didn't say anything until we were in there."

"He's hopeless sometimes." I picked up my key ring from the coffee table, ripping the beer cap off with my bottle opener and holding it up to do the same for her.

Ella shrugged. "We have to get used to one another."

I leaned back. "How well do you think this is going to go?"

Her eyebrows dipped in confusion. "What do you mean?"

"Sam and Ella." I paused as her brows crept back up. "Salmonella. You two are poison. Says a lot."

She tilted her head, twisting her mouth, and I grinned at her obvious struggle to come up with something smart to say. "Oh ha ha."

I shook my head. "Is that the best retort you can come up with?"

Ella shrugged. "Maybe it's not worth a response."

"Oh, come on. That was pretty good."

"Maybe, by your standards." Now she grinned, and my heart flipped as those ruby red lips raised at the corners for me.

"Ouch." I held my hand over my heart.

Ella rolled her eyes.

"I've been holding that one in all week." I held up my beer to clink with hers, and she shook her head as the bottles gently collided.

"It was better in." She leaned back, focusing on the television. I turned my head to watch the rugby.

We sat quietly, with only the sound of the television in the background, and I didn't care.

Having her there was nice. *Too nice.*

CHAPTER 4

MATT

By the end of the following week, Ella was all but moved in with us. And when I say 'us', I mean she took over the house. The stockings she wore every day under the vintage dresses she favoured hung on the towel rail in the bathroom. I'd open the hot water cupboard to find her underwear staring back at me.

On the upside, the house was spotless, and she cooked dinner nearly every night for all of us. There wasn't much left of the year, and we'd soon be graduated and headed into the job market.

I struggled with my attraction to her. It was at least as strong as it had been that first night I saw her, made worse by her constant presence. Seeing her happy and carefree, the smallest of dimples appearing in her cheeks when she grinned, filled me with joy. Seeing her entangled with Sam on the couch did not.

In response to that, I tried my best to pay no attention to her, or to them. I went into protection mode. If I ignored what went on around me, it didn't exist. It wasn't always so easy.

I'd always been active, and running had always helped me take my mind off the tough stuff. When I was younger, it had helped when Mum and Dad went through a rough patch. I'd run, and keep running, with no thought of turning back and going home. Dad usually came looking for me. There was only one road out of the coastal town I lived in, and he was guaranteed to find me somewhere along the way.

Now I did the same thing, pounding the pavement to drive distraction from my mind. I stopped to stretch along the way, giving girls running in the opposite direction a flirty smile. Anything to avoid being home with *them*.

I ran into the house and straight into the bathroom. Opening the cupboard to get a towel, I spotted Ella's bra hanging over the shelf above it. Sighing, I pulled out the towel, flicking the shower on and stripping off, throwing my clothes in the washing basket in the corner.

The hot water felt good on my tired muscles. Tomorrow was crunches at the gym. Since any job I might get out of my computer science degree was likely to be deskbound, now was the time to make a routine to keep fit.

I closed my eyes, standing with my head under the water, washing away the sweat and soothing my soul. For the millionth time, I wished we had a bathtub.

I'd better not use all of the water.

Grabbing the bath gel, I lathered up and washed myself off. Exercising made me feel alive, invigorated. Although, after all that, I'd end up veging out on the couch in front of the television or the computer. Maybe even have a nap.

After washing my hair and a final rinse of my body, I turned the water off, stepping out of the shower.

The door flew open, and I grinned at the sight of Ella, her jaw dropping as she fixed eyes on me. She'd been holed up in Sam's room, and with her earbuds in, clearly hadn't heard the shower running.

"I ... I'm sorry. I didn't know anyone was in here."

She pulled the plugs from her ears as she dropped her gaze, her cheeks blazing red. I tilted my head, watching her. Despite her best intentions, her line of sight was right where it really shouldn't have been.

Thank god I wasn't jerking off.

"I'm nearly finished. I have to get dressed." Her eyes shot up to my face. Oh, this was funny, and cute as she struggled to stop looking.

"Thanks. Um. I mean, okay." She turned on her heel, closing the door behind her. I laughed, shaking my head as I grabbed the towel, drying myself off and wrapping it around my waist.

I opened the bathroom door. Ella sat on the couch, her face buried in her hands. Even with her face hidden, I could see the blush on her skin.

"Ella. We good?"

Her head jerked up, her embarrassment still plain to see. She nodded as Sam walked out from the kitchen. He eyed me suspiciously as I stood there, clad only in a towel, gazes locked with his girlfriend.

"What's going on here?" he asked, sitting on the couch beside Ella. He flung his arm around her shoulder protectively, cocking one eyebrow at me.

"Ella didn't look too happy. I wanted to make sure she was okay," I said. No point embarrassing her further if she didn't want to tell him.

"Can you do that with a few more clothes on? I doubt my girl wants to see you half naked." He laughed, kissing the top of her head as she snuggled in against him.

"Sure." I headed off toward the bedroom to get some clean clothes on, turning as I got to the door. Sam was already engrossed in the television, but Ella had turned her head, tracking my movements, a small smile on her face.

I winked at her, grinning at the blush returning, and pushed open the door, closing it quietly behind me. Maybe she'd gotten a fright at catching me like that, but she wasn't too prudish to keep looking.

I liked that far too much.

My clean shirt and jeans were on the end of the bed where I left them, and I pulled them on over underwear before running my fingers through my hair. Sam was bound to be eating crap and drinking beer. It was a waste of a workout if I joined him, but at the same time, I kinda liked the idea of watching Ella squirm. Not because I wanted to torment her, but the thought of her liking what she saw took up so much space in my mind right now. Might as well go out and live the fantasy.

They were still cuddled up on the couch when I came back out, and I flopped on a nearby chair, crossing my feet as I sat back.

"What's on?" I asked.

"League. Warriors are playing the Panthers. It's just started."

I nodded. It wasn't my favourite sport, but it was entertaining to watch.

Ella stood, walking to the kitchen. I watched as she moved, appreciating the sway in her hips. She returned with three beers and a smile on her lips as she handed me one. Her eyes told me it was a peace offering.

"Thanks, babe," Sam said as she returned to the couch, handing him the second bottle.

"You're welcome." She leaned her head on his shoulder.

"Don't I have the perfect girl, Matt?" Sam had that shit-eating grin on his face, and for a few seconds I wanted to tell him to eat shit. I didn't need the reminder that she was his.

"Someone's punching above their weight." I grinned at Sam, and he rolled his eyes in response. Not Ella. She gaped at me, clapping her hand across her mouth and running for the bedroom.

"Damn it." He growled, glaring at me.

"What? What did I say?"

"She thinks you mean her, numb nuts."

I stood, my heart pounding in my ears at my screw-up. "I'll go and talk to her."

"Yeah, you'd better. She's a good one, Matt. I want this to work."

I held up my palms. "I'm going to apologise now. You know that's not what I was saying."

"I know. Give me all the shit you want, but she's really sensitive. You have to make it clear it's me you're hassling and not her."

Nodding, I turned, heading for Sam's room. I tapped on the door, turned the handle and pushed.

Ella sat on the bed, her head in her hands, but not because of any embarrassment this time. She cried softly, and seemed completely oblivious to my presence.

"Ella." I took a step toward her, and she shook her head. "I'm sorry."

She dropped her hands, her eyes filled with tears, her lips downturned. "You don't like me ... do you?" Her voice was soft, pained, and she stabbed me in the chest with her tone.

"I like you fine."

"So why are you so mean to me? I didn't mean to walk in on you in the bathroom, and then you go and say something nasty."

I sighed, closing the distance to the bed and sitting to face her. "I know you didn't, and I'm not trying to be mean. I never meant to hurt you. I meant Sam was punching above his weight being with you."

Her nose twitched, and I had this sudden urge to plant a kiss on it. This was getting ridiculous. The more time I spent around her, the more I wanted her. Despite who her boyfriend was.

"Are you sure? I mean, you don't laugh and joke with me like you do with Sam. You go all quiet and moody. I adore Sam, Matt, and you're his *best* friend, so it's really important to me that we're friends, too."

I grasped her arms, steadying her as she shook. She seemed nervous, but determined for me to get the message. Her eyes were so blue and deep, I got lost in them for a moment before waking myself up. Her lips were so close, and more than ever I wanted to taste them, run my tongue along her lower lip and not only kiss her, but also possess her.

Instead, I swallowed.

"If I made you feel I don't like you, I apologise. Sam and I have known one another forever, and neither of us have had a long-term serious relationship yet. You being around is taking some getting used to."

She licked her lips in a slow, deliberate gesture, which on anyone else I would think was flirtatious, but I'd seen enough of Ella to know this was her being herself.

"Thank you, I appreciate it. I know you two are close, and the last thing I want is to come between you."

"I don't think you could ever do that, Ella."

For a moment we stayed there, locked in space and time, as if nothing would ever move us. My heart beat so fast and my head spun, but I couldn't take my eyes from hers.

She nodded, dropping her gaze. "Thank you."

"You already said that."

She peered back up, her eyebrows inching up as she took in my grin. "So now you're teasing me?"

I raised my eyebrows. "I'm good at that. I thought you'd realised that by now. I give Sam enough crap."

"I don't like being teased."

She pouted, and I lost all sense of myself. When Ella looked sad, it was as if the skies grew dark and rain began to fall. I never, ever wanted the rain to fall. Not for her.

In that moment, I knew I was in love.

CHAPTER 5

MATT

It became Sam, Ella and I. The three of us spent so much time together it was crazy. And even though I loved spending time with both of them, I struggled as I watched them fall in love with each other.

We all graduated, and went onto our first full-time jobs. I went to a software development company as an intern, Sam taught computing at a nearby high school, and Ella went to work as a business analyst. Life was good.

When it came to the way I felt about Ella, it wasn't fair to give myself false hope, remembering the girl in the tight dress sucking her drink through a straw. But I couldn't help it. No matter how close her and Sam got, some part of me hoped for the day that she'd turn around and see me in another light.

Not that I didn't date. Ella tried to take care of that.

First, she set me up with Carla, a perfectly lovely woman who was actually pretty sweet. We had absolutely nothing in common, except for knowing Ella. She hated everything I said I liked, and the only time we were in tune was over dinner when we selected the same meal.

One date.

Then there was Marissa. That got to two dates, but only because she felt ill during the first one and had to go home early. I figured she was ditching me, only for her to ask me out again. I didn't know why. Last I saw her, she'd been fleeing the restaurant having been horribly offended by me wanting to order steak. I didn't know she was a vegan.

"I'm not doing this anymore," I said to Ella over dinner at home. She'd cooked lasagne, and it was the most amazing thing I thought I'd ever eaten.

"Not doing what?"

"Dating your friends. I'm sorry, they are very lovely, but not for me."

She smiled half-heartedly. "I'm the one who's sorry. I was only trying to help."

"Matt's always been a slow mover. It takes him at least six dates to even kiss a girl," Sam said.

I picked up my fork and pretended to throw it at his face.

Ella's eyes were on me from under those long eyelashes. "Is that true?"

Sam roared with laughter while I shook my head. "No. Sam is full of shit. I will admit I don't tend to jump into bed on the first date; I like to treat a girl better than that."

Blush crept from Ella's neck up to her cheeks. I watched, intrigued as she licked her lips, glancing between us as if unsure if she should say anything else. Sam didn't notice, too wrapped up in his joking dig at me to pay attention to her, while I didn't miss a thing.

"Me? I move fast." He waggled his eyebrows at her, grinning as she laughed, her eyes now fixed completely on him. There was that look, the one of total and utter devotion. I was momentarily forgotten.

Ella leaned over, kissing him, and he sighed as they parted.

"Love this lady," he said, stroking her face.

"Do you want me to leave you alone?" I asked.

"You don't have to leave. Have some more dinner." Ella always made me welcome, even when I was clearly the third wheel.

"Thank you, Ella." I flashed the nicest smile I could at her, leaving Sam rolling his eyes.

"Do you two want to get a room?" he asked.

This was the usual banter between us. I felt almost like an equal in their relationship. Except I didn't get the love and affection.

"Any time. I'm sure Ella would love to spend some moments alone with me." I fluttered my eyelashes, Ella spraying the mouthful of juice she'd sipped all over the table.

"Great. Orange lasagne." Sam laughed.

That was the problem. I loved both of them far too much to try to screw with the thing they had.

"You might have someone to spend time with if you went out with girls more than once." Ella poked her tongue at me, and I returned the favour.

I shrugged. "I guess I won't know what I want until I find it." Our eyes met, and she smiled as if she understood. I guess she did, given the way her relationship with Sam had gone.

"Good for you," she said quietly.

Sam rolled his eyes. "Let's finish dinner, then we can have a beer in front of the television. What's on?"

Ella picked up her phone, scanning through the television guide. "Oh. There are re-runs of *Thunderbirds* on channel four. I haven't seen that for *ages*."

"What on earth do you want to watch that old crap for?" Sam flicked a glance between us. "Oh, let me guess. I'm outnumbered. Matt likes that show, too."

She grinned. "Seriously?"

"I love all those old shows. Dad and I spent hours watching them when I was a kid."

Her eyes widened. "Me too. My dad was a huge fan. Let's watch it."

Ignoring Sam's groan, I nodded. "Sounds good."

"I am totally changing my ringtone for you to the *Thunderbirds* theme." She pressed buttons on her phone, finding what she wanted and playing it triumphantly.

"Dude, you're totally killing me right now," Sam said.

"You can always go and watch something else in your bedroom." I laughed as Sam threw a teaspoon, missing my head by about an inch.

He sniffed, putting on a show. "Maybe I will. Leave you to your puppets."

"Marionettes," Ella said, not skipping a beat.

Sam laughed. "Trust you to make that distinction."

"She's right though." I winked at Ella, who gave Sam a smug smile.

"Still puppets. Anyway, I'm out to watch a movie in my room." He pecked Ella on the cheek. "You can always join me if you get bored with your puppet show."

She laughed as he stood, grasping his hand as he slowly pulled away.

"I'll help you clean up," I said.

Ella shook her head. "I can do it." She smiled. "I appreciate you guys letting me move in."

"Doesn't mean you have to clean up after us." I stood, picking up my plate and Sam's.

"I like looking after you two. You're so easy to take care of."

"I guess Sam needs food and beer to make him happy."

She picked up the lasagne dish. "What makes you happy?"

I shrugged. "The same."

Following her through to the kitchen, I couldn't keep my eyes from her hips. The way she walked was an aphrodisiac, let alone everything else about her.

I opened the dishwasher, slotting the plates in and going back out to the table to collect her plate and any leftover cutlery. On the way, back I caught her eye, smiling as she opened the fridge, taking out two beers.

"Are you going to get Sam one?" I asked.

Ella shook her head. "If he wants one, he can come and get it. I'm going to turn the TV on."

I joined her on the couch, right as the show started. That distinctive theme tune commenced, and we were laughing, saying the words in time with the television, mimicking the music.

She might not have been my girlfriend, but spending time with Ella was fun.

And I kept falling in deeper.

PART II

I couldn't breathe

CHAPTER 6

MATT

The bad thing about being in love with someone so utterly unattainable who also lived in the same house as you was that they were always around. The good thing was that they were always around.

I dated. Not a little, but a lot. Woman after woman entered and left my life. Anything to get my mind off the fact that the woman I was in love with loved someone else.

Two years into their relationship, Ella and Sam bought a house together. Her parents contributed a large amount of money for a deposit, and our cosy villa was too much for me to cope with by myself. They moved out to Hobsonville, a suburb to the west of Auckland city. I found a small apartment in the city. The idea being to move on, find my own way and maybe meet someone special.

Not long after moving, I sat on a bench to catch my breath after running, only to be joined by a tall, slim brunette, with long legs and the deepest brown eyes I'd ever seen. She stood with one foot on the bench, stretching, and gazed down at me judgmentally.

"I saw you run as far as the bench and sit down. Shouldn't you be stretching or something?"

I shrugged. "I got sick of running."

She grinned and sat down on the bench beside me. "Fair enough. I was thinking about going for coffee. Want to join me?"

How could I resist such a tempting proposal? She was gorgeous.

We crossed the road, entering the coffee shop opposite the bench.

Her name was Christie. From that first day where we'd gone to share a coffee to now, six weeks later, I'd enjoyed her company. We both worked in IT, shared a sense of humour, and from our second week together, the sex had been off the charts. And frequent enough that I'd not seen anything of Ella or Sam.

I still thought of them often, and when they invited me to dinner because they hadn't seen me for so many weeks, I leapt at the opportunity to introduce them to Christie. She was funny, smart, sexy—everything that should have clicked. And it did, when we were together. Alone, I still thought of Ella sometimes. I'd never had the same initial reaction to anyone else as I had to her, and I wondered if I ever would.

The evening started pleasantly enough. We got to Ella and Sam's, and I knocked, nervous but excited. If Christie hit it off with these two, it'd be good for all of us. Especially me.

Ella opened the door, screeching at the sight of me. Christie stepped back as Ella flung her arms around my neck, hugging me tight before I even got in the door. My nostrils filled with that familiar scent, which my heart responded to uninvited. *Down boy.*

"Matt. It's been forever. You need to tell me everything you've been doing. We've missed you so much." Ella's cheeks were flushed, her dimples coming to life as her genuine warm smile lit up the front step.

"Sounds great. Ella, I'd like you to meet Christie. My girlfriend." I'd told Ella on the phone I'd be bringing someone, but hadn't gone too far into details, wanting to surprise them with the fact that I now had a life.

Ella blanked. Her face was unreadable, then slowly the corners of her mouth curled up into a smile. What that was about, I didn't know, but she seemed to force herself to wave to Christie. "Hi, Christie. Come in. We've heard *nothing* about you." Just like that, the previous

Ella reappeared, and she was all smiles and sunshine. She led us into the house where Sam stood in the living room. Guess I'd caught her by surprise.

"Matt." Sam grinned, and his expression didn't change as he cast his eyes over my girl.

"Sam, this is Christie. Christie, this is the famous Sam you've heard all about," I said.

Sam laughed, extending his hand for her to shake. "Please ignore anything Matt's told you. It'll all be lies."

She stared at him with wide eyes. "But he had so many good things to say." She deadpanned, and I roared with laughter. Ella now clung to Sam's side and took a closer look at Christie.

"Oh, you are good. Matt, I can already tell you this one's a keeper."

I met Christie's eyes. "Maybe."

Christie grinned in response, grabbing my arm and swinging it in hers.

"Beer?" Ella spoke, her eyes focused on me.

"Sounds good. Christie?" Beside me, Christie nodded, and I leaned against her.

"You're driving," she whispered.

"One, and then we'll have dinner. I'll be fine by the time we go home." I kissed her temple. "Promise."

"Great," Ella said brightly, smiling at both of us. Whatever had crawled up her butt was clearly gone.

"So, Christie, what do you do?" Sam held out a hand to indicate she should sit on the couch, and I nodded.

"I'll help Ella." Maybe I could find out what was wrong, that swing from flat to happy. Living with the two of them, I'd seen the ups and downs of their relationship. It had been mostly ups until now, but that didn't mean they hadn't argued. The arguments would hit Ella the hardest; Sam was always one to bounce back and move on.

Have they had a fight?

I followed the direction Ella had gone into, pushing the door open that led to the kitchen. She stood over the stovetop, stirring something in a pot, the aroma of roasting chicken making my mouth water. I peeked over her shoulder, but she didn't hear me, or wasn't reacting to my presence. In the pot appeared to be good old-fashioned homemade gravy.

With her head bowed over the pot and her hair tied up in a bun, I noticed for the first time a mole on the back of her neck below her hairline. It was mesmerising. The urge to lean over and kiss it came out of the blue, and I couldn't take my eyes from it. From her.

"Sam, I can feel your breath on the back of my neck. Behave. We have guests." She turned, her eyes that dazzling blue that caught me every time, and they widened as she saw it was me.

"Matt." Her smile widened, her cheeks flushing as I grinned at her.

"I came to see if you needed some help."

"I was checking on the food. It's nearly done. If you want to grab the beers, I'll be back in the living room shortly."

I nodded. "Of course."

I opened the fridge door, taking three beers and carrying them back out to the living room. Sam sat on a chair facing the couch, and seemed to be deep in conversation with Christie. I grinned. He didn't notice I was on the way back, and I moved slowly, pressing the cold beer against the back of his neck. He shrieked, Christie bursting out laughing as I chuckled. Sam leaped out of his chair and stared me down.

"Dick," he said, grinning as he took the beer from me.

"You two are both dicks." Ella came out from the kitchen, passing me and sitting with Christie on the couch. She turned to her. "This is what I put up with for two years; can you believe it?" She really was back to her usual charming self now, smiling brightly at my girlfriend. Maybe she hadn't been feeling well earlier.

"I bet they kept you on your toes." Christie was equally warm, and I locked gazes with her, giving her a reassuring smile. The thought of coming here had made her nervous, especially given how long I'd known Sam. She'd fretted that he wouldn't like her. Even though he was committed to Ella, being female gave Christie a huge advantage. Sam was guaranteed to be a fan.

"Ella kept us on our toes. I spent two years tripping over her underwear, and she wasn't even *my* girlfriend," I said.

Ella shrugged. "I had to keep my things somewhere."

"I couldn't get a towel from the bathroom without a bra falling on my head." I sat on the other side of Christie, Ella reaching over and slapping me on the arm.

"It's true." I knew Sam would back me up. "Ella used to stash them at the top of the cupboard to dry them naturally. She still does. Watch out if you need a towel."

Christie laughed. "I'll keep that in mind."

"Just so we can get off the topic of my underwear, dinner is nearly ready," Ella said.

"Do you cook?" Sam asked Christie.

Christie shook her head. "Kind of. I can boil water." She gave me an affectionate smile. "Matt's been doing a lot of cooking for us."

"Matt's a good cook. He makes such a good mac and cheese." Ella stood, taking a couple of steps toward the kitchen door.

"I don't eat a lot of carbs. He hasn't made me that. Maybe I'll give it a go."

I squeezed Christie's hand as Ella disappeared again. From where we sat, I could see the table was set and ready for dinner. In typical Ella fashion, she'd gone to great lengths to make everything perfect.

Over dinner, the banter continued. Christie got the rundown on almost everything, from the time Sam and I had met as children, through to our uni days. The food was amazing, and the company superb. For the first time since we'd arrived, I relaxed and enjoyed the evening.

"We have something to tell you." Ella grinned, glancing at Sam. He had a silly smile on his face as well, and I eyed both of them suspiciously.

"What are you two up to?"

She took a deep breath, glancing at Sam again, and waved her hand around. "We're getting married."

"I thought I spotted a ring earlier," Christie said with a smile.

For just a moment, I let the mask slip. I couldn't help it. Ella and

Sam were too wound up in their own excitement to notice, but Christie saw. The pain in her eyes was unbearable as I put that smile back on my face to cover the hurt I felt that Ella was lost to me for good. Not that she'd ever been mine, but I guess in my own selfish heart I'd held out some hope that if things didn't work out with her and Sam, I could be there to pick up the pieces.

"That's fantastic, you two. Congratulations."

I turned my head back toward Christie. She sat, staring at her plate, looking up and blinking as if she'd been asleep. "That's wonderful."

Ella grinned, holding her hand still so we could see the ring. The diamond solitaire glinted in the dining room light, and she snuggled against Sam. "Thank you."

"When did this happen?" I asked.

"A few days ago. We decided to save the news for tonight. I hope you'll be my best man," Sam said, fixing his gaze on me.

"As if I'd say no. When's the wedding?"

"In a few months. Ella has her heart set on the church near her parents' place."

I nodded. "That's up north somewhere, isn't it?"

"Kerikeri."

Out of the corner of my eye, I caught a glimpse of Christie sparking a conversation with Ella, taking a closer look at that glistening ring. Maybe she hadn't seen what I thought she had; maybe she was feeling a bit like the odd one out, seeing as we all knew one another so well.

It was weird, watching the woman I'd been in love with for what felt like forever with the woman I hoped to love. This was exciting, freeing, and at the same time it completely contradicted the suffocation that made it hard for me to breathe. Deep down, I was devastated that Ella would soon be tied to Sam for the rest of her life, even though I had known this would come one day.

Truth was I didn't know how to feel.

CHRISTIE SMILED as I jumped into bed beside her, pulling her into my arms.

"Thank you for tonight. I had fun," she said, kissing me on the nose.

"So did I."

She took a deep breath, averting her gaze.

"What is it?" I was almost afraid to ask, but if I said nothing that might make things even worse.

"Did you and Ella ever ...?" She raised her eyes to meet mine, and I saw that sadness I'd seen at dinner.

"No. She's only ever been with Sam."

"She told me that if I hurt you, I'd have to answer to her."

She blinked back tears. This wasn't what I'd been expecting. To me, it had seemed like they were getting on well.

"We've been friends for a while now, and Sam and I have been best friends my whole life. Ella has a big heart. She worries."

"I hope that's all it is."

I rubbed her arm. "It's not anything else. Those two have been joined at the hip since the night they met. Trust me."

She nodded, dropping her gaze. "So, how long have you been in love with her?"

I froze, the question punching me in the face.

"Christie, I ..."

"You love her." Christie's voice sounded so small.

"Don't do this. You know I want to be with you."

I was lost in those deep, dark eyes. They were sad, and I knew the simple act of responding the way I had to Ella's announcement had broken her heart. I could see it.

"Do you?"

"Taking you to meet my friends was a really big thing. I haven't taken a girlfriend to meet them before. Hell, I've not had anyone who I've called my girlfriend in ages."

"Because you love her."

I grasped my forehead with my fingers, rubbing it, knowing I'd have to be completely honest or find a better way to lie. So far, she'd seen right through me.

My mouth was dry as the desert, and I licked my lips, trying to summon up some courage. "When I first met Ella, I had feelings for her. But she's with Sam, and now they're getting married. I'm with you."

"So you don't have feelings for her anymore?" I could tell from her tone that Christie already knew the answer.

"I'd be lying if I said I didn't. But I'm happy for her and Sam. Their happiness means just as much to me." I flicked a lock of straight brown hair from her shoulder. "The feelings I have for you are growing all the time."

"You can't say you love me yet, though." She had that puppy-dog look, the hopeful one, the one that had made me ask her out in the first place.

"Only because it's been *six* weeks. I like what we have; I'm enjoying us getting to know one another."

Christie frowned. "What if Ella and Sam break up later on? What about me?"

"Maybe we need to not overthink things, and see how it all goes." I slid my fingers under her chin. "You're amazing."

She smiled a little, but I could see it in her eyes—she wasn't sure if she should stick around to see what happened. She took a deep breath. "You're pretty awesome yourself. That's why I don't know if I can do this."

I shook my head. "No. This isn't the way to deal with this. I'm here with you, right where I want to be."

"Because she's with him."

I could try my hardest to fight this, but she was right, and not giving an inch. It wasn't because I didn't care about Christie, and I wasn't lying about wanting to be with her, but there was someone who was that much more important to me. Someone who, despite my attempts to keep my distance from, I'd still come running to if she clicked her fingers.

I hated this feeling, and I loved it, torn between my heart that told me she might one day still be mine, and my head which told me the only way that would happen would be for Sam's heart to break. That was the last thing I wanted to happen.

Christie backed out of my arms and my bed, and as she dressed and walked away in silence, I knew there was nothing more I could do.

So I let her go.

CHAPTER 7

ELLA

Ella missed Matt.

She hadn't realised how much until he stood on their doorstep with a woman she didn't like. Ella didn't know what it was about Christie, but there was something that gnawed at her from the moment she laid eyes on her. Maybe it was because she was tall and slim, everything Ella had always wanted to be. Maybe it was because she slotted nicely under Matt's arm, falling easily into his embrace.

When the three of them had been living together, Matt had been the calm to Sam's storm. When they'd argued, Matt had been the peacemaker, soothing things over and making both Ella and Sam smile again. Living with only Sam had been hard to adjust to, but six months in, and they were happier than they'd ever been.

Seeing Matt at the door all loved up with someone she didn't know was plain weird.

She'd set him up on dates with several of her friends, but this was different. Part of her had known Matt wouldn't end up with the women she set him up with, but from what he'd told her, he'd been dating this one a little while and seemed serious.

This wasn't right. Sam had proposed, and she was the happiest she'd ever been with him. Becoming his wife would be the proudest moment of her life. But a black cloud had hung over her as she'd watched Christie and Matt, laughing and joking. No. This didn't feel right.

"Christie seems nice," Sam said, wrapping his arms around her waist when they'd gone.

"She does."

It was so stupid. What on earth did all this mean? It wasn't like she was about to give up Sam to pursue Matt; she loved Sam and was going to marry him. Everything she ever wanted was in place—the man she wanted, the home she'd craved, and soon, the wedding she'd thought about her entire life.

This was the man she would spend the rest of her life with, gladly and without reserve. When he'd asked her, she hadn't hesitated to say yes, despite her father's ongoing misgivings about their relationship. He hadn't said why, wouldn't, but there was a general unease between Sam and her father she didn't understand. Sam doted on her.

Her parents had helped them into their own home, given them their blessing. Ella had made it crystal clear that Sam was who she wanted, who she loved, and they had been supportive, regardless of whatever was going on with her father.

"Matt's a lucky man. Not as lucky as I am, though." He bent his head, kissing her, taking her breath away, as he'd always done. She relaxed into him, closing her eyes as she buried her face in Sam's chest.

"You okay?" Sam whispered.

"Happy. I can't wait to marry you."

"I can't wait to marry you. You'll be such a beautiful bride. And then we'll make beautiful babies."

She raised her face for another kiss, and he obliged, this time gentle and lingering.

"I plan on making you so happy. I want to grow old with you, Ella Brown."

Those were the words that made her melt. The words that made up for the rough times. When she was down, she thought of these moments between them. These were what made their life together worth it.

"That's what I want too. Can we go to bed now?" She pursed her lips for another kiss.

"The dishes aren't done."

She laughed. "Does it matter?"

He wrapped his arms around her waist, twirling her around while she giggled. "I guess not. I'm not looking forward to the mess tomorrow if I do what I really want to do."

"What do you want to do?" She widened her eyes, trying to make herself appear as innocent as possible.

Sam kissed her earlobe, nuzzling her neck. "Celebrate our engagement in style."

"Oh, Mr Mason. Whatever can you mean?"

He took gentle bites of her neck, and she moaned, her whole body tingling in anticipation.

"I think you know what I mean."

Sam let her go, taking her hand in his and pulling her toward the bedroom. Not that it took much for her to move. Sam was the star that shone brighter than any other in the sky, the man who had brought more to her life than anyone else had.

She'd seen them both in her class; the two men were inseparable. When she'd found out about their parties, she'd decided to brave it and turn up. Sitting in the corner, she'd spotted Matt. He always had a smile on his face, and seemed so easy-going. Sam was more outgoing, and when Matt had disappeared partway through the evening, it made her decision about who to make a move on much easier.

Ella had taken her opportunity, and never regretted a thing. Matt was her other best friend, gentle to Sam's rough. All she wanted was for all of them to be happy, and right now she was, content to hold Sam's hand and be led to the bed they'd shared for two years—the one they'd sleep in as newlyweds and beyond.

In the bedroom, Sam's kisses grew more urgent, his fingers dancing over her skin as they undressed one another. He was beautiful naked. Ella had never been thin. Sam had boosted her confidence to not care about any lumps and bumps. He loved her for her, and she revelled in the way he touched her, kissed her, and loved her.

"Damn it, Ella. I could be half dead and you would make me hard." He grinned, kissing her again, gripping her hair tight in his fist. Every nerve in her body was alive. His lips brushed down her neck as she closed her eyes, losing herself all over again. Her earlier discomfort was forgotten as her husband-to-be gave her the warm glow in her chest she'd become addicted to, and she surrendered completely to him.

She laughed as they fell into bed, and he buried himself between her thighs, using his tongue until she cried out his name, bucking her hips toward his face. He moved over her, planting kisses on her neck in his favourite spot, where the line of freckles from her shoulder to her neck blazed a trail, and she gasped as he thrust into her, meeting his every movement with one of her own.

As he sped up, Matt entered her thoughts again, uninvited, but not unwanted. Sam was everything, but some little part of her wondered what Matt's lips would be like touching hers, grazing her skin. Sam sucked gently on her neck and she snapped back to reality, stroking his hair, losing herself in thoughts of him. Guilt sat on the surface for her rogue musings, but she pushed it down, focusing on Sam and their mutual pleasure.

Sam groaned, smothering her with kisses. Ella giggled, gazing into those blue eyes she knew so well.

"I love you," she whispered. Sam rolled her to her side, pulling her in close to spoon.

His hand on her breast told her this would be no early night.

CHAPTER 8
MATT

Ella and Sam were marrying in a small country church, not far from her family home. Sam hadn't been keen on the venue, he would have been happy with the registry office, but seeing as Ella's parents were paying for the wedding, he soon gave in.

I trailed along behind them on their way to Kerikeri. Ella had insisted I stay with them in the lead up to the wedding. Her parents had a farm with a big old house on it, and we were all staying there. I smirked at the thought of Sam in the country. He had been the one to fall in love with the noise of the city, and being out in the middle of nowhere was not his thing. Not that he'd ever tell Ella that.

The farm had sheep and a handful of cows, and I drove slowly as we approached the house, taking in the view. Sam and I both came from small towns, but neither of us had spent much time in the country other than on school trips. One thing was clear—Ella had grown up in what seemed to be paradise.

It wasn't so far out of town to be inconvenient. Schools and shops were only minutes away, but the air was clean and sweet. We arrived so early that the grass was still covered in dew, and I shivered as I climbed out the car.

"Did we have to leave at five a.m., Ella?" Sam wrapped his arms around himself as he joined me.

"I wanted to avoid the traffic. We're here now; stop complaining." Ella exited the driver's side of their car, walking around and pushing her hands through the gap between Sam's arms and his body, snuggling up to him.

"I'm not complaining. Did I sound like I was?" He bent his head while she rested hers on his shoulder.

"You're always complaining." I grinned and winked at Ella.

"Oi. You'll have to stop that flirting in a few days. Once the delectable Ella is Mrs Mason," Sam said.

I laughed. "That's in a few days. Right now is open slather."

"Slather? I don't think I like the sound of that." Ella's throaty laugh echoed in the quiet morning.

"I'll protect you." Sam tried to glare at me, but failed with that silly grin on his face.

He pulled away from Ella, turning and wrapping his arms around her. Bending his head, he kissed her in a big open-mouthed movement that left Ella blushing and me dropping my gaze.

"Is that right?" She gasped when he broke contact.

"You can count on it."

I didn't need to see his face to see that loving look he had for her. I'd seen it enough over the past couple of years. There was no denying how happy I was for the pair of them, even if I did wish I were in his place.

"Come on, you sappy lovebirds. Let's get inside and out of the cold before Sam freezes to death."

Ella laughed. "You need to come and meet my family, Matt. I promise they'll love you."

"Maybe your sister will love him, too," Sam said.

My ears pricked up at that, though I didn't know if hooking up with Ella's sister was a great idea.

"Don't you dare try to push them together. She's too young, and besides, if I've learned anything from my failed matchmaking, it's that Matt needs to find someone himself. Apparently I have no idea about who's compatible with him." Ella winked at me, and I laughed, shaking my head.

There hadn't been anyone serious since Christie four months ago. I'd been out a few times, but nothing had come close to being serious. That suited me for now.

I trailed behind them as we walked to the front door, Ella tapping twice before pushing it open and calling out. In an instant, her family surrounded us, all crowding to hug and congratulate Ella and Sam.

"Third wheel, huh?" Ella's dad shook my hand. He had a strong handshake, and weathered skin, his years working outside obvious. "You must be Matt. We've heard all about you."

I nodded. "It's good to meet you, Mr Brown."

"We weren't sure for a while which one Ella was with, she spoke about you both so much."

"Dad." Ella rolled her eyes, gritting her teeth.

"Matty's my best friend, but you're stuck with me." Sam laughed.

"We're happy to be stuck with you, Sam." Ella's mother spoke. I could see where Ella got her looks from; she shared features with her mother.

Not so much could be said for the young woman who now stood in front of us. "Hey, Smella."

That must be the sister Ella had spoken about. She was the polar opposite of Ella, with light brown hair hanging in plaits, hazel eyes, and a sparkling nose piercing, not to mention the jeans and cut off T-shirt she wore, exposing her flat, tanned stomach. I wanted to ask her if she was cold, but bit my tongue.

"That doesn't work as well as Rubella." Ella laughed, reaching for her sister to hug.

"Not all of us are as creative as you." Ella's sister peeked over her shoulder at me, one eyebrow popping up. "So this is Matt?"

"Yes, it is. Matt, this is my little sister, Vanessa."

Vanessa let go of Ella, raising her chin to me. "Hey."

"Hi."

"Why don't you set me up with him, Ell?"

Ella laughed. "Because you're sixteen and he's twenty-five?"

"Pfft. Since when does age matter?"

I grinned, shaking my head. "I like your sister, Ella. Quite the comedian."

Vanessa winked. "I aim to please."

"I'm sorry, I'm not into younger women. Especially children." I tried to straighten my expression as much as possible, failing as my lips refused to stop smiling.

She pulled away from Ella, straightening up to her five-foot nothing height. "I'm no child."

Ella tugged at my arm and laughed. "I'm sorry for my little sister. She's jealous of me."

Vanessa rolled her eyes. "As if." She put her index finger to her mouth, swaying as she looked me over. "If you need anything, let me know."

"There is one thing you can help me with."

Ella and her sister had identically cocked eyebrows, I swear.

"What's that?"

"Put a jumper on. You'll get hypothermia with all that skin exposed."

Vanessa grinned. "I like this one, Ella. You can keep him."

"Thanks, I think," I muttered, as she waltzed off up the hallway. To get changed, I assumed.

"She's such an attention seeker sometimes. Ignore her." Ella said.

I'd been here for five minutes, and it already felt like home.

"I'm on the way out to check on the sheep, Matt. Want to come?" Ella's dad spoke. In my peripheral vision, I saw Sam roll his eyes. Clearly not his thing.

"Sure. Sounds great, Mr Brown."

"We'll go after a coffee. You look like you need something to warm you up. And it's Eric."

I nodded, Ella squeezing my arm harder. It was obviously important to her that I got on with her family. They seemed really lovely.

Eric didn't ask Sam if he wanted to go, turning and walking back to the living room instead.

"Dad's been up for hours already. He's got a few dairy cows to take care of. You'll have really fresh milk in your coffee." Ella laughed, pulling me toward the living room to the couch. Her mother arrived seconds later, with a tray full of coffee cups and a jug of milk.

"Help yourselves. Have you had breakfast? I can put some bacon and eggs on."

"Sounds amazing, Mum." Sam appeared in the doorway, having been left behind by us.

"Matt?"

I nodded. "Sounds great. Ella was in such a rush, we didn't stop for breakfast."

"Ella was excited to be here to get ready for her wedding, and for her family to meet you," Ella said.

"It's so creepy when you refer to yourself in the third person." I picked up the milk jug, pouring a generous helping into my coffee.

"She is creepy." Vanessa sat on the floor, now covered in a thick woollen jumper. She spooned three heaped teaspoons of sugar into her coffee and poured milk in, sitting back, cradling the cup in her hands.

"I don't know. She's usually pretty alright." I winked, and Vanessa grinned.

Yep. I could get used to this.

~

I'D CLIMBED into Eric's four-wheel drive and we'd headed out across a couple of paddocks before we got to the sheep. As we walked the last few metres to the gate, it dawned on me that he was checking on them because it was nearly spring. Soon there would be lambs, judging by the heavily pregnant ewes standing around chewing on the grass.

This whole place would be teeming with new life, how beautiful it must be then.

"Some of these girls are real close," Eric said, confirming my thoughts. "I check in the mornings to see if we have any newcomers."

"Must be rewarding, taking care of them."

He shrugged. "It has its moments." He looked up at me. "It's good to finally meet you. I wasn't kidding when I said Ella speaks about you a lot."

"Ella's a good friend. I'm glad to be here."

He licked his lips, and in that moment, I knew this invitation wasn't about showing me around. "Do you think she's doing the right thing?"

Could he see how I felt? I swallowed. "Sam and Ella love one another deeply."

"I'm the kind of man who speaks my mind, as you'll come to know. I helped her when she wanted to buy the house and move in with him, but I have my doubts about him looking after my girl. I know she dotes on him, but he never seems to do anything for her. I trust you will keep this confidential."

"Absolutely." I nodded. Lord knew I had enough secrets at this point—one more wouldn't matter.

"They don't seem to have a lot in common. When she first brought him home, he spent a lot of time being fed by my wife while she talked about you. That was behind my comment about not knowing which one she was with."

I grinned. "We've all spent a lot of time together, especially when she and Sam were first together. We lived in the same house for two years. I got used to tripping over your daughter's clothing."

He roared with laughter. "We've all had to deal with that. When Ella first moved out, Vanessa said she was glad that none of her underwear would fall out of the hot water cupboard anymore."

"I can relate to that. Go to grab a towel and end up with a bra."

Eric patted me on the back. "I want to make sure my girl is making the right choice."

I swallowed down every doubt I had. Sam needed me to back him up. What else was a best friend for? "She is. He's a good man. He'll take great care of her."

Eric turned his back on me, looking toward the sheep. But not quickly enough for me to miss the words he uttered. "More like she'll take care of him."

I leaned on the fence, watching the animals move around, squinting into the distance. "Is that a lamb?"

"Where?"

I pointed, and he narrowed his eyes. "I think you're right. Let's take a closer look."

In the centre of the paddock, with sheep all around it, was a lamb. It shook on its thin legs, but bleated loudly as we approached. Eric laughed, slapping me on the back. "Good spotting. For a city boy."

I grinned as he scanned the paddock for signs of any others. It appeared this little one was it, and I swear Eric was as proud as a new father himself as he checked the lamb over, nodding as he went.

"They'll come thick and fast now. Won't all be as good as this one, but it's a start."

"It's so cool it happened now. I've seen lambs in petting zoos, but seeing one like this is a bit different."

He laughed. "We can call this one Matt, then."

"Great. My mother will be so proud I've had a sheep named after me."

Eric stood straight, shaking his head as he led me back to the gate. "I like you."

He didn't say anything else on the way back to the house, but I liked him, too.

By the time dinner rolled around, I was well and truly at home.

Sam had been inside the house with Ella most of the afternoon. I had been out and about to see the farm animals. We'd gone to see the cows after lunch, and then Vanessa had taken me to see the chickens. She might not have resembled Ella physically, but she never stopped talking, and we got on like a house on fire, just like Ella and I.

"Do you like living in the city?" she asked.

"It's okay."

"I hate it here." She scowled as she scooped up the eggs into a bowl.

"I like it. It's nice to get real fresh air."

Vanessa stood. "It's so quiet and boring. I'll be going to the city in a couple of years when I go to university. I can't wait."

I held the gate as she came back out, closing it again after her. "What are you going to study?"

"Medicine, I think. Dad and I have very different ideas. I don't know why. He let Ella do what she wanted."

We walked up the path that led back to the house. From the slight elevation, I could see over the farm, down to the paddock we'd gone in the morning over to the one I'd seen this afternoon. It seemed big, but it really wasn't. Enough space to feel free.

"Your dad is a good guy. I bet you he thinks you're more capable than you realise."

She stopped, rolling her eyes at me. "You're either on my side, or you can't be my friend."

I laughed. "I think you're probably the kind of person who could do anything."

She grinned, turning back toward the house. I followed her down the path and into the kitchen. Ella stood inside with her mother, her eyes sparkling with happiness as they sipped coffee, and she kept glancing at her engagement ring while they talked. The closer she got to being a bride, the more beautiful she was, I swore.

A sharp pain in my side reminded me that Vanessa stood beside me. She grabbed my arm, dragging me into the living room. "Sit there. I'll make you a coffee."

"Yes please, Ness." Sam smiled at her.

"So, one coffee for Matt. What about you, Dad?"

Eric chuckled. "Sounds good. Get one for Sam too."

Vanessa flipped her plait over her shoulder and disappeared back into the kitchen. I glanced sideways at Sam, but he was engrossed in his phone again, playing some game.

~

DINNER WAS AMAZING. Ella's mother had cooked a beef roast that fell apart; it was that tender. She'd grown the potatoes herself, and the vegetables. It had to be the best food I'd eaten in a long time.

After dinner, Sam disappeared to have a shower. Ella grabbed my arm. "Do you want to get us a drink each, and we'll go outside for some fresh air?"

"Sure. What are we drinking?"

She leaned in. "I'll get the vodka, you get the Coke from the fridge."

I found the glasses in a cupboard, and retrieved the mixer. Ella produced a bottle of alcohol from another cupboard. "You mix them. I'll help Mum load the dishwasher."

"I can do that," I said, turning toward the bench.

"Don't you worry about a thing." Ella's mum tapped me on the shoulder. "You're our guest."

I mixed the drinks and headed out the back to the deck with them, leaving Ella with her mum. The evening was cooling quickly, but it was still early enough that it wasn't too cold yet. We'd get maybe half an hour out here before having to go inside.

"Over here." Ella appeared in the doorway, and led me to a swing-seat. It was comfortable, and if it wasn't chilly, I could have gone to sleep on it after that dinner. It had settled in my stomach, and I struggled to keep my eyes open as we sat. Ella smiled as I handed her the glass.

"I barely saw you today," she said.

"I think I've been everywhere. Spending time with your dad was cool; I got to see a new lamb."

She grinned. "I love this time of year. So much new life." She clamped her lips together. "Sorry if Vanessa is a bit too much."

I shrugged. "She's fine. Full of energy, but I guess being a teenager on a farm might be a little boring."

Ella took a sip of her drink, closing her eyes briefly. In the dim light cast from the house, she looked beautiful. She was only inches away; I could lean over and kiss her. I licked my lips and swallowed hard. This could be my last chance to make a move, to tell her how I felt, but at the same time it would be a dick move. Her fiancé, my best friend, was right inside the house.

Ella breathed deep, opening her eyes and fixing her gaze on me. Uncertainty flickered across her face.

"I'm glad you're here. I can't imagine doing this without you."

"I'm glad I'm here. For both of you."

"So ..." She ran her finger around the rim of her glass. "What happened with you and Christie? You never told me." Her sapphire eyes drilled through me. During the wedding planning, she'd asked me a couple of times. I'd managed to change the subject up until now, or find a distraction. It hadn't been hard with everything going on. There was no getting away this time.

I shrugged. "It didn't work out."

"She seemed *really* into you."

I couldn't take my eyes away from hers as they scrutinised my reaction. "Do we have to talk about this?"

Ella frowned, not dropping her gaze. "You and Sam are my best friends. I care. And I thought you would have been more hurt than you were when you two broke up. I always thought it was weird for you not to be that upset."

I swallowed hard, trying to get rid of the lump in my throat. Of course I'd been upset at Christie leaving, but what could I do? There was no hiding from the feelings she'd unearthed, and it wasn't as if they were about to change overnight. Not after all this time.

Once Christie knew, there was no way we could face the future together.

"I was hurt. We ran out of steam."

Now, she looked away. "I'm not trying to interrogate you. I want to see you happy."

"I am happy. My two best friends are getting married."

Ella looked back up at me, a smile spreading on her lips. She held up her drink and I brushed my glass against it. "To you and Sam. And to happy endings." She took a sip, screwing up her nose this time. "There is far too much vodka in that."

"Maybe I'm trying to get you drunk. There are still two days before you get that second ring on your finger." *Maybe I was half joking.*

Ella snorted. "Just as well I can handle my drink then, isn't it?"

"What a shame." I grinned as I sipped my glass, pulling the same face she had. "Oh, I see what you mean."

"I'm going to drink it anyway. It'll help keep me warm." She laughed, leaning back in her seat, looking up at the sky.

It was beautiful out here. There seemed to be about a million more stars in the sky on the farm than in the city. I closed my eyes; it was so calm and peaceful. We were far enough off the road not to hear any traffic that might have been out there. The only sound was the hum of talking coming from inside and the crickets, singing loud and proud in the dewy grass.

"I love this place." Ella put down her drink, linking her arm in mine and leaning on my shoulder. My concentration broke at the fruity scent of her hair as she snuggled up, and I fought the urge to pull my arm away and wrap it around her. She was only being friendly, but it screwed with my head big time.

"It's lovely. Why did you leave?"

She shrugged. "I wanted to study, and experience the big city. Maybe one day we'll come back up here."

"I can't see Sam living anywhere like this."

She tilted her chin, facing me. "No?"

"He's a city boy, through and through. He faked glandular fever to get out of going camping when we were in high school."

"What about you?"

I shrugged. "Thinking of swapping out your groom?"

Ella laughed. "No. I'm being nosy. Would you live somewhere like here?"

"Can't see why not. It's quiet and peaceful. The city's busy and noisy, and I love that, but sometimes it'd be good to have a break."

She went back to leaning her head on my shoulder. "I want to make him happy, Matt."

"If he's not happy by simply being with you, he's an idiot."

My circulation nearly cut off. She squeezed my arm so tight. She didn't say anything more, just clung to me, and I guessed the squeeze was her way of saying thanks. I meant every word. For the last two years, Ella had run around after Sam, taken care of his every wish. He was lucky to have her, and not only because I loved her too. Because she was so kind and caring. I could sit out here with her on my arm forever. "Can I ask you a personal question?"

She rested her head on my shoulder. "You can ask me anything."

"What's the deal with you and your sister? I didn't realise there was such a big age gap."

Ella nodded. "It goes back to when my dad took over this place. He inherited it from his grandfather, not his father. My grandfather didn't want to be a farmer. It caused a huge rift in the family. He fell out with his father, moved to the city and made it big in property, earning a lot of money. Dad loved the farm and took it over. Grandad was disappointed Dad chose the farm over following in his footsteps and cut Dad off. Dad and Mum decided to have one child, because they knew there would be ups and downs and didn't want to have a huge family to support if things went really bad."

"So they had you."

She nodded. "That's right. When I was eight, they did have a bad year. Dad sold some of the land, but it was tough, and then Mum found out she was pregnant. So, my father swallowed his pride and went to Grandad for help. I think it was the push they both needed to make amends. Grandad helped him out financially, and I got to know him. Vanessa was born, and we had maybe three years with him around before he died."

She picked up her drink, taking another sip.

"The farm's shrunk further since then. Mum and Dad don't need the money from farming; they do it because they love it. It's how they helped us into the house."

I tilted my head, resting it on hers. It all made a lot of sense. And I got it. If I'd had my hands on this place, I wouldn't let it go either. No wonder Ella loved it so much.

The rest of the world didn't exist as we sat together, I'd do it all night if I could.

Still, it was time to let go.

CHAPTER 9
MATT

In the morning there were more lambs and sheep to be moved around. I'd been asked again by Eric to join him, and this time, had a chance to get plenty of exercise while we moved the sheep and fixed some fencing.

By late-morning, sweat dripped from places I didn't know existed, and Eric patted me on the back, chuckling. "Go have a shower and a cup of tea. Reckon you've earned it."

I grinned. "Thanks for letting me help. It was a great workout."

"Thank you for helping. You're a good man, Matt."

"You're welcome." I looked around the paddocks. "It's so nice being here."

He chuckled. "You're welcome here any time."

"Thanks." I took a deep breath. This was amazing. How had I never explored anywhere like here?

His expression changed in an instant, from smiling to frowning. "I asked Sam to come out, too. He didn't seem interested." Eric clamped his lips together. "Don't get me wrong. It bothers me that he's inside with the ladies, while you're out here. Ella will inherit part of this place one day; I want to know it'll be in good hands."

I shrugged. "I've always been more active than Sam. He's lucky he has a good metabolism."

"It's close enough to lunch time. I bet both of you could do with a beer."

That was better. A smile and a laugh told me we'd steered back to a good place. One where he wasn't making me feel like he thought Sam was the wrong choice for his daughter. "That would be fantastic. Though I think I need a shower first."

He chuckled again, nodding as I turned back toward the house and headed for the bedroom. Stripping off my clothes, I twisted the mixer in the shower to run the water warm.

As I soaped up, I thought again about what he'd said. There was something hanging over all of this, from the moment we'd arrived. The wedding was tomorrow, and Ella's family seemed welcoming, but what was with the doubt? Surely her father'd had time to settle any bad feelings he might have about Sam.

The water was soothing against my tired muscles. While I regularly worked out, working on the land had been an effort and a half. And I'd enjoyed it.

Maybe I could make it on a farm after all.

I stepped out of the shower, plucking a towel from the railing and wrapping it around my waist. Inside, the house was warm; it wouldn't take long to dry off.

Walking back into the bedroom, I opened my bag, pulling out fresh jeans and a T-shirt. I threw them on the bed and turned toward the door to close it.

"I timed that right, then." Vanessa stood in the doorway, in an even shorter shirt than earlier. This one barely covered her breasts. She had that eyebrow raised again as she looked me up and down. I'd never felt so naked.

"Timed what?"

"Arriving in time to see the view."

"Are you flirting with me, Miss Brown?" I laughed.

"Whatever gave you that idea?" She took a step into the room, pursing her lips as she looked me over again. "I already know you're a lost cause. You're in love with Smella."

My heart stopped as I looked at her. Was it that obvious? The past two years I'd tried to hide it, and even made Ella think I didn't like her at the start. Had her sister seen right through me?

Vanessa laughed. "You should see the look on your face. Totally knew it. Everyone's in love with Ella."

I exhaled a breath that I felt as if I'd been holding forever.

"Are you jealous of her?" It was my turn to cock an eyebrow.

"Little Miss Perfect? Sure. Though I'm not jealous she's getting married. Your boy Sam is a douche."

I narrowed my eyes. What had he done to deserve that? He adored Ella. "What are you talking about?"

She ran her finger across the foot of the bed until she stood inches from me and shrugged. "I don't know. Just a feeling."

"Your dad said something similar. Has Sam done something?"

Vanessa shook her head. "No. Dad gets feelings about these things. I trust him. I think he's a bit psychic."

"Has he ever liked any of your boyfriends?"

She looked up at the ceiling. "No."

"I think he's more dad than psychic, then."

Her eyes met mine, and she twisted her mouth. "I guess you're right."

I smiled. "Sam loves Ella. He'll take good care of her."

"I hope my sister isn't being a pain in the butt." Ella's voice came from the doorway. I didn't know how much she'd heard, but I hoped I'd said the right thing.

"She's fine. We're having a chat."

Ella moved toward us, hooking her arm around her sister's shoulders and looking down at her. "As long as you're not being mean to Matt."

"I might take you seriously if you were looking him in the eyes. They're not in the middle of his chest, Ella." Vanessa smiled triumphantly and I grinned as Ella went a deep shade of pink.

"I'm not married yet. I'm allowed to look." She flicked her hair back over her shoulder, catching my eye. That mischievous twinkle made my stomach do flips. Damn it. And then she winked, sending a signal in my body that went from my brain directly to my cock. I needed both of them out before anything further happened.

"Neither of you are allowed to look right now. I have to get dressed," I said.

"I think he's telling us to leave, sister dearest." Vanessa smiled sweetly, and I rolled my eyes as Ella joined in. They might play like they didn't like one another, but their unity told an altogether different story.

"That's exactly what I'm telling you. Some privacy would be nice."

"We'll leave you to it. Want me to make a coffee?" Ella asked.

"Your dad offered me a beer. I'll take you up on that coffee suggestion later though."

She pulled Vanessa toward the door. "Good. I want you to feel at home here, too."

"Can he be my roommate?" Vanessa asked her.

I laughed, shaking my head as Ella closed the door behind them. I did feel at home.

I pulled my shirt over my head, drying myself as I put the remainder of my clothing on. Fresh jeans and a clean shirt made all the difference as I walked out to the kitchen.

"Have you got any dirty clothes, love?" Mrs Brown asked.

"I've got a few changes of clothes; I'll be fine." I smiled at her.

"I'm doing a load of washing this afternoon. I'll grab them and get them washed if you want me to."

"I don't want to put you out."

She looked at me with those same eyes that Ella had, the ones that opened up her soul, and I saw kindness and motherly caring.

"I do washing nearly every day. Another pair of jeans and a shirt aren't going to make a difference. Are they on your bed?"

I nodded.

"I'll grab them and give them a wash. No point in storing stinky clothes away."

I turned at the sound of footsteps. Eric was right behind me with a bottle of beer in his hand, chilled and open. "Here you go. I bet this'll go down a treat after today. Thanks for the help, Matt."

"No problem. I enjoyed it."

We made our way into the living room, where Sam and Ella were curled up on the couch together.

"Any time you want to come and help out, you're more than welcome. Any friend of Ella, and all that," he said, grinning at me as he sat.

"Thanks. I'll keep that in mind."

"Matt always did like getting dirty." Sam laughed, and I held in my exasperation. There it was, written all over Eric's face. He thought Sam was looking down on him, and I couldn't do anything now that particular horse had bolted.

"Not my fault you're too precious to do a bit of hard work." I laughed. That pleased the old man; he was smiling again. Something told me that this wasn't an easy time for him, his daughter about to marry someone he clearly didn't like very much.

"Hey, we went down the road and took a look at the church while you were gone," Ella said, nudging me as I sat on the couch beside them.

"I'm assuming it's still there."

She poked her tongue at me. "Yes, smarty pants. And it'll be amazing tomorrow."

I looked down at my beer. In twenty-four hours she would be Mrs Mason, and I really would have to get over her.

But I had a plan for that.

IN A REVERSAL of the night before, I helped Ella's mother with the dishwasher before heading outside. That dazzling sky hit me again with its beauty, so simple with the tiny pinpricks of light peeping through the darkness.

"I'll be glad to go home; my hayfever goes nuts out here." Sam's voice came from the doorway, and he meandered across the deck toward me.

"What hayfever?"

"That's what I mean. I never got it before I started coming here."

I rolled my eyes as he sat beside me. "I love this place. I could see myself living somewhere like this."

"You can have it." He leaned back, closing his eyes. "I do sleep like a baby, though. Must be all the fresh air."

Shaking my head, I smirked. "You do cry like a baby. It's fitting."

Sam punched my arm. "Hey, you're not allowed to pick on me. I'm getting married tomorrow."

Don't I know it.

"To you and Ella," I held up the coffee cup I'd brought outside, and he touched his beer against it.

"Thanks, bro. It means everything that you're here. And Mum and Dad being here in the morning will be awesome. They've never met Ella's folks. Maybe then her dad won't give me such a dirty look. Pretty sure he's in love with you."

Sam stretched his legs out, yawning. Bed wasn't far away for all of us, tomorrow being such a big day. In the afternoon, there had been a marquee assembled, and meat had arrived for the dinner. There would be a pig on a spit, and the thought of that alone was enough to make my mouth water.

"He's a nice guy. I can see where Ella gets her charms from."

Sam spat his beer all over the deck, laughing. "From her mother. Her dad is a cranky old bugger."

"Maybe with you."

He sighed. "Anyway, what are you doing after the wedding?"

I took a sip of coffee. "I'm going to travel for a bit once you two are safely married. I've got a trip planned for the UK and beyond. I didn't want to drop it on you, but I figured I should tell you before I disappear."

He cocked his head, narrowing his eyes. "You've never mentioned travelling before."

"It was always something I was going to do eventually. Feels like the right time."

Sam nodded, slapping me on the shoulder. "Fair enough. We'll miss you."

"Besides, how would you and your lovely wife start your life alone together with me tagging along?"

He laughed. "She's lovely, but I'm not?"

"Sorry, man, my heart's not in it for you. I'm not that type of guy." I patted his shoulder in return, grasping it tightly. "Be happy, and take care of that lady of yours. I'll be back."

Sam took a deep breath, grinning like the damn Cheshire cat. "I'm getting married. Never thought I'd say those words. Couldn't have found a better woman than Ella."

"You two are good together. Keep it that way while I'm not around to get you out of trouble."

He laughed. "We are going to miss you. Ella's family love you. I can't quite put my finger on it; they're nice and everything, but I don't know if they like me much."

I shrugged. "I don't know about that. Ella's mum seems to like you."

"I think Ella's mum likes everyone." He looked at me slyly. "You seem very cosy with Vanessa."

"She's sixteen."

He grinned, taking a swig of his beer. "Nearly seventeen. Still legal."

"That's gross, man. She's a kid."

"Yeah, but she's stacked. Sweet little thing, too. Bit mouthy though."

I took a deep breath, holding in the anger that was building. I could punch him now, but the last thing I wanted to do was to ruin Ella's wedding and fall out with her. No matter what, I still wanted her as a friend.

"What's wrong with you? She's Ella's sister, and she's a child."

He rolled his eyes. "When did you get so uptight?"

"When my friend started perving on sixteen-year-old children."

We stared one another down, his lips twitching as if he was trying to decide if I was serious or not.

"Sam." Ella's voice came from inside, and Sam put his hands up in surrender.

"Fine. Whatever. It's not like I'd go there anyway."

Ella walked toward us, perching between Sam and I on the seat. She'd showered, the scent of honey stronger than ever, and I smiled at her, ignoring Sam.

"Hey, Ella. After your groom?" I asked.

Her cheeks pinked as she grabbed Sam's hand. "Just a few things we need to sort out."

"He's all yours."

Her eyebrows dipped as she looked back and forward between us. "Are you two okay?"

No.

"We're fine." Sam kissed her on the cheek.

He stood, pulling her up by the hand. As they got to the door, Ella looked back over her shoulder, one eyebrow raised, clearly still puzzled by what she'd walked in on.

And then I was alone, left with my thoughts and the stars. Of all the time we'd spent leading to this moment, this was the hardest.

Tomorrow I'd say goodbye to any last hope.

CHAPTER 10

MATT

The wedding day. The day I would watch my best friend marry the woman we both loved.

I'd skirted around it so much in my head, but there it was. I was in love with Ella, and had been from day one. It wasn't enough to be her friend; I still wanted her.

We'd got to the car when I stuck my hand in my pocket, grabbing Sam's arm with my other hand in panic. "The rings."

Sam rolled his eyes. "You're an idiot. Go back and get them, and hurry. If we throw off the timing for today, Ella will kill me."

I laughed. "Whatever. Pretty sure she'd forgive you anything."

He climbed in the car while I turned back toward the house. The rings were on the cabinet beside the bed in my room. They'd given me one job, and I'd nearly failed at it.

Inside, women were everywhere. Vanessa, a couple of other ladies I didn't really know but I'd been told they were old friends of Ella's. Sam's mother and Ella's mother were in the kitchen, laughing at me as I came running back into the house.

"I forgot something." I shrugged, heading up the hallway to the bedroom. I breathed a sigh of relief as I spotted the two little boxes I was supposed to be responsible for.

"Matt." Ella's voice came from her room as I went back toward the kitchen and the back door.

I poked my head in the room. "What's up? I have to run."

Her back was to me, and she slowly turned with the biggest smile on her face I think I'd ever seen. "What do you think?"

My heart fell to the floor. Her dress was similar to the one she'd worn the night I'd first seen her, with the heart-shaped neckline that showed off her cleavage. It was clinched at the waist and then flowed outward in material of the purest white.

Ella looked like an angel.

"Matt?"

"I ... you ..." She frowned as I fumbled my words, unable to form any at the sight of her. "You look incredible, Ella."

Her smile lit up the room when it returned, and she studied my expression closely. "Are you sure? I want it to look perfect."

"I've never seen anything so beautiful in all my life," I blurted out, meeting her eyes as her mouth fell open, uncertainty crossing her face. "Uh, I have to go."

I raced the rest of the way to the car, jumping in the back seat and pulling the door closed behind me.

"Everything okay?" Sam's eyebrows were raised.

"Fine." My heart pounded so hard, he must have been able to hear it. Surely. If I hadn't been a goner before I would have been after seeing Ella in her bridal gown. I could complain about how unfair it was, but she loved him as much as he loved her. It wasn't as if he was forcing her into this.

Sam's dad was driving. He had some talkback station playing on the radio, we couldn't even listen to music to relax. Not that Sam needed to. I was much more stressed than he was.

I fiddled with my tie, running it through my fingers, the image of Ella still playing through my mind.

"Are you sure you don't want to hook up with Vanessa?" Sam said.

I closed my eyes. "I told you, she's young and not my type."

Sam laughed. "I'm beginning to think that no one is your type."

I nodded. "Forever alone." I looked out the window to rolling paddocks as we passed. It really was beautiful out here, peaceful.

He grinned. "I'm really doing it, Matt. I can't believe today I get to marry Ella. I love her so much, man."

I swallowed down any resentment. Sam did love her, and he would take good care of her. I couldn't fault him for that.

We pulled up outside the church. It was small and beautiful, like something out of a country postcard, with ivy growing up the walls, the roof reaching up into a steeple.

I'd never thought about my wedding day, never planned for anything or had any dreams of what it might be like. This was perfect.

"Cool-looking place," he said, as if reading my mind. "Ella had her heart set on it. We were lucky we got it this weekend; it's pretty solidly booked. There's a big garden out the back that's popular for photos. Perfect."

"It looks fantastic." I patted him on the back. "Congratulations, my friend. Let's get you married."

As hard as it was to see Ella marrying someone else, I was happy for Sam. My emotions were conflicted, but one thing was true. I loved Sam, too, and wanted him to get his happy ending.

We walked up the old stone steps and into the church. The minister stood up near the altar, and smiled as we approached.

I hung back while Sam went to speak with him. It was homely in here—small wooden pews, embroidered cloths everywhere. It was so like Ella to like something a bit old-fashioned.

"Matt, we have to wait around here, and we'll get plenty of warning Ella's coming."

"If she doesn't stand you up." Even if I didn't feel the way I did, I needed to give him as much crap as I could. He would be doing the same for me.

"I wouldn't blame her if she did." He grinned. Turning serious, he squeezed my arm. "Thank you for being here. There is no one else I'd rather have by my side. We've been through everything together, haven't we?"

"School, university, puberty ..." I laughed.

"Sometimes I think we're stuck on that last one."

"Speak for yourself." I sat down in the front pew.

"Are you really going away?"

I nodded as he sat beside me. "Europe. I've got a job lined up in the UK for a while, and then I'm going to travel. I don't know how long for."

"It'll be weird without you around." He fiddled with his tie rather than meet my gaze.

"I haven't been around for ages. It's been you and Ella. I'll miss you two, but I need to do this."

"It'll still be weird. I always thought we'd do some big overseas trip together, but Ella turned the whole world in its head." He smiled, that satisfied smile that tied my stomach in knots. I wanted what he had, but I couldn't hurt him to try and get it.

Sam stood as his parents arrived, and I took another look around before joining them. I don't think I'd ever seen his mother so happy.

Ella's mother wasn't far behind, and she smiled at me as she took her seat. No matter what, I'd enjoyed my time here, getting to know Ella's family. They were such good people.

"Ella's right behind me, love," Ella's mother said to Sam, and he nodded toward me. We took our places at the front of the church and waited for her to appear.

Vanessa appeared in the doorway. Ella and Sam had kept the bridal party small, with me as the best man and her as the bridesmaid. It went with the simplicity of our surroundings and the small congregation.

Vanessa was dressed in a dark blue dress with her trademark plaits brushed out. Vanessa couldn't be less like Ella if she tried, her hair completely straight, and she looked out from under her fringe, catching my eye and smiling as she walked toward us.

In the background, Ella appeared.

Sam gasped at the sight of her. Smiling proudly, she walked up the aisle, her gaze fixed on Sam. I glanced at him. He was as trans-fixed as I was at the perfect woman who now came toward us.

Jealousy burned in my veins, but I held it in, smiling at Ella as she drew closer. She took a deep breath, joining Sam at the altar as he took her arm.

I'd never wanted her so much.

Her father stepped aside, and I forced a smile as they exchanged vows, promising to love one another for the rest of their lives. My only contribution was the handing over of the rings. I hated this feeling. Hated that I still wanted her.

Afterward, as they made their way down the aisle hand in hand as man and wife, Vanessa took my hand in hers and squeezed it, giving me a reassuring smile as we followed them out of the church

We stood through photos, but all I wanted was a drink, something to take away this shitty feeling.

When we sat in the marquee for dinner and toasts, I gulped back the glass of champagne waiting for me, the waitress spotting me and rushing over to refill it quickly. No one else noticed, and I sat as the bride and groom made their entrance, Sam sitting next to me with Ella on the other side.

And then it was time for me to speak. I'd spent weeks writing my speech over and over again, trying to sum up how much I loved both of them. It was so easy, and yet one of the hardest things I'd ever had to do.

I stood. "For those of you who don't know me, I'm Matt. Sam is my brother, or at least the closest thing I could have had to one. We grew up together, and I was there the night Sam and Ella met. Although, I kind of wish I wasn't."

Sam and Ella both looked at me with raised eyebrows. I chuckled to myself. "They were drawn to one another immediately, and you would have needed a crowbar to pull them apart."

Gentle laughter filled the tent, and the smiles on everyone's faces told me they saw how much Sam and Ella loved one another.

"Ella quickly became both Sam's great love and my friend. I couldn't ask for anyone better to be marrying him. She's about as perfect as they get." I looked down at Ella. Tears welled in her eyes, and her mouth was twisting as if she was torn between smiling and crying.

"I've missed them both since they moved into their own place. Especially Sam's annoying habit of taking my last beer, and Ella's cooking. But I know that they'll be happy in their life together, even if I'm not around to bug the hell out of them."

At that Ella grinned, burying her face in Sam's chest as he stroked her shoulder

"I love you guys, and I would like to ask that everyone join me in a toast to Sam and Ella."

"Sam and Ella." The sound went up throughout the marquee, and everyone raised his or her glass.

Vanessa sat on the other side of Ella, eying me as I smiled at her. *What about me?* she mouthed.

"Oh. And I can't forget Vanessa for being such an exceptional bridesmaid. If I do, she might kill me in my sleep."

At that Ella smiled, and Vanessa sat back, a satisfied look on her face. As I sat, Sam slapped me on the back.

"Thanks, man. That was awesome."

"I mean it. I'm really going to miss you two."

Ella narrowed her eyes. "Why? We're not going anywhere."

Sam kissed the top of her head. "Matt's going away for a couple of years. Around Europe or something. I don't know all the details. He sprang it on me last night."

She swallowed hard as she said nothing, her gaze fixed on me, the colour fading from her cheeks.

"What?"

"I want to do something different for a while. I'll be back."

Stabbing pains grew in my stomach at her sudden change in demeanour. I hadn't planned to tell her this way, but now Sam had brought up the subject, there was no getting around it.

"Where are you going?" Vanessa's voice came from behind Ella. Trust her to be listening.

"England at first, then I'll do some backpacking. Find my way around a few more countries until I run out of money and it's time to come home again."

"Jealous," she exclaimed.

I leaned over to kiss Ella on the cheek, her head still resting on Sam's chest. "I'll be back," I murmured.

"I know. It's so out of the blue. You surprised me." She gave me a small smile, lifting her head to look at her husband. "Guess we'll just have to put up with one another."

Her grin returned as he kissed her.

"I think we can manage that."

WITH THE BRIDAL dance came my chance to escape the suffocating marquee. Ella and Sam only had eyes for one another, and I slipped out, sitting on the grass at a distance from the big tent. One side had been rolled up, and I could see the dancing from where I sat.

I took deep breaths, and leaned back on my arms, looking up at the sky. Not a cloud in sight, and I got yet another stunning view of the stars.

"It sucks, huh?" Vanessa's voice came from behind, and I turned to see her approaching, a can of Coke in each hand.

"What sucks?" I took one can as she offered it to me. "Cheers." I popped the tab and clanked my can with hers. It fizzed over the edge and onto the grass.

"Idiot." She laughed, sitting down beside me. "Ella marrying a douchebag. That's what sucks. I know you think it too." She smiled. "I guess you don't know a lot of people here—most of them are my family's friends."

I nodded. "I know Sam's parents obviously, and a couple of their friends. But me? I'm forever alone."

Vanessa grinned. "I'm glad you came to stay with us. You're the best part of this whole thing." As I sighed, she touched my hand. "I'm not flirting with you; I'm really glad Ella has you as a friend. And I think you're my friend too now."

"For sure, squirt." I tapped her on the nose as she laughed.

"Besides, I have a kind-of boyfriend at school."

"Really? Why isn't he here?"

She took a sip of her drink. "I'm playing hard to get."

I nudged her shoulder with mine, smiling at her sudden shyness as she looked at her feet. "Good for you. Keep it that way."

"Can I keep you while they go back home?" She leaned her head on my shoulder, and we watched the wedding reception at a distance. Sam and Ella danced slowly, wrapped up in one another as if no one else was around them. I couldn't help but smile at two people so in love and happy.

"Sorry. I'm going on a trip."

"Is it because of *them*?"

"No. Well, maybe a little. I've spent the last couple of years with those two, but now they're married; they need time to settle into that. So I can stay and feel like I'm in the way, or I can go out and see the world."

Vanessa sighed. "I want to do that some day."

"Grow up a little more and you can."

She raised her head, rolling her eyes. "I wish I was a couple of years older, then you might take me seriously."

I grinned. "I take you very seriously, Vanessa. I'm sure in time, when you're allowed to spread your wings, you'll soar." I yelped as she squeezed my arm tightly. "You've got one really firm grip."

"I wish you were marrying Ella." She sighed as she leaned her head back on my shoulder.

I turned, kissing the top of her head. In the distance, the music played, reminding me of where I was, but I could have easily slept under the stars even with the chill in the air.

I had to go.

CHAPTER 11

ELLA

"Are you coming back to bed?"

Ella closed her eyes as Sam's voice came from the bedroom. It was day three of their week-long honeymoon, and in the beach house they'd rented, they'd spent those first three days in bed.

"I need food," she yelled back, a smile on her face.

She also needed a break. Their celebrations had gone late into the night every night since they'd been married, and what she really craved now was sleep.

Sam's footsteps padded toward her on the tiled kitchen floor, his arms wrapping around her waist. He nuzzled the back of her neck. "Damn it, I got a mouthful of hair," he said, laughing as he pulled away.

"That's what you get for being impatient."

"What are you cooking?"

She turned, pushing past him to get to the fridge. "French toast. I'm starving after expending all that energy."

"I don't think we've expended enough." Sam grabbed her wrist, pulling her closer, tugging at the hem of the T-shirt she wore.

"Sam, I mean it. We need to eat."

"Let's have a baby, Ell."

She caught her breath, staring at him, searching his eyes for some sign of a joke. He was straight-faced, his blue eyes staring into hers.

"Where did *that* come from?"

"We've got the house, and if I pick up some adult night classes we can live on my salary for a while. I want us to have a baby."

Ella bit her bottom lip, looking at him, still unsure if he was joking or not.

"We talked about this being a future thing."

"You said you always wanted kids. So do I. I can't think of any reason to wait," he said, his lips twitching, giving her a small smile.

"Yes, but ..." Ella trailed off and glanced out the window. On the beach was a family, parents and two young children. They ventured into the water before running back to their mother and father screaming. "I just didn't think we'd have them so soon. I thought we'd spent time being us first."

"I don't want to wait. You'll make an amazing mum."

She took a deep breath, meeting his gaze.

"Ella? Please don't leave me hanging."

"I don't know."

He wrapped his arms around her waist, pressing his body against hers. She rolled her eyes as his erection pressed against her stomach. "Again?"

Sam grinned. "Again. Always. Come on, wife."

Ella switched off the stove element as she followed her husband back to the bedroom. He lay on the bed, waiting for her as she stripped off her panties, and impaled herself on him.

"Can't wait either, huh?"

She giggled, leaning over to kiss him as he pushed her T-shirt up to her neck. She flipped it over her head as he stroked her skin, placing his hands on her shoulders so he could kiss her breasts, lapping at each nipple before letting her up again.

"I love seeing you naked," he murmured.

She blushed, her cheeks an inferno at his compliment.

"Do you remember that first night we were together?" He cupped a breast in each hand, running his thumbs over them. Ella closed her eyes. This was the same position they'd been in, always Sam's favourite.

"How can I forget that. The living room floor?"

"Matt walking in."

If Ella's cheeks had been hot before, they were blistering now at the memory of the cool air that had hit her body as the front door had opened. But that hadn't woken her out of her dreamy haze as she rode Sam. It was Sam speaking up, asking Matt to shut the door that had stopped her.

Matt had stood there, not knowing where to look as she'd crossed her arms. Afterward, Sam had taken her to his bed and said one sentence that had sealed the deal.

"Don't ever be embarrassed at someone seeing your body. It's a work of art." It might have sounded trite, but he'd been sincere in his delivery.

He groaned as he came, and she leaned over, kissing him softly.

"Yes," she said.

"Yes what?"

"I want to have a baby with you."

Sam grinned, rolling them both onto their sides facing one another as he kissed her.

"I want to give you the world," he said, pushing her hair back off her face.

"I still want breakfast."

MATT WAS LEAVING. It was the one thing on Ella's mind as she returned to normal life. Everything seemed to happen at once. No sooner were they back from their honeymoon, but Matt was packed and ready to go.

What if he didn't come back?

It wasn't even so much that he was going, but that he'd never said a thing about it. The way she'd found out stung.

Matt was supposed to be one of her best friends.

She drove to his apartment, wanting to know more about his journey without giving Sam the chance to derail the conversation and distract her from what she wanted to know.

Ella knocked, and Matt smiled as he opened the door. "Ella. What are you doing here? Is Sam with you?"

Behind him in the small living room were stacks of boxes. This was really it.

"No, only me. I wanted to see you before you left."

He nodded, stepping back to let her inside. She followed, closing the door behind her. His apartment was small, just the living room, kitchenette, bedroom and bathroom. With everything packed, it looked so much bigger.

"Sorry, all the furniture's gone. I sold it. Two more nights in this place and then I'm out of here, so I'm camping on the floor."

She shrugged. "It's fine. I won't stay long. I had some things I wanted to ask you."

"Shoot."

"Why are you going?" She searched his face for a sign, something to indicate how he was feeling. Damn Matt and how good his poker face was. There wasn't a hint of his emotion. This man was her other best friend, and she was bewildered at this feeling of loss. She shouldn't feel this way, not this strongly. She'd given her heart to Sam forever.

"It's something I've been thinking about for a while. Broaden my horizons."

"But why didn't you say anything? This is so random."

"Maybe to you, but like I said, it's been on my mind for some time. I'm sorry if you're unhappy about me not sharing it with you."

Ella frowned. In the time they'd known one another, she'd been sure Matt had been as open as he could be with her and Sam. "I'm sorry, I don't mean to press you on it. I'll miss you."

Matt's right hand landed on her face, palm to cheek in such an intimate gesture she closed her eyes. His thumb traced the lower lid of her eye, right below her makeup, wiping the tear that had gathered.

"Ella," he said mournfully. "Don't make this harder than it already is."

He raised his other hand to the right side of her face, wiping the tear on her cheek. Ella opened her eyes to see him only inches away, his dark blue gaze full of emotion, now searching hers.

"I don't want you to go. Just because Sam and I are married now doesn't mean we don't want you nearby."

Matt's Adam's apple bobbed as he swallowed, and his expression blanked again. What was this? What was going on with him?

"I need to do this for me," he murmured.

"I'm going to miss you. You and Sam are my best friends."

Matt sighed, his right thumb tracing down her face to her lips, his fingers stroking her face as if committing it to memory.

He dropped his left hand to her back, firmly pulling her closer to him, and she was lost in his eyes like she'd never been before. They told her everything.

"Ella," he whispered. In one swift move his mouth claimed hers, his tongue pressing between her lips. It was a desperate kiss, a goodbye kiss, and instead of pushing him away she kissed him back, tasting him for the first time, gently pressing her tongue against his.

No.

She shoved his chest, backing away with wide eyes. Where had *that* come from?

"This. This is why I need to go." His voice cracked as his gaze stayed on her, fixed to her face as if looking for how she felt.

"I didn't know," she whispered.

"It's you, Ella. It's always been you. I don't want anyone else."

He took a step forward, and Ella inched back as far as the wall behind her would allow.

"I have to go and clear my head of you. I don't know how to do it, but I do know I can't do it here. Not when you're so near."

Unable to form coherent words, Ella saw the anguish for the first time, the knowledge that he couldn't have her. How had she never seen it before?

"Matt?"

"I need some time. And some distance. I'll come back over this, and we can all pick up where we left off. As friends."

Her heart ached to see him so tortured. To think when they'd first met she'd thought he didn't like her.

I don't know how to feel.

"I need to finish packing. I've got a moving company coming to pick up the rest of my things and take them to Mum and Dad's place."

Ella closed her eyes, fighting back tears. The thought of her friend going away had been hard; knowing his feelings made it even harder.

"Okay," she whispered. "Do we get to say goodbye at the airport?"

She opened her eyes to his smile, his gaze sweeping her face. "Of course you do. I hope you're there to greet me when I come back, too."

"How long will you be away for?"

"I've got a two-year visa, but I'll see what happens. I want to travel around, and I'll work where I can. I've got a job lined up over there with an old friend for the first few months, and then I'll play it by ear."

"Two years," she whispered.

His hand landed on her shoulder. "I'll miss you guys. But you and Sam don't need me hanging around while you work out your new life together. Besides, I'll still be online when I can. We can catch up over Facebook."

She nodded; there was no talking him out of it. He'd clearly had it planned for a while to have his visa. Ella let out a big sigh, wrapping her arms 'round his waist and burying her face in his chest.

"I don't mean to upset you, Ella. I have to do this for me." His arms tightened around her, the steady beat of his heart reassuring.

How easy would it be to run away with him right now? Jump the plane to Europe and disappear? If she didn't love Sam so much, she might do it. The loss of Matt from her life was an unbearable thought.

"I should go," she said.

"I know."

Her heart thrummed at a million beats per minute as he let go, and she turned to go toward the door.

"Ella?"

She looked back over her shoulder.

"I'm going to miss you. You and Sam. I love both of you. That's what makes all of this so hard."

"I'll miss you too," she croaked.

Ella closed her eyes as she closed the door behind her.

It didn't matter what Matt said—nothing would ever be the same.

CHAPTER 12

ELLA

One year later …

At first Ella hadn't worried. She'd moved on and waited, but after a year of trying for a baby, her heart was ripped out, month after month. Sam's laidback attitude to nearly everything wasn't helping.

"I looked it up on the internet. It said because of our age and how long we've been trying that maybe we need some help." Ella leaned her head on Sam's shoulder, squeezing his hand.

"What kind of help? Doctors?"

"Yes. It's been over a year, Sam, and we're not old enough to have issues conceiving. There must be something going on."

He turned, wrapping his arms around her. "Surely we can wait a bit longer. There's no hurry."

"I thought you wanted to have a baby." She sighed. *This was your idea to start with.*

"I do, and I would be happy if you told me you were pregnant tomorrow. But maybe we just have to be patient."

"What if something's wrong?" She fought back the tears that

threatened and tried to force her lips into a smile. They wouldn't co-operate, and Sam frowned with her.

"Fine. Whatever. If you think we need to see a doctor, we'll see one." He smiled. "I can't wait to have a baby with you, Ella."

Now her lips did what she wanted, and curled into a smile. She planted a big kiss on his lips. "I can't wait, either."

He leaned in, nuzzling her neck, and she moaned at the contact. Sam always did know how to touch her, how to make her feel as if there was no one else around.

"Let's go to bed now," she whispered.

"It's the middle of the day."

"So? Who are we going to get in trouble with?" She giggled, accepting his kiss, leaning back on the couch as it grew deeper. This—this was perfect.

"Rugby's on." Sam kissed her on the nose, sitting back up and grabbing the remote. She stared at him in disbelief as he flicked on the television and she seemed forgotten.

What the hell just happened?

"Get some chips, Ell. The game's about to start."

Ella placed her hands in her lap, unable to move. The television transfixed Sam, and he completely ignored her sitting there. She was not moving, not saying a word. What was there to say? One moment, a serious conversation about their relationship, the next minute, discarded for sport.

As each month had passed, Ella had wept because there was no baby. At first, Sam's suggestion, his idea consumed her. It kept her awake worrying, but now he seemed disinterested and only going along with it because she wanted it.

She closed her eyes. How had they ended up like this? There was settling into marriage, and there was this, whatever this was, where he'd planted this seed but now didn't seem to care.

Matt wandered uninvited into her thoughts. If she tried hard enough, she could still feel his kiss, burned on her lips for eternity. The kiss of unrequited love.

But maybe, had he still been around and Sam as neglectful, things might not have stayed that way.

No.

Her eyes flew open. It didn't matter whether Matt was there or not. She could never return his feelings, not in that way. Even if sometimes she thought of the kiss and wondered what it would be like to go further, to be touched by him, to be loved by the sweet, gentle man who was in some ways the opposite of the man she'd married.

No matter how many times those thoughts filled her head, they could never come to anything. She hadn't told Sam for fear of him being hurt.

She loved Sam.

"Ella? The chips?"

"Sure."

Chips in front of the television with the man she adored. Life could be a lot worse.

She retrieved the bag of potato chips and settled them in the centre of the couch, jumping as her phone vibrated in her pocket. It was Vanessa.

What are you up to?

Ella smiled. Vanessa now studied at Auckland University, turning down her sister's offer of a place to stay and living in student accommodation in the city.

Watching TV. You?

Standing on your doorstep

Ella squealed. Even so close, seeing Vanessa was a real treat. Ella had adored the straightforward, often sarcastic teenager from the day she was born.

"Babe," Sam muttered.

She stood, running for the door. Pulling the handle, she found Vanessa on the other side, grinning, with two pizza boxes in hand.

"I saw there was rugby on, and figured you might need something else to do given that Mr Boring will be glued to the TV."

"He is." Ella grinned.

"I heard that," Sam called.

Vanessa rolled her eyes. "You were supposed to."

She walked in past Ella, placing the pizzas on the table.

"I'll grab us a drink. There's Coke in the fridge."

"Can you get some for me too please, babe?" She heard Sam as she got to the cupboard where the glasses were stored.

"Why don't you get off your butt and get your own drink?"

Ella laughed, shaking her head as she heard her sister.

Sam chuckled. "Always nice to see you, Ness."

Ella grabbed three glasses and the Coke from the top shelf in the fridge. Vanessa sat at the table, watching her as she placed the items on the surface and opened the bottle.

"So what have you been doing?" She placed a glass of Coke in front of Vanessa, and took one to Sam on the couch. He wrapped one hand around the glass, pulling her down for a kiss.

"Thank you," he murmured.

"Any time."

She turned with a smile on her face, and laughed at Vanessa's eye roll. "You do that far too much, young lady."

Vanessa shrugged. "It's habit." She lifted the lid of one of the pizza boxes. "I got your favourite—Meat Lovers."

"Thanks. I appreciate it." Ella sat next to Vanessa, her back to the television. "So, what have you been up to?"

"Study, study and more study. It's not as full-on as I thought it would be, but we're just starting. So, I'm trying to get ahead."

Ella nudged her sister with her elbow. "Good for you."

"You might have to brush up on that bedside manner before you become a doctor, Ness," Sam said.

"Ignore him," Ella whispered.

Vanessa grinned. "I'm good at that. What have you been up to?"

Ella reached for a piece of pizza, closing her eyes as she took her first bite. She'd been trying to be good and lose a bit of weight. This wasn't helping, but it was so good.

"Same old. Working. Trying to make a baby."

Vanessa's eyebrows dipped as she gazed at her sister. "How's that going?"

"It's not." Ella shrugged, tears coming to the surface. "Can we change the subject?"

"Heard from Matt?" Vanessa took a bite of her pizza. Ella's heart thumped—the other subject she didn't want to think about.

"Not for a while. He was in semi-regular contact with us while he was working in London. Now he's travelling, I think access to the net is sporadic." *I haven't been online as much either.*

Ella had started avoiding the net at home. The temptation to pore over fertility and childbirth sites was too tempting. It was too easy to self-diagnose her failure to fall pregnant.

"I haven't heard from him either. He accepted my friend request on Facebook, but I wasn't sure if he was not posting, or posting and hiding it from me." Vanessa twirled a stringy piece of mozzarella between her fingers.

"Matt's probably out there sexing up all the ladies." Sam waggled his eyebrows as he approached the table, reaching for a slice of pizza. Vanessa slapped his hand, shaking her head.

"Matt's not like that."

"How would you know? You met him once. I've known him his whole life. He's not a monk." Sam grabbed a slice, taking a big bite out of his. "Thanks," he mumbled with his mouth full.

"Gross. I didn't think he was that kind of guy," Vanessa muttered.

"He's not. Sam is trying to get you to bite." Ella slapped Sam's arm, and he swallowed, pursing his lips to give her a kiss.

"Don't eat too much, it's not good for you," he said as he pulled away.

Ella narrowed her eyes as he turned back toward the television.

Vanessa slapped Ella's arm, frowned and nodded toward Sam.

Ella shrugged. He only said it because he cared. Right?

CHAPTER 13

ELLA

It was funny how something so perfect could go so wrong. How one little aspect of your life not being right could turn everything upside down.

The struggle to have a baby had weighed on Ella's mind far too long.

Sam hadn't seemed worried, but she'd made the appointment with the fertility clinic anyway, to give herself peace of mind more than anything else. The tests had seemed to go on forever, but the results would be in tomorrow. She and Sam had an appointment with the fertility specialist, Dr Goodrich.

"I hate doctors," Sam said.

"Maybe everything is okay. I need to know," she said quietly, resting her head on his lap.

He stroked her hair while she closed her eyes, the sound of the television fading as she became drowsy.

"We'll find out tomorrow," he whispered. "Whatever happens, I love you, Ell."

"Love you too," she mumbled. She could stay like this forever, loved up with him on the couch. Push all the bad thoughts aside as to what was going on.

In her dreams, she held her baby—their baby. The stark reality of the truth only burdened her in the daytime when she could think about it.

Dreams were nicer.

~

"We call it unexplained fertility," Dr Goodrich said.

Ella looked at the floor. "So what now?"

"Well, there's no medical reason for you two to not be able to conceive a child. Either time will tell, or you could explore the possibility of IVF."

Sam squeezed Ella's hand, and she raised her head to look at him.

"What's involved in that?" Sam asked.

"There are a few things we can look into first. I think for the moment, I'll give you some reading material, and we'll make another appointment so you can ask any questions that you might have."

"Okay." Ella's voice cracked. Even though they didn't know the root cause, the responsibility was on her. It had to be her fault.

"Ella, this isn't the end. You have a lot of options. You might find that as we work through them, it happens naturally. Sometimes when the pressure is off, it seems to make a difference." The doctor smiled, and Ella nodded slowly. She had to get control of herself, not let it pull her down. They'd get on top of it all; it was a matter of taking it one day at a time.

Sam buried his head in her neck, kissing her softly. "At least we know that nothing's wrong, babe. We'll get there."

The car ride home was quiet, Ella poring over the documents the doctor had given them. They had two choices for IVF—the public system, where they'd have to wait, but be funded for up to two attempts, or going private. Private equalled money they didn't have, but was the much faster of the two. They could be starting the process in a matter of weeks rather than months.

Ella's parents had already helped them out with a sizeable

amount of money to get them into the house. She didn't want to ask for more, but that could be the only way they could try sooner.

"What do you think?" Sam broke the silence.

"We could be waiting a long time if we don't go private."

He sighed. "What choice do we have?"

"We've got a bit of savings."

"Not enough for this."

She clamped her lips together in an attempt not to cry. It seemed these days, she did that a lot. It wasn't always because she was unhappy; her life with Sam was close to perfect. They were only missing the one thing she now wanted desperately.

"Don't cry, babe. We'll work it out somehow."

"I'm sick of waiting."

"I know."

Pulling into the driveway, he sighed as he turned off the car, placing his hand on her knee. "Let's go and have a nice evening. Curl up on the couch together."

She leaned her head on his shoulder. "That sounds nice."

"Give me the folder, and I'll read through all this. I suspect you've read most of it on the internet."

Ella kissed him on the cheek. "Thank you. I wasn't sure if you were in this with me or not."

Sam grinned, making her heart flutter. "You bet I'm in it. We kinda need to do this together."

An hour later, Ella cleaned up after their steamed fish and vegetable dinner while Sam immersed himself in the fertility clinic paperwork.

"It says here that the chances of conceiving are better if we're both at healthy weights," Sam said, waving around the paper he was reading.

"Why do you think I've been on a diet these past weeks? I've read up about it." Ella flopped onto the couch beside him, lying down with her head in his lap.

"You have?"

"If you came home for dinner more often, you'd notice."

He put down the paper, running his fingers through her hair. "I'm sorry, babe. I know it's tough. I'm trying to take the opportunities I can when I can. The adult computing classes are really popular right now. Believe me, I'd rather be with you than spending my evenings with people who can barely turn on a computer."

Ella laughed, turning her head to nuzzle his leg.

"You could try that a bit farther up if you want."

She sighed, sitting back up.

His blue eyes twinkled with mischief. "How about we snuggle up in bed and watch a movie? Then ..." he ran a finger from her throat down to her breasts, "we can see what happens."

Ella grinned. For a couple trying for a baby, the sex had become less frequent, and when it did happen, it wasn't always the crazy, passionate sex they'd enjoyed for so long. Sam was usually tired, and Ella scared to get her hopes up.

"Sounds wonderful," she whispered.

"You're wonderful." He pressed his lips to hers, exploring her mouth with his tongue while she relaxed into him. His hands cupped her breasts. "Don't lose too much weight. I wouldn't want you to get rid of these."

His eyebrows shot up as her body shook with laughter. "I don't think there's any chance of that. Besides, once we make a baby they'll get bigger again."

"Oh." He kissed her again and took her breath away as only he could.

"I love you, Sam."

"Love you too. Come on—I say we watch the movie naked and take it from there."

Ella laughed. "What movie did you have in mind?"

"*Transformers*. The latest one."

She shook her head, standing and taking him by the hand. "Let's go. But it had better be me giving you a hard-on and not Optimus Prime."

He grimaced. "I can't promise you that."

Ella rolled her eyes. "Dick."

"I know you'd rather watch something soppy, but what can I say? The robots do it for me."

"You do it for me," she said.

His eyes grew sad, as if overwhelmed by emotion. "No matter what happens, you mean the world to me. You know that, right?"

"Of course I do," she whispered. Maybe things were tough, but the one thing she could count on was Sam's love for her. The ring on her finger said everything.

"Let's forget the movie." He grinned, his eyes scanning her features, excitement on his face as if he were discovering her for the first time.

Ella chuckled, running for the bedroom, pulling Sam behind her.

That was what really mattered.

CHAPTER 14

ELLA

Another month of no baby.

Ella sat on the couch, a bag of potato chips by her side, huddled up in front of the television. She seemed to spend a lot of time there these days, hiding from all the things in her life she didn't want to face.

Cranky from dieting and a healthy dose of PMS, she sat staring at the screen, stuffing her face with one of her favourite comfort foods.

The front door opened, and she didn't look up. Sam sank into the couch beside her, kissing her cheek.

"You okay?"

"What makes you think I'm not?" she snapped, immediately regretting her tone. Sam hadn't done anything wrong.

"Let me see. My gorgeous wife is sitting in her trackpants and sweatshirt, stuffing her face with potato chips, and her eyes are all red from crying."

Ella fought the urge to cry again, her lower lip quivering as she met his gaze. Sam looked at her with so much understanding and love it was impossible to be bitchy with him.

"I'm not pregnant."

He pulled her into his arms, that familiar soap powder smell of his shirt enveloping her. No matter how upset she was, he made her feel safe, wanted.

"We have a plan for that. Now we have to wait our turn."

"I don't want to wait," she whispered.

"Babe, we talked about this. It's too expensive to do it privately."

She sucked her lower lip through her teeth. His eyebrows knitted as he looked back. "Ella?"

"I've told them we want to go private. It'll still take some time to go through everything, but it'll be so much faster."

Sam let her go, standing, pacing back and forward, his head buried in his hands. He stopped, glaring at her, his palms up in surrender.

"How the hell are we going to pay for it?"

Ella stood, moving toward him and placing her hands on his. "Mum and Dad will help. They want this, too."

"They can't pay for everything. It's enough that they got us into this house. I want us to live our own lives."

Ella closed her eyes, holding in the tears trying to break free. "I want a baby. We need help. I can't keep going the way I am. This is getting harder and harder, and it's doing my head in."

Sam's strong arms wrapped around her neck, and he pulled her in tight against him. "I know it is. This whole thing is killing me, seeing you like this month after month." He hooked his fingers in her hair, running the auburn strands between them. "I know I'm not the easiest person to live with at times, and I know I'm not always as supportive as I should be. But I love you, Ella, and I want what's best for both of us."

"What do you think that is?"

"Maybe we need to take a break for a few months. Forget about trying for a baby. Maybe it'll stop you having so many mood swings."

She pulled back, shaking her head to free it from his fingers. "I don't know if I can switch off like that."

Sam smiled. "I'll make dinner. Forget about everything tonight."

"Aren't you working?"

He shook his head. "Classes were cancelled this evening. Those grotty classrooms we're in are being fumigated. I'm all yours for the night."

Ella licked her lips. Sam growling in response brought a smile to her face that felt long overdue. "Oh. So you're choosing me over the cockroaches?"

"Every time."

The *Thunderbirds* theme playing made that smile bigger. *Matt.* She snatched up her phone, sitting back on the couch.

"Hello?"

"Hey, sis."

"Since when does my phone play *Thunderbirds* for you?" Her irritation was tempered with the welcome sound of Vanessa's voice.

"Since I screwed with your phone last time I was there." Vanessa laughed. What her life must be like to not have the stresses Ella had. But at the same time, she was hard at her studies.

"I'm going to change it again once I hang up. Can't have you stealing someone else's ringtone."

"I thought it might make you smile."

Ella laughed. "It did. What's up?"

"Checking in. You by yourself tonight? Or is Douchebag home?"

"Sam's home." Ella caught his eye, winking as his eyebrows dipped in confusion.

"Good. I'm glad you're not alone."

"Make up your mind."

Vanessa laughed. "I don't care. Whatever makes you happy. I miss you smiling. I'm supposed to be the bitchy one."

Ella leaned back in her chair, gazing at the ceiling. "I'm over being like this. I want to hold my baby. Sam's baby. We only need one."

"I know, sis. Chill out and maybe it'll just happen."

"I don't think it's that simple."

"Maybe not, but if you're not yourself, is it worth all of it?" Vanessa sighed. "Have you heard from Matt?"

"You ask me that every time, and you stand as much chance of talking to him as I do. Sam had a call the other night. He was in Amsterdam and travelling back toward England."

Sam sat, and pulled her sideways, resting his chin on the top of her head.

"I've got to get going. Sam's going to cook dinner."

"Oh. Lucky you. Give Douchebag a punch in the face for me."

Ella raised her face, pursing her lips for Sam to kiss. He grazed his lips against hers, leaving her smiling as he stood. "Don't be so mean," she murmured down the phone.

"Catch up with you later. Maybe I'll go stalking Matt on Facebook."

Ella laughed. "You do that. Talk to you soon. Love you."

"Yuck. Byeee."

Ella closed her eyes, putting the phone on the table. The nagging throb in her head wouldn't leave her alone and she rubbed her temples, leaning forward.

Sam's thumbs pressed into the back of her neck as he rubbed her shoulders. "Feeling sick?"

"Just a headache. I think I'll have something quick to eat and climb into bed."

Sam yawned, and Ella couldn't help but follow suit.

"Sounds like we're both tired," she said.

"I'm glad for even a small break. The school is so busy—they want to do another two evening classes."

Ella groaned. That was good and bad. The money was good, but the evenings alone weren't helping the situation.

"I'll chuck some canned spaghetti in a pan and cook that up for dinner," Sam said.

"At least I've managed to progress you past coffee and toast."

He grabbed her by the hand, pulling her to her feet. Reluctantly, she rose, turning to face him.

"Only just. I mean, I wasn't *that* good at coffee and toast to start with." He pecked her on the lips. "Was that Ness on the phone?"

Ella nodded, trailing behind him to the kitchen. She stood at the end of the kitchen bench, watching as he took a tin of canned spaghetti and opened it, tipping the whole thing in a pot.

"What did she want?"

She shrugged. "The usual. Wants to check on me. Wants to know if I've heard from Matt."

Sam shook his head. "You know, if she was a bit older, she'd probably know exactly where Matt was. She'd be literally following him around Europe."

Ella laughed. "I think you're right. She's right, though. Apart from that short phone call, we have no idea what he's been doing."

Sam placed the pot on the stovetop, flicking on the element.

"If he knows what's good for him, he'll be having copious amounts of sex with hot European girls."

Ella looked away.

"Ella?"

"Do you ever wish you'd gone with him?"

Sam frowned. "What are you talking about?"

"He's probably with all those girls, and you're here with me. Being miserable."

He covered the distance between them, kissing her so hard she squealed with laughter. His lips were so warm and comforting as always, his hands tight around her waist.

"I would rather be here with you than anywhere else on the planet. No matter who I could be with."

Ella ran her fingers up his arm to his shoulder. "Even Optimus Prime?"

He raised his face to the sky. "Even him." Sam dropped his gaze. "Want toast with your spaghetti?"

"Sounds amazing. As long as you don't burn it."

Sam looked at her in mock horror. "Such an insult."

She grinned. "I might put up with a bit of charcoal because I love you."

He laughed, turning back toward the cooktop. "As long as you love me, all is right with the world."

SAM MANAGED NOT to burn the toast or the spaghetti. Ella lay on the couch as he brought the plates into the living room, placing them on the coffee table.

"Dinner."

She smiled. "You did well."

Sitting, she picked up her plate, leaning back. Sam sat beside her, sitting so close his thigh touched hers.

"All this space, and you nearly sit on top of me."

"I want some close time with my girl. I don't see enough of you right now."

Ella plucked the fork from her plate, twirling the spaghetti around on it. "Things aren't what they should be right now."

Sam nudged her knee with his. "We'll get there. Nothing's ever perfect. Do you know what I'm going to do after I finish this amazing meal I cooked?"

"What?"

"I'm going to sleep. It's the other thing I don't get enough of."

Ella laughed. "Poor, tired baby." She leaned on his shoulder. "Why don't we go away for the weekend?"

"Where?"

"To see Mum and Dad. I miss them." She chewed on her lips. "Maybe we can talk to them about helping us with IVF?" She didn't miss his eye roll, the way he turned his head not to look at her.

"Uh, maybe."

She licked her lips, staring past the television to the curtains. This house was suffocating at times, reminding her of the early days, when they'd moved in and she'd put her stamp on it. All the decorations were so much hers, and so very little Sam's. It was something she'd never noticed before. Ella had sewn her own curtains, made her own cushions, and decorated everything the way she wanted.

Turning her attention back to the plate, she cut the corner off her toast with a generous helping of spaghetti. It went down easily, and she moaned, smiling at Sam as she swallowed.

"That good, huh?"

"Not bad for someone who can't cook."

He grinned, rolling his eyes as he scooped in a mouthful of food.

This was nice, a small quiet moment with her husband. Something they didn't get enough of.

As they finished, she stood, holding her hand out for his plate, and Sam put his feet up on the couch, lying down and closing his eyes. For a moment, Ella watched him, envying the ease with which he fell asleep. Within moments, he snored softly, and she shook her head, smiling at him.

Ella walked into the kitchen, filling the sink with hot water and rinsing off the dishes. It hadn't been much, but it had to be the best evening they'd had together in a while. The most peaceful at least.

She returned to the living room, sitting on a recliner next to the couch and putting her feet up. Sam might have fallen asleep, but he was there with her and not working.

Closing her eyes, she jumped at a tap on the door.

"Who on earth could that be?" she grumbled.

"Probably some door-to-door salesperson." Sam yawned, rolling over.

Ella rolled her eyes. Trust him to leave her to sort it out.

She got up, going to the door and pulling the handle. A tall, young, blonde woman stood on the other side.

"Is Sam here?"

Ella turned her head. Sam's eyes were still closed.

"Babe, it's for you?"

"Who is it?" He opened his eyes, squinting at her.

She shrugged, nodding toward the door.

Sam sighed, dropping his feet to the floor and standing, walking toward her, his eyes already glazed over with sleep. They widened as he approached and saw the young woman.

"Petra? What are you doing here?"

She smiled. "I wanted to return this." In her hand was a battered old textbook. Ella had seen that kicking around when they'd moved house. How did this girl know where they lived?

"Thanks. You could have done that in class. There was no hurry." He took the book as she handed it to him. "Ell, this is one of my adult students, Petra. Petra, my wife, Ella."

Petra smiled sweetly. "Nice to meet you. I won't be in class for a couple of weeks. Family stuff. I wanted to make sure I got it back to you."

Sam looped his arm around Ella's waist. "Well, thanks. I don't think you should be coming by my house though. It's not really appropriate."

The young woman swallowed hard, her expression hardening. "I'm sorry. I thought I was doing something helpful," she snapped.

"It's fine. Thank you."

She nodded. "Thanks. See you when I get back to class."

"Sure."

Ella watched as Petra walked back down the path leading to the street. She smiled as the young woman turned at the gate, looking back at the house. "That was weird."

"She's weird. I'll have a chat to the school. There is no way I want any students showing up uninvited."

Ella nuzzled his cheek. "Was it even urgent?"

"No. She was struggling with some of the more basic concepts I was teaching. The book is so ancient, it's only just useful. Thought it might help." He shrugged, kissing Ella softly on the lips. "I'm going back to sleep on the couch."

She laughed, wrapping her arms around him as she pushed the door shut. "I won't make any noise, my beautiful, hard-working husband."

Sam grinned, kissing her again, his hands slipping down her back. "You're worth all the work, Ella Mason."

He threw the book on the coffee table, letting her go and flopping back on the couch. "We could always snuggle together."

"I think we'll need a bigger couch for that."

Sam's right eyebrow crept up. "I bet we can both fit. Easy." He crooked his index finger, beckoning her with that look she knew so well. "Come here, wife."

If only life were always this good.

SAM'S next night off was due at the end of the week. After their earlier evening together, he'd promised more of the same. There had been far too many letdowns for Ella lately.

That one evening had sparked something in her. It was time to reclaim her life, what she had before all of the attempted baby-making happened. Tonight, she'd rebel and do something different.

And there was nothing like a bit of *Rage Against the Machine* when you need to rebel.

Screw the diet.

Ella pressed the volume up a couple of notches, pressing her earbuds in tighter as her iPod pumped out the music. She needed real food tonight, and real music as she danced around the kitchen. She paused, breathing in the aroma of that wonderful meaty, cheesy lasagne she'd been working on for the last hour. Not long to go now.

She pulled open the oven door, impatient now. Her stomach grumbled.

"Ella."

Sam stood in the doorway, his face crossed with frustration. Smiling as she pulled out her earbuds, she pushed the oven door shut.

"Babe. Dinner's nearly ready."

"I've been standing here for about five minutes calling your name."

She grinned. "Whoops. I'm sorry, I had the music a little too loud."

Sam sighed, walking toward her. "What's for dinner?"

"Lasagne. I haven't made it in forever, and I thought we could be a little naughty."

"Are you allowed that on your diet?"

The words and the snarky tone they were delivered in deflated

Ella. Her shoulders slumped as she looked at her husband. "I wanted lasagne."

"Yeah, but we're supposed to be in good health and physically fit for our best chances to conceive. That's not going to happen if you keep cooking shit like this."

Ella's cheeks blazed with a mix of anger and embarrassment. She'd been living on salad and protein for weeks, and being called out by Sam for one carb- and fat-rich meal hurt her to her core. Especially when she'd spotted burger wrappers in the bin. He'd tucked them under other rubbish, but he'd not hidden them well.

"It's one night. I've been good for weeks. And I don't think I have to justify myself to you. I wanted us to have a nice dinner together, but apparently two in one week is too hard." She breathed hard, her anger growing by the second as she glared at her husband.

"Well, whatever. I've got a class to teach tonight; I came home to change."

Ella's hands tingled in irritation. "But you promised we'd have dinner together."

"And I got the chance to earn a bit more this week. I can't win. I'm doing this for us. So we have savings when we have our baby, and to help pay to have a baby."

"But you promised," she whispered.

He smiled. "I'll make it up to you, I swear."

Kissing her on the cheek, he disappeared up the hallway toward the bedroom to get changed.

"After all these evenings alone, this *was* making it up to me."

She slammed the spoon in her fingers on the bench, flicking up the hot sauce on it onto her hand. Tears rolled down her cheeks as she twisted the cold tap, running the water over the reddening skin. The last few weeks had been the worst. Everything seemed too hard.

"Ella? You okay?" Sam appeared in the doorway, watching her standing there with her hand under the tap.

"I'll be fine. I burned my hand."

He strode toward her, and put his hand on her shoulder, squeezing gently. "Want me to get anything?"

"A new life?" She turned her head toward him, seeing the concern in his eyes.

"I know this is hard." He leaned his head on hers.

"I'm so over everything."

"Not over me, I hope."

She turned to him, flinging her arms around his neck. "Never. I know I can be up and down, but you're the one thing I know I can count on."

"Always." He planted a kiss in her hair, pulling her hands to his chest. "How's your hand?"

"It's okay. It was only a few spots of hot sauce."

"Want me to kiss it better?"

Ella smiled as he covered her hands in kisses.

"Did you talk to the school about that student?"

He placed his hands on her arms, smiling warmly. "I did. She's no longer in my class. Sounds like I'm not the first person she's done that to. Serves me right for trying to help."

"You're a good man, Sam Mason. We really didn't need a stalker to deal with on top of everything else."

Sam raised a hand, pushing her hair back behind her ear. "Anything that causes you stress, I'll do my best to sort out. You have so much to deal with already; the last thing I want is for you to worry." He kissed her tenderly. "I've got to get going. I'll try to be home early."

She nodded.

"Save some of that lasagne for me. It smells amazing." Sam squeezed her arms before letting go. "Love you."

And you think I have mood swings.

THE LASAGNE WAS everything Ella had dreamed about—rich, cheesy, and it left her more satisfied than she'd been by any meal she'd had in a long time.

I can't go on living like this.

Afterward, she lay in bed, staring at the ceiling, waiting for Sam to come home. If he followed his normal pattern, he'd come home late and smelling faintly of beer. School wasn't always his only hangout.

I wonder what bar you go to?

In her dream house, married to the man she loved and trying to create a family with him, she was all alone.

PART III

I couldn't believe it was true

CHAPTER 15

MATT

What do you do to get away from heartache? The pain that tears your insides apart while you smile and pretend nothing is going on.

I was drawn to Ella like a moth to a flame, but also repulsed by my feelings for her. I was Sam's best friend, but not worthy of the love he bore me. Every day I'd betrayed him with my heart. That same heart broke when she became his wife.

So, I ran. I ran as far as I could. Watching them marry was the last straw for my battered emotions. Every morning for the rest of her life, the woman I was in love with would wake up in bed next to my best friend. I should have been happy for him; instead, I was miserable.

Now, on the other side of the world, in a small English village, I was in bed with this beautiful woman. She had long blonde hair and even longer legs. Any other man would have been in paradise. Me? I'd dragged her into my hell.

Inside her, my body tightened, ready for release. That amazing moment every sexual encounter inevitably leads to. Groaning as I let go, floating in a world all of my own, I said one word that screwed everything up.

"Ella," I whispered. A bit too loudly. My eyes flickered open to see the blonde's big blue eyes gazing at me in return.

"What did you call me?"

"Shit, I didn't mean ..."

She pushed me off and I rolled to the side, cradling my head in my hands. "Amy, I'm so sorry."

"First rule of screwing anyone is to get their damn name right if you're going to call it out." She looked at me, that little wrinkle between her brows growing as she frowned.

"I'm sorry. I'll go."

"What was that about?"

I swallowed. Hard. In all this time, I'd never admitted my feelings for Ella to anyone else. I'd never said how thoughts of her had consumed me at times, how despite the time and distance, if she'd needed me, I'd be there without a second thought.

"Call it unrequited love. I don't know. Something I shouldn't feel."

Amy's eyes were so sad. We'd known one another two days, and my heart ached at calling her by the wrong name. Starting again was hard when all I could see was Ella.

"Who is she?"

I couldn't stand being under her stare as her eyes bore through me, seeing my heartache. I focused on an imperfection in the ceiling, a tiny mark on a tile, rather than looking back at her.

"My best friend's wife."

"Oh." Her voice broke on that one little word, and I knew if I looked back she'd be looking at me with pity. That wasn't what I wanted. What I wanted was Ella out of my head, once and for all.

"I'm trying to get away from it. That's why I've been travelling. They are blissfully happy, and I'm the arsewipe who wants her but doesn't want to try and break them up because I love them both."

Amy sighed, but it wasn't a frustrated sound, and I turned my head to look at her. There was no pity in her eyes, just the faraway look of romance. Weird.

"That's beautiful. Fucked up, but beautiful. I mean, I didn't think we were any great romance, and I would have appreciated it if you'd been thinking of me, especially when you came."

"I'm sorry."

"You've said that about three times. It's too late to kick you out, so you might as well sleep here."

"Thanks. I'm—"

"If you say I'm sorry again, I'll push you out the window." A satisfied smile crossed her face, like she'd told me off but understood. It didn't help how badly I felt, wondering if I was ever going to get over this.

Maybe it was time to admit defeat.

IN THE MORNING, Amy barely looked at me as we ate the breakfast I'd cooked. Making her food was the least I could do for the way I'd behaved.

I studied her across the table. We'd met in the pub, and it hadn't taken long for her to invite me into her home. She had long blonde hair in big curls, so much like Ella's but the wrong colour. Her skin was so soft and smooth, and her cheeks rosy.

Why couldn't I fall in love with this girl? I liked her. She'd been a lot of fun. But, whatever I did, my heart belonged elsewhere, and as much as I couldn't rein it in, I also didn't know if I wanted to.

"Can I use your computer?" I asked. It had been a few weeks since I'd checked in on Facebook. I'd been living on next to nothing for so long. All I'd logged in from was from the odd internet cafe.

"Uh sure." At least I hadn't totally pissed her off the night before.

I made my way to the computer in the living room, logging into Facebook to a whole lot of notifications.

118 unread messages, all from Vanessa. They all seemed to be the same.

Matt, are you there?

Matt, you need to come home.

Matt, Ella needs you.

Douchebag is being douchey.

Come home.

Over and over again. I stared at them. Douchebag is being douchey? There was only one person she called that, and my stomach fell to my knees as I read the repetitive messages a second time. Then again, Vanessa was good at exaggerating.

I clicked on Ella's profile. She was barely posting anymore, when barely a day used to go by that she didn't post some goofy picture, sometimes of herself. I clicked through her photos. She hadn't posted a selfie in forever.

What had changed?

I messaged Vanessa.

I've been travelling and not on Facebook. I'm coming home soon; I've got no money left.

Seconds later came the reply.

I miss you. Ella misses you too. Sam is a dick.

How is Sam being a dick? I replied.

They've been trying to have a baby, and it's not happening. Ella is miserable. I don't think Sam is being very supportive.

I sighed. I had to remember that Vanessa didn't like Sam. She was hardly going to see it his way.

Have you seen her? I asked.

I'm going to university and living in an apartment block near them. When you come back, you can stay with me. My bed isn't very big though. She posted a big wink emoticon after the message, and I roared with laughter. Some things never change.

We'll see. I'll message you when I know what my plans are. Give my love to Ella and Sam.

What? None for me?

I miss you too, squirt.

You need to stop calling me that. I kinda grew up while you were away.

Fine. I've gotta go. I'm using someone else's computer, and I think she's not far off kicking me out.

I got the sad face.

I'll be home soon, and we'll catch up. You can tell me all the goss.

Ciao. Come home safely.

I moved back to the table, lost in thought until another buttered slice of toast landed on my plate. Amy cheered for herself while I rolled my eyes.

"So, what are you doing today?" she asked.

"I think I'm going to sort out my ticket home. Time to go back and be a grown-up."

Amy lifted her slice of toast to her mouth, grinning. "Are you going to tell Ella how you feel about her?"

I shrugged. "She knew before I left."

"Chin up, Matt. Who knows? Maybe she'll see you again and realise she's made the wrong choice."

I shook my head. "No. Apparently they're trying to make a baby. I doubt there's much hope for me."

She winked. "You never know. You could always come back here."

"Thanks." She was nice. It wasn't her fault my heart was elsewhere.

"But next time, call my name."

CHAPTER 16

MATT

Flying into Auckland was bittersweet. Part of me dreaded seeing Sam, knowing that despite my efforts, the love I had for Ella could flare up again. Not that it had ever really left me.

I closed my eyes during the descent, the plane shuddering in the windy conditions.

Hopefully this is the only turbulence today.

At the bump of the landing gear hitting the tarmac, I opened my eyes again. *Home.* The sound of air rushing past as the plane braked filled the cabin. I'd never heard anything so glorious in my whole life. All this time away, and being right outside the airport made me more homesick than I'd been in months.

As we slowly made our way through customs, my head filled with questions about who would meet me on the other side. Sam would be there, and Vanessa had messaged me to say she'd be with him. From Ella, only silence. The desperate need to see her filled me, Vanessa's messages churning through my mind. I wouldn't be satisfied she was okay until I saw her for myself.

The male customs officer's expression was neutral. This must be the most boring part of the job, having to sit there and ask that question a million times a day.

"Do you have anything to declare?" *Yes, I'd like to declare I'm in love with my best friend's wife.*

"I've got chocolate in my bag." I pulled out my backpack, unzipping it so he could see. All packaged up, I already knew it passed all the rules.

He stuck a finger in the bag, pushing things around. "Is that all?"

"Yes."

"Go through the green door."

I waited until I was out of earshot to breathe a sigh of relief. Now my feet were on the ground, the last place I wanted to be was going through an X-ray, even if I had nothing to interest them. That could literally take forever.

I spotted Vanessa, waving her hands in the air to get my attention. She jumped up and down as I came through the last door, throwing herself into my arms as I came to a stop. I wrapped my arms around her, kissing her cheek as Sam came up behind her.

"Bro," he said, a huge grin across his face.

"Hey, man."

"I'd hug you, but it looks like Vanessa has that covered."

I laughed as she let go, standing back a little. She'd filled out since I last saw her, and she wore makeup. Most unlike the girl I left behind.

"Well, look at you. You went and grew up."

She slapped my arm, grabbing hold of it while Sam bumped knuckles with my other hand.

"Where's Ella?" I looked around, just in case I'd missed her. Vanessa's grip tightened as Sam sighed.

"She's at home. She really wanted to come, but she's not in the right frame of mind today."

"He's trying to say she had another negative pregnancy test. Only he's too douchey to just say that." Vanessa's tone was bitter, enough for me to raise an eyebrow at Sam.

"She's upset, and I'm trying to give her a little space. So we'll drop off Vanessa, drop your gear at home and go out for a drink."

Vanessa's fingernails dug into my skin. She didn't need to say anything further for me to know she wasn't happy. And if I knew Ella, she just needed someone to hold her through the tough times. But I couldn't judge. I'd been gone long enough to know that changes happen, that what was true when I was home before may not hold now I'd returned.

"So what's this?" Vanessa raised her other hand to my face, running her fingers through my beard. Even I had to admit it was impressive, the result of not shaving for several months.

I shrugged. "I was travelling the last six months. Just got easier not to spend money on razors and other unimportant things."

She raised her eyebrows, looking at me like I was crazy. "You need to get rid of it."

"Listen to you, Miss Bossy." Sam laughed.

Vanessa snuggled against my side. "I liked him better the way he was. We need to catch up. I have so much to tell you." She grabbed my arm, squeezing it as we walked.

"I'll look forward to it. Why aren't you coming back to Ella and Sam's place with us?"

She grinned. "I've got a test tomorrow and a whole lot of studying to do. First year medicine at Auckland University."

"Wow, that's so cool. Are you going to be a doctor?"

She nodded. "Made up my mind at the last minute, but yeah. Dad wanted me to become a vet so I could go back home and work, but I couldn't inflict myself on the poor animals."

I roared with laughter. "Good for you. I'm sure you'll be an amazing doctor."

"I hope so."

Vanessa jumped in the back of the car while Sam and I put my bags in the boot. To her obvious disappointment, I sat in the front with Sam, while she pouted behind me.

"The wind will change, and you'll be stuck with that face," I said, looking over my shoulder.

She laughed, turning to look out the window. Sam started the car, backing out of the park and driving into the street.

"Ella will be glad to see you," Sam said. "You know I said she's not having a good day? She's not having a good time in general."

"I'm sorry to hear that." I looked over my shoulder again at Vanessa. Her gaze had shifted back to me, and there was sorrow in her eyes as she nodded slowly.

"Yeah, we saw a doctor and they can't tell us why. We signed up for IVF, but we have to go through all this shit to get to it. It's been a real strain." He took a turn onto the motorway, heading toward the city.

"Sounds like it."

We drove to an apartment block near the university. This must be where Vanessa lived.

"I'll see you tomorrow afternoon if you want to catch up," she said.

"That would be great. I'm in town for a couple of days before I visit Mum and Dad. Good luck with your exam."

She leaned forward between the front seats, pecking me on the cheek. "Thanks. It's good to have you home."

As she leaned back and opened the rear door, Sam turned toward her. "Hey. Where's my kiss?"

"Go get one from my sister. She probably needs it about now." Her tone was clipped

She slammed the door after getting out, Sam visibly recoiling at the sound. What had he done that had upset Vanessa so much?

Douchebag is being douchey.

The words had stuck with me since I saw the message. *Please don't let Sam have hit on Vanessa.* The idea popped into my head, uninvited, unwanted, but it stuck as my best friend indicated and pulled into the traffic.

"I don't know why she wanted to come and pick you up so much when she was going to go home again," he grumbled.

"I dunno—I think it's kind of sweet. She didn't have to take time away from studying to say hello. Anyway, why are we talking about this? How are you doing?"

He flicked a glance at me. "Me or Ella?"

"You."

Sam shrugged. "I don't know. Confused. Tired. I want things to be the way they were before you went away. If I could rewind and erase everything I've done ..."

We stopped at a traffic light, and this time when he looked at me, I saw the pain in his eyes. If he was hurting this bad, I didn't know if I wanted to see Ella. She'd be off the charts.

"I'm sorry to hear that. You two were so happy when I last saw you."

"We're okay, but it's getting a bit too much. One minute she's coping, the next minute she's off the rails. I don't know what is going through her head half the time."

We travelled the rest of the way in silence, along the north-western motorway where I could breathe in the familiar smell of home and see the sights I'd not laid eyes on for so long.

Ella and Sam's little house looked much more lived in than it had when they'd first bought it. Then it had been a shell, waiting for Ella and Sam to put their mark on it. Now it looked like a home.

"Babe, we're home," Sam called as we walked in the front door.

The silence was deafening as we ventured further into the house. I'd lived in the same house with Sam and Ella for two years, and never known it to be quiet. This wasn't right.

We both turned our heads at the same time as a sob broke the quiet. It came from somewhere in the hallway. Sam gritted his teeth in what appeared to be irritation.

She needs help.

"Sorry, man. I thought by the time I got you and came back she'd be okay again."

I closed my eyes at the sound of her weeping. "Sam, I'll go out somewhere and you can take care of Ella."

Sam sighed. "I want to get out of here."

"She's upset. What the hell is wrong with you?" The bile rose in my throat. Regardless of my feelings for Ella, no man should leave his wife so upset. Hearing her utter despair was agonising.

"Nothing. It's another month where nothing happened. She has to let go and see what happens next month."

My head swum as I stared at my best friend.

Sam shrugged and picked up his jacket. "Look, Matt. We deal with it in different ways. Of course I'm upset, but I can't let it control me."

"I can't believe you're leaving to go to the pub. You need to be here with your wife." The anger was building. I fisted my hands in frustration at him. *When did you become such an arsehole?*

"I've been here. I am here. She knows that. Believe me, I'm the last person she wants right now. All we do is argue when she's like this. I'll come home after a few drinks and handle this so much better." He nodded toward the hallway. "She'll be in our bedroom. Go in and say hello, and we'll get out of here."

I nodded, swallowing down my irritation at him, and knocked on the bedroom door. "Ella? Ella, it's Matt. Can I come in?"

"Yes," she said, almost too quiet for me to hear.

I turned the handle and pushed. She sat on the bed, holding tissues over her eyes. My heart lurched at the sight. This was so wrong. If I thought at all that my feelings had lessened, I was proven wrong when I laid eyes on her.

"Hey," I said, tilting my head and smiling at her. She lowered the tissues, her eyes rimmed red, swollen from crying. My chest tightened, and I resisted the urge to grab and hold her.

"Hi."

"I wanted to say hello and make sure you were okay."

She nodded, frowning as she looked away. *Far from okay.*

"I'll be fine, Matt. Thanks for checking on me."

More than your husband is doing.

"Any time. You know I'd do anything for you two."

Slowly, she raised her head again, the tiniest of smiles crossing her face. "Thanks. It's so good to see you."

I sat on the bed, facing her. "Good to see you too. What's all this about?"

"I ... I'm not pregnant."

I'd known the answer; I'd just wanted to make sure it was that and nothing Sam had done. His attitude pissed me off. "Sam told me. I'm so sorry, Ella."

She shrugged. "Guess I should be used to it now."

"You wouldn't be human if you were used to it. You wouldn't be you." I opened my arms and she leaned over to hug me.

"I'm glad you're back. We didn't hear enough from you when you were away. Tell me how your trip went. Did you meet any nice girls?"

"Hundreds." I grinned, kissing the top of her head.

Her shoulders shook as she giggled, and she leaned back, a smile growing on her face. "We've missed you."

"Is that the royal we?"

Her smile grew into a grin. "Okay. *I've* missed you."

"I missed you, too. We'll catch up soon. Sam wants to go out for a drink, but I'll crash here for the night."

She nodded. "The spare room is ready for you. I didn't know Sam was planning to go out." That grin had vanished. Her cheeks were bereft of colour, and her lips in a straight line. This wasn't the same Ella I left behind.

"We don't have to go out. I'm happy to stay right here."

Ella shook her head. "No. You two need time to catch up, too. I'll see you in the morning."

"I don't think we'll be late."

She dropped her gaze. "Yeah, you will be."

My heart ached. Clearly Sam had done this before. She knew the routine, from the look on her face.

"Then we'll catch up tomorrow. I'm not going anywhere for a few days, and then I'll go and see Mum and Dad and come back. I need to find a job."

"Are you back for good?" Her eyes pleaded with me for the right answer.

"Sure am. I've had my adventures, and now I'm home."

The corners of her mouth twitched, and she gave me another small smile, running her fingers through my beard. "I'm glad. This so needs to go."

I laughed, placing my hand on hers. "Vanessa said the same thing. I guess you have similar taste."

Ella rolled her eyes. "Maybe some of the time." Her eyes lit up as she looked me over, and I could see how much she'd missed me. Not helping my situation.

I reached out with my other hand, grasping her shoulder. "Are you going to be okay while we're gone?"

She nodded slowly.

"Do you know what I think?"

"What?" she asked.

"I think you should lie down and get some sleep. You look exhausted. Can't be good for you."

She nodded again, launching herself at me for a hug. "Thank you."

"For what?"

"For checking on me. For caring."

I hugged her tight. "Always. Get some rest."

As I shut the door behind me, Sam grinned. "Ready?"

"I don't know. I feel guilty leaving her here. Are you sure she'll be alright?"

"She needs to calm down and get some rest. She'll be fine in the morning."

Reluctantly, I followed him out the front door, taking one last look toward the bedroom. My skin crawled with discomfort. It wasn't right to leave her in this state, but this was my chance to get to the bottom of what was going on.

"BOURBON AND DRY." Sam tapped his fingers on the bar impatiently as the bartender mixed the drink. When the glass arrived, he took a deep sip and wrapped his fingers around it as he placed it back down.

"You okay?" I'd never seen him drink spirits. Sam had always been a beer man.

Sam shook his head. "This whole baby thing is driving me insane. I don't know how much more I can take. Ella's so damn moody. It's like living on a rollercoaster."

I placed my hand on Sam's shoulder. "What about what it's like for Ella?"

"Oh, I know she's not happy, but then she is. One minute she's up, next minute she's down with this constantly wanting sex to make the baby, not because she wants me. The sex is so mechanical, like we're doing it for only one reason, and I hate it. I hate feeling this way. Every month it gets worse."

He picked at his fingers, his lips twitching. Sam's face contorted in pain, as if he was ready to burst into tears, and my heart broke for him. It wasn't fair that either him or Ella had to go through the agony this was causing.

This whole situation sucked hard.

"You two have come so far. It's hard, but it's worth it, right?"

Sam shrugged. "I don't know what else to do. My dick responds because it's Ella. She's the hottest woman I've ever met. I could be in Antarctica freezing my gonads off and I'd still get hard seeing her naked. And the way she smells. It drives me abso-fucking-lutely wild. I can't get enough of that. But then I remember she only wants it so much to make a baby, and I lose my momentum." He shot a glance at me. "Maybe you should sleep with her. Maybe your swimmers are more powerful than mine."

My mouth went dry at the thought of one night with Ella.

Shit. No.

"Come on, man. You know Ella would never go for it, and shit, this is yours and hers to the end. You'll get there."

"Maybe you're right. I'm so tired and stressed, and you need to come around and spend time with us. Help take the pressure off. Ella loves you."

Platonic love, maybe.

"I love you guys. That's why I want you to get through this in one piece." If I said it enough, maybe one day I would mean it. "Remember all those things about her you loved in the first place and get through it together."

Sam sighed. "Oh, I remember. But back then we were constantly screwing because I wanted inside her, and she wanted it as much. Now all she's interested in is getting my boys to crack an egg."

I shoved his shoulder with mine. "Come on. You know she just wants you both to be happy."

He picked up his drink, cradling it in his hands, staring at the amber liquid. "I don't know what I want anymore."

"But you want her, right?"

Sam took another mouthful, holding the answer back as he took his sweet time swallowing. "I love Ella. I don't know if it's enough. I don't know if I'm enough."

I placed my hand on his shoulder, squeezing it. "She loves you. She always has. This thing has to play out, one way or another. Are you doing IVF?"

He nodded.

"She needs you more than ever right now, Sam."

He frowned. "I hate it when you're right."

"You should be used to it by now." I grinned, and beckoned the barman over. "Can we get a couple of whiskey shots?"

Sam cocked an eyebrow. "You're going to get me into trouble."

"Who, me? I was born trouble."

CHAPTER 17

MATT

I yawned and stretched, opening my eyes and forgetting for a moment where I was. The floral wallpaper and lemon bedspread gave it away.

The unmistakable smell of Ella filled my senses. This whole damn house smelled of her. Sunshine and honey.

My mouth was drier than the desert, the taste of bourbon and dry still hanging around unwanted. It wasn't anywhere near as nice the morning after.

I nestled down into the pillow, breathing in the aroma I'd avoided by leaving the country. Damn it. As hard as it was to be around, there was no way I'd be away from it now.

At a gentle tap at the door, I leaned up on my elbows. "Come in?"

Ella bounced into the room, full of life as always, her long dark hair piled on top of her head in a bun with spirally curls escaping from it. Her makeup was immaculate. I couldn't help but wish that she was about to bounce into bed with me. I'd ruin that makeup in seconds.

"What *are* you doing?" I asked.

"I've cooked breakfast. Sam's still snoring, so I thought I'd see if you wanted something to eat."

I grinned. "I could do with some more sleep. Sam's got the right idea." I dropped down onto my back and pulled the blanket up to my chin.

Ella grabbed hold of the blanket, pulling it back like a Band-Aid. "It's time to get up."

Her eyes widened as she saw me, naked to the waist wearing only a pair of briefs. Briefs that resembled a tent with that early morning wood, no doubt stimulated by her presence. But it wasn't that her gaze was fixed on.

"What's that tattoo?" She'd seen it, the small symbol I'd had engraved in my skin. The result of one drunken night in Amsterdam. My way of showing my love for her in a place barely anyone ever saw. It was on my hip, and sat above the waistband of my underpants. A small yellow and black bee. Somehow, it had seemed appropriate.

Ella leaned over, brushing my stomach with her hand, softly stroking the skin near the tattoo as she looked closer. God damn it, if I was hard before, every sense was now in overload as I could smell her, feel her touch. If she noticed, she gave no indication, and she smiled. "That's so cool. But why a bee?"

She stood straight, her warm hand no longer touching my flesh. She looked at me with such a wide-eyed and innocent expression, a big part of me wanted to pull her down on top of me and defile her.

"I ... it's personal." *It reminds me of you.*

Ella's lips quivered as she seemed to try to hide her disappointment. Did she really want to know that much?

She nodded. "It's okay. You don't have to tell me" She paused. "I thought we were friends."

"Did you really pull out the friendship weapon?"

Ella ran her bottom lip through her teeth in the cutest gesture I'd ever seen from her. If I hadn't known better, I'd think she was flirting.

"Do you really want to know why I have a bee tattooed on me?"

Nodding slowly, she smiled shyly. *Life is so not fair.*

I crooked my index finger beckoning her closer, and she narrowed her eyes but came near.

"Closer," I said.

Now she leaned right over me, our faces inches apart, so I could tell her my secret. But I said nothing, gazed into her eyes and smiled.

"So ..." She sounded unsure, confused.

I pounced, grabbing her by the waist and tickling her, pulling her down onto the bed with me. She shrieked, trying to get away, but I wouldn't let her, my grip on her tightening as she wriggled.

"That's not fair." There were peals of laughter that made me smile. A complete 180 from how she'd been the day before.

It took a moment to realise she was pressed against me, my erection pushing against her legs, and I think I registered it right around the same time as she did.

The giggling stopped, and she panted at the effort of trying to get away from me but stilled.

"Ella." There, I whispered the name of the woman I loved, and this time she was right in front of me.

Ella searched my face for something, maybe a sign that I was still kidding around. The laughter in her eyes drained as she met my gaze and she pulled away from me, rubbing one arm uncomfortably as she backed up.

"Ella?"

"I'm sorry. I shouldn't have asked such a personal question," she said quietly, retreating back into her shell and scuttling from the room.

I buried my head in my hands, sighing at what had happened. Nothing had changed. If anything, my time away had clearly made my feelings for her stronger

I slipped out of bed, pulling my jeans on and grabbing my T-shirt from the floor. They still smelled of the night before, and I wrinkled my nose in disgust. All my clothes were buried in my bags among the gifts I'd brought home, but this'd do until after breakfast. I'd deal with my grumbling stomach first and then shower.

Sighing, I pulled open the door. The house was still, but I could smell pancakes.

This felt like coming home. Going out with Sam the night before hadn't. It was all about him, to get him out of the house and away from his distraught wife. That still grated.

Ella stood at the cooktop as I came in, the pancakes piling up on a plate beside her. She'd gone overboard.

She smiled as I sat at the table.

"Smells amazing." I beamed at her, so grateful to be taken care of when I still felt so seedy.

"I tried to wake up Sam, but he's out to it. So he'll have to miss out."

"Ella, about before ..."

"It's okay. It's good to have you back." She flicked off the element, carrying the plate full of pancakes with her. The table was already laid out with white linen and white plates. Everything was so light and fresh and matching in Ella's world. I felt so gross in comparison, sitting here hungover in my dirty clothing.

"It's good to be back. Sorry if we were out a bit late last night."

She shook her head, picking up a fork and piercing pancakes to move to my plate. "Don't worry about it. It's normal around here."

"He goes out a lot then?" I studied Ella's face. Her focus was entirely on the food, and whatever I did, I couldn't get her to meet my gaze.

"He works hard. We're trying to get ahead. One day we'll be down to one income and we need savings, so he teaches night classes at the high school. You know, adult education classes in computing." She shot a glance at me, long enough to give me a brief smile, and went back to staring at her plate.

"Oh? Good for him."

"I ... well, I wished he didn't. We don't get a lot of time together. How do we make a baby when he's home late and drinking even when he's said he won't, and ..." She looked at me again, this time long enough for me to see the sadness, the despair in her eyes. Whatever was going on between them wasn't good.

I scratched my beard. "I'll get rid of this today." That brought a smile to her face.

I'd do anything for you.

"Morning." Sam appeared in the doorway, dressed in a T-shirt and boxer shorts. He approached the table, pecking Ella on the cheek as he sat next to her.

"Sleep well?" he asked.

"Like a log."

"Did Ella wake you up? She tried hard to get me to move, but I didn't want to. Not until I smelled the food." He turned his head toward her. "Looks amazing, babe."

It was like a transformation came over her. The woman who sat across the table lit up, and she leaned against him as he kissed her temple. This was what she'd wanted. Sam's affection.

Why couldn't he give her what she wanted?

"He's right, Ell. This is amazing." I cut off a piece of pancake, closing my eyes at how good it tasted. She always had been an amazing cook, and this was hitting the spot after a night out on the booze.

"Good for soaking up leftover alcohol." She grinned, the dimples in her cheeks twinkling with the genuine smile on her face.

The love she had for Sam was written all over her, and my heart ached at the way he'd acted the night before.

Alarm bells rang in my head, and I didn't know whether to be wary or embrace them.

CHAPTER 18
SAM

Matt was right. Ella deserved nothing but the best. She deserved a husband who would love and protect her, no matter what. Sam had tried, but at a distance.

There were so many things he'd done during the past few months that he'd deeply regretted. Harsh words he didn't mean. The easy jibes about her diet when she was simply the most beautiful woman he knew. Her curves drove him wild, and yet he'd thrown crap at her when he was down. It wasn't fair

He watched her sleep, her dark hair flowing around her head on the pillow. He'd never loved anyone the way he loved Ella, had never been so obsessed with making another person so happy.

That was why he'd spent every moment he could with her, and why he'd suggested having a baby in the first place. It was the kind of thing that would make her happy.

Instead, it had made her sad.

Sam had never been good when it came to real intimacy. Every month, Ella needed him more and more, and instead of embracing the situation and taking control, he'd backed off, burying himself in work, finding things to do that didn't involve spending time with the woman he loved.

Now, he saw her at peace. Her eyes were puffy from crying, but she was still the most beautiful sight he'd ever seen. Sam smiled, raising his palm to her cheek. Ella stirred, opening her eyes, her lips curling up slightly.

"Hey, beautiful."

She licked her lips. He caught his breath at the simple act. No matter what, everything she did had an immediate effect on him, his body rousing as he gazed at her.

"Hey." Her voice was raspy from sleep, and probably from crying. He hadn't been there to see it, but it was obvious from her appearance.

Sam ran his thumb down her cheek. Her skin was flawless, soft and warm, and she closed her eyes to his touch. He appeared to have the same effect on her as she did him.

"Damn it, Ella, you're beautiful," he whispered.

She opened her eyes, gazing at him with the deep blue he'd fallen into so many times before. It seemed like forever since she'd looked at him that way.

"Sam."

He didn't give her a chance to say anything else as his mouth claimed hers and he kissed the lips he loved tasting. It had been so long since he'd kissed her this way, like a man not only in love with his wife, but in lust. Where had that gone?

From that first night, when they'd tangled for four rounds, neither of them could keep their hands off one another. Somewhere, that had gone by the wayside. The sex was still there, but there was no passion, only the never-ending hope for Ella that she'd become pregnant.

How quickly it had all gone downhill.

Now he kissed her like a man possessed, and he cupped one breast in his hand, running his thumb over the nipple, leaving her gasping at the contact.

"Where is this coming from?" she asked. He didn't know the answer, just that he'd had enough of things being the way they were. Maybe it was partly guilt from neglecting her, and burying himself in other things to take away the pain of what seemed to be their relationship dying.

From the way her body reacted to his touch, nothing was dying here.

"I've missed you." He meant the words, no matter how corny they sounded.

"I've missed you, too." She ran her hand down his back, the joy in her eyes unmistakable. This was what his lady needed.

He kissed her again, long and deep, as he dropped his hand to pull up the hem of her nightgown. Ella moaned as he touched her, stroking her clit with his fingers, her eyes rolling back in her head at the first orgasm he'd given her in, well, he couldn't remember how long.

This was how she deserved to be treated.

Maybe his idea from the other night wasn't that bad. Matt could help them out.

"We could invite Matt for a threesome," he whispered.

Her mouth fell open in horror, pain taking over her eyes in a way he'd never seen. She froze, her eyes wide.

"What are you talking about?"

"It might be one way to make a baby, and if we end up with a sperm donor, I can't imagine anyone we'd want more."

Her eyes pleaded with him, but he meant every word. If Matt could help them achieve this where Sam had failed, it was worth it.

"But I want *your* baby," she said.

"I know. But if you can't have my baby, Matt would be every bit as good. I'm sure he'd say yes, Ella."

"Why do you always have to ruin everything?" she whispered, tears rolling down her cheeks. "This was the most amazing night in ages, but you dragged it somewhere it shouldn't ever go. I love you; I want you. Matt means to the world to me, but not like you. You're my husband."

Sam lost the ability to speak. He'd tried to do what he'd thought was the right thing, hurting her all over again.

She rolled over, turning her back on him. This was it. Either go back to square one or make the effort.

"I love you so much, Ella. I want to give you what you want, but it's not working. I want you to be happy again."

Ella rolled back to look at him. "I want to be happy again, but it's so hard. It doesn't help when you come up with ideas like that when things seem good between us."

"I'm sorry." He nuzzled her cheek, pulling her close.

"I'm sorry, too. I know this whole thing has driven me a little nutty, but we'll get there."

He swallowed, hard. "Yeah. I'm sure we will."

She wrapped her arm around his waist, snuggling in against him. He'd done it, broken the moment between them with his silly musings. He was sure Matt would have been eager to join Ella in bed. Who wouldn't? She was the most beautiful woman he'd ever known, inside and out.

But once again, Sam had screwed up everything.

CHAPTER 19
MATT

It hadn't taken long to find a job and a flat. My work experience overseas left me in good stead back in Auckland, and I landed a job with a software development company making apps.

I lived not far from Sam and Ella, which was good in some ways, but not in others. Vanessa's messages still haunted me, and the way she'd begged me to come home for her sister. I watched from a distance.

I'd been back a month when Sam invited me over for dinner. I hadn't seen either of them since those first few days I'd been back, I'd used work as an excuse to stay away.

This time though, I thought it might be good to check in and see them. Maybe if I kept my distance but still kept in touch it'd make it easier to get over it all.

I was due at their place at five-thirty, when Ella came home, but the guys at work were having a boozy late lunch, and I bailed instead. I could always wait outside their place.

Her car was in the driveway, and I parked outside, puzzled at its presence. She hadn't called to change plans, so assuming she'd finished work early, I headed to the front door.

I knocked, looking around at the garden. It had flourished while

I'd been away, Ella taking it from basic to blooming with colour. She seemed to have the magic touch with everything, whether it be plants or people. A woman of many talents.

I turned at the sound of the door opening. My smile drained from my face as I looked at those bloodshot raw eyes. She was always one to wear her heart on her sleeve, but I'd never seen her quite so forlorn.

Every month it gets worse.

Sam's words echoed in my head, but now I saw it for myself. Ella was heartbroken, as she had been last month, and the month before no doubt.

All the time I was away, I'd had no idea things were this bad. My chest ached at how alone she must feel. Sam would still be at work, but after his previous response to her tears it didn't take much to work out Sam still wouldn't be here for her.

"Hey," I said softly.

"Hi. Sorry, I must look a sight."

My eyes searched hers for some sign of spirit, that twinkle. It was nowhere to be seen. "You look amazing, as always. What's going on?"

She flapped her arms as she turned and walked back into the living room, sitting on the couch. "Same old story. Another month where I'm not pregnant."

I followed, sitting beside her, scrutinising her as she sniffed, a screwed up tissue between her fingers. Judging by the pile on the other end of the couch, she'd been here a while.

"Tell me what's going on. Don't you start your treatment soon?"

She nodded. "We're booked in, but I hoped in the meantime ..." She trailed off, staring at the tissue.

"Where's Sam?"

"Working." She checked her watch. "He'll be home in about an hour."

I closed my eyes. Surely he must know. Was he that out of touch, or did he not care?

"Why are you putting yourself through this, Ella? Is this for you, or is it something you're trying to do to please Sam?" I opened my eyes, fixing my gaze on her, frustrated by her anguish, torn by her pain.

"What do you mean?" she asked the question with her eyes so full of confusion.

I took a breath, working out how the hell to word this without upsetting her more. "One of the things I truly love about you is how much you try to take care of everyone. Including me. You're a people pleaser. And that's not a bad thing at all. I think it's wonderful. But are you driving yourself this crazy over something *you* wanted?"

Understanding registered on her face, and Ella dropped her gaze. She didn't need to reply for me to know the answer.

"So you're turning yourself in knots in an attempt to make him happy."

"He suggested it, but I want it, Matt. I want it more than anything."

I raised my hand to touch her face, the contact I'd vowed to stay away from. But she was right there, and she needed me, needed a friend.

"I know you do, but this is eating you alive," I whispered.

With my thumb, I wiped the tears rolling down her face as she blinked, her lips parting and then closing as if she struggled to find anything to say. Eighteen months I'd stayed away, distancing myself from the feelings I had for her, and now they punched me in the gut as we gazed at one another. I didn't want to simply love her anymore —I needed to love and protect her.

All I wanted right now was to take her in my arms and kiss her. Kiss the tears away, kiss the pain away, and take every little bit of hurt from her eyes. Instead I held her tight, wrapping my arms around her as she cried on my shoulder.

I stroked her hair, burying my face in it, breathing Ella in.

I love you.

I didn't dare say the words. She'd run a mile. No matter how hurt she was, no matter how indifferent Sam could be, she was so fiercely loyal. By confessing my love, all I would do was drive her away. That was the last thing I wanted.

"Sam even suggested ..." She trailed off, as if lost in thought.

"Suggested what?"

Ella's eyes darted from side to side. Her cheeks blazed red. She did that thing where she sucked her bottom lip through her teeth, like she was holding something back.

"I thought we were going to be okay. Sam was so affectionate. And then he suggested that ..." She stopped again, dropping her gaze, closing her eyes. "He said we could invite you for a threesome, that maybe you could father our child."

Desire coursed through my veins at the thought of being with Ella with no guilt. But that didn't work for me—it had to be all or nothing. I would never be able to walk away from her.

"What did you say?" I had to know.

"I shouldn't even be telling you this, but I don't know who else I can talk to. Vanessa would freak. I know he said it with the best of intentions, but it hurt that he threw it out there."

I ran a finger down her cheek, tilting her chin so she couldn't look away again. "He's about as subtle as a brick sometimes."

Her eyes searched mine, and I was lost as we sat so close, looking at one another.

"Ella," I said softly.

"Don't." One word was all she whispered. At least some of the feelings I had for her were reflected in her eyes. Ella was always such an open book, and right now I could see all the way into her heart.

I didn't stop myself, I couldn't, despite my vow to stay away, and I bent my head, kissing her softly at first. Her shoulders slumped as she sank into it, kissing me as I ran my hands down her back. This was wrong, so wrong, but it felt more right than anything had in forever.

"Ella," I said again as we broke apart.

"We can't do this," she whispered.

"I can't help the way I feel about you."

Tears welled in her eyes again. She opened her mouth as if to speak, but no words came out. There was only one thing left for me to say, despite my misgivings.

"I love you."

She blinked back her tears, letting out a squeak as she took in what I'd said. The torment in her eyes was unbearable, but my relief from finally saying the words to her face was indescribable.

"Matt." Her pained tone told me everything. She couldn't say the words back, couldn't think it, but somewhere in her heart was a space for me. More than there should be.

"You don't have to say anything more. I can see it in your face. Another time, another place, and all of this could have been different. I'm not stupid; I know you love Sam more than anything. I hope you have the baby you want, and you're happy for the rest of your lives together."

She leaned in to me, and I closed my eyes as her tears wet my shoulder. Maybe this was what she needed—a literal shoulder to cry on. I hadn't meant to pour all that out on her, but everything was so screwed up already. How long had Sam brushed off her despair for? He loved her, that much was true, but when had his breaking point been? He glossed over the sadness that now filled his wife.

All I knew was that I wanted to hold her in my arms for the rest of my days.

I wasn't back to where I'd started.

I was much, much deeper.

SAM WAS due home around six, and I'd volunteered to help Ella. Normally, she would have refused, running around after the two of us and making sure everything was to her perfect standards.

Maybe it was because she was so down, but she'd accepted, and I stood at the kitchen bench, peeling potatoes.

"Ella, about before ..." I said, tipping the chopping board up to drop the potatoes into the steamer.

"Don't worry about it."

"I don't want it to screw things up between us."

She sighed, wiping the bench down with a clean sponge. "Everything's so screwed up right now. I just want things to be the way they used to be."

"I know."

Ella walked away, back into the living room, and I followed her, watching as she picked up the discarded tissues. She'd stopped crying, but her eyes were so tired. She looked up at the clock. It was now a little after six, and she frowned.

"We might as well eat. I'm not sure what time Sam will be home," she said.

"He can't be that far away."

She gathered the remaining tissues and walked back into the kitchen, dropping them into the rubbish bin. I fished my mobile out of my pocket and dialled Sam.

It rang a couple of times before going to voicemail.

"I'll just get us some food, Matt. He can have his whenever he gets home." Her tone was flat, disappointed, but she was calm, as if she'd accepted this a hundred times before.

"He knows I'm coming for dinner, doesn't he?"

"I told him. Maybe he forgot." She shrugged, turning to the oven. I grabbed the dinner plates out of the cupboard they lived in, and placing three on the bench, I smiled as she lifted the roasting dish with the crumbed chicken pieces out.

"That smells amazing. I miss your cooking."

She shrugged. "It's nothing special."

"Everything you do is special."

The words were out of my mouth before I could stop them. I hadn't meant to say anything to make her uncomfortable. She was, I could see it, as her eyes widened for a moment before she turned her head away from me.

"You can't say things like that," she said.

She worked in silence, placing the chicken, potatoes and peas on the plates, handing me one without a word.

I trailed behind her, back to the dining table. The quiet was unnerving in a house that used to have a lot of noise and laughter.

This was my fault. I never should have said the words, never should have told her what was in my heart.

A few minutes passed, but it seemed like an eternity in the silence. Ella jumped as the front door opened, Sam shoving it shut behind him.

"Hey, babe. Matt, what are you doing here?"

He drew closer to the table, leaning over Ella to kiss her cheek. She screwed up her face, turning her head away. The overpowering smell of beer filled my nostrils.

"You two invited me for dinner. Remember?"

He frowned, his eyebrows dipping as he obviously tried to rack his brain. "Oh. Sorry. I went for a couple of drinks after work. What's for dinner?"

"Crumbed chicken," Ella said flatly.

"Nice." He stood there, looking at her plate until she rolled her eyes.

"I'll go and get you some. Sit down." She picked up her plate as she stood, taking it back to the kitchen.

"Ella makes the most amazing fried chicken. She just needs to stop eating it." Sam slurred the words, and sat beside me with a stupid grin on his face. He wasn't just drunk; he was toasted.

"I'm glad she didn't hear that," I grumbled.

He shrugged. "I can't give her what she needs. It's not like she really wants me that much anymore."

"Stop being a dick." I glared at him, shoving his arm to wake him as his eyes fought to go to sleep. "Did you drive home like this?"

"I got a taxi. I'm not *that* stupid."

"Stop acting like it, then."

Ella returned, placing Sam's dinner plate in front of him. He grinned at her, still fighting his eyelids. "Thanks, babe."

She sat next to him, watching as he fumbled with the knife and fork, checking him over. I'd seen him drunk, but this was ridiculous. What on earth had he been thinking?

A few mouthfuls, and he was nearly asleep in his food. "Want to go to bed?" Ella stroked his hair.

"I thought you'd never ask." He laughed, resting his head on her arm and locking his gaze on me. "Didn't I tell you that I have the perfect girl?"

He lurched forward, and I caught him before he fell from his chair. "Whoops."

"Come on, mate. I think it's time to get you to your bed." I stood, pulling him up with me and looping my arm around his waist to keep him upright. I took a few steps, dragging him with me into the hallway and toward his room.

"No offence, but I don't want to go to bed with you." He laughed, trying to steady himself and failing as I dropped him in the doorway and onto his bed.

"Feeling's mutual. Get some sleep."

He fell asleep almost as soon as he hit the bed, at some awkward angle. I shook my head as I closed the door behind me. He'd regret that in the morning.

Ella stood out in the hallway, her arms crossed defensively, her brow furrowed in concern.

"He's sleeping sideways in your bed. I don't know if there's room for you."

She nodded. "It's okay. I'll sleep in the spare room. Thanks for helping him."

"All the time I've known him, I've never seen him that drunk."

Ella shrugged. "I know he goes for a drink sometimes after class. Never in the day time and never that bad. I don't know what's going on with him."

She led me to the front door, looking at her feet as I turned to say goodbye.

"Sorry dinner was so awful," she said.

"Dinner was fine. I'm sorry things got so heavy."

She met my eyes, sucking me in with the sadness in hers. This was a woman who seemed to be fighting to keep her head above water, only to be dragged back under by everything going on around her.

"Have a good night's sleep. Give me a call if you or Sam need anything else."

"Thank you."

For a moment we just stood there. I had no idea what to say, and I guess she didn't either. So I nodded, turning back toward the car and walking away.

She stood in the doorway, watching me until I pulled out into the road and drove away.

All I could do was give them space.

CHAPTER 20

ELLA

lla yawned. It had to be the longest day ever, and all she could think about was going home to snuggle into bed and sleep. With Sam would be nice, too, but there was no point holding her breath over that.

The more strained things were between them, the more time he poured into his work. He hadn't repeated his drunken arrival home, and he'd put it down to going out with his co-workers to say goodbye to one of them. Maybe it was time to admit defeat. Time to heal the wounds in their marriage and change things to be the way they used to be.

When they were friends as well as lovers.

Not that long ago, they would laugh together, often falling into bed, unable to keep their hands off one another. As Ella closed her eyes, memories of all those happy times overwhelmed her.

"Are you okay, Ella? You look like shit."

Trust Holly to notice. She and Ella had bonded the instant Ella had started working with her. They'd had very little in common, at least at first. Holly was a single mother with a young daughter. She understood Ella's need to have a baby. But did Ella really look that bad?

"Feeling a bit off today. Really tired. I think I'm coming down with something."

"Do you start IVF soon?"

Ella sighed. "There's still so much to do before we get to that stage. My parents said they'd pay if we wanted to go private though; that'd speed things up."

"You don't sound very excited."

She shrugged. "I think I know better than to get my hopes up now. I haven't told Sam yet, but I don't think I can take more than one go. Maybe it's time to admit defeat if it doesn't work."

Ella shuffled the papers on her desk, flicking through what was left to do for the morning. She'd been working as a business analyst with the same company she'd worked for since she'd left uni, and was currently assigned to a large IT project. One that had far too much paperwork.

"How long have you had that coffee on your desk, Holly? It stinks to high heaven. Enough to make me want to puke."

Holly cocked an eyebrow. "I bought it this morning. Are you sure you're not pregnant?"

Ella leaned back, rolling her eyes. "Positive."

"That was the first thing that went when I was pregnant with Lexie. My ex switched to tea, because the smell of coffee made me want to hurl."

Ella stared at her. *I can't get my hopes up.*

"Maybe I'm just off colour."

Holly's lips curled into a sneaky smile. "Maybe you should try a pregnancy test."

Tears pricked Ella's eyes. "I'm not pregnant, Holly. I'm never pregnant."

"You're tired, and feeling gross. I know how hard you're trying, Ella, and I don't want to upset you, but what if you are and you don't realise?"

Ella was late. But she was always late, her body on this big hormonal rollercoaster. It didn't seem to know what late was anymore.

"It's only a suggestion. I'm sorry if it upsets you." Holly moved around her desk, slipping her arm around her friend, hugging her tightly. "I know you, and this isn't normal. There's something going on."

Ella shrugged. "I think I might stop trying to be honest. I want a baby so much, but I don't know how much more Sam and I can take."

"Does he still have that gorgeous friend?" Holly cocked her head.

"Matt?" Ella swallowed down her guilt at the memory of his kiss. She hadn't initiated it, but it burned on her lips as a reminder. "Why? Do you want me to hook you up?" The thought of him being with someone else made her sick to her stomach, but at the same time he had to move on.

Holly laughed. "No. But you said that when he went away, Sam changed. Just a little, but he changed. Maybe you need to get them together a bit more."

Ella nodded. "Anything to get Sam away from that damn night school. I swear, he's teaching so many classes; he'll exhaust himself."

Holly squeezed her arm. "There you go. Invite Matt over more often. Like the old days."

The old days. When the three of them were always together, always laughing.

When did the fun go out of our lives?

"And seriously, Ella, get a pregnancy test."

Ella bit down on her bottom lip. "I've got some in my bag."

"Some?" Holly's right eyebrow inched up.

"The doctor gave us a whole pile of them last time. Rather than me wasting money at the pharmacy. I've got some of those little pee-on-a-stick ones."

Holly grinned. "Then go and do it. If it's a no, you can come drinking with me after work. If it's a yes, then you go home and celebrate with your man."

Ella nodded. With heartbreak after heartbreak, it surely couldn't get any worse. She reached down for her bag sitting beside her desk, clinging to it as she stood and made her way toward the bathroom. Really, what was the worst thing that could happen? If it was negative, again, she'd get on with her day. Although, going home to sleep was mighty tempting either way.

The bathroom was empty, and Ella headed straight for the cubicle right at the end. The one with the dodgy lock on the door that no one ever used. She'd be tucked out of the way in a place where no one would ever look.

She took a deep breath, reaching into her bag and pulling out the little box the doctor had given her. Inside were maybe thirty sealed strips. This box had gone everywhere with Ella—a pregnancy test had never been far from her side in the past year. If she gave up the dream, it would be weird not to carry it around.

Hanging her bag on the hook at the back of the door, she pushed down her panties, tearing open the packaging and holding the test under her. She closed her eyes, some tiny part of her begging for those two little lines to appear. Not the one that had been on every other test. The single line was the one that broke your heart.

Ella pulled it back out, placing it on a wad of toilet paper she'd collected with her other hand. She gazed at the ceiling, trying so hard not to stare at the test, convinced it would never change if she so much as took a peek.

The silence in the bathroom was comforting. The only person she had to deal with was herself and how she'd handle the inevitable disappointment this would bring. And yet, there was a tiny glimmer of hope she was too soft-hearted to let go of. And that hope sat in her hands, on the tissue, waiting for her to look at it.

One, two, three ... Ella counted in her head, resisting the urge to peek. The longer she waited, the more the anticipation built, the harder to deal with the gut-wrenching negative result.

She closed her eyes, taking two deep breaths and took a chance.

Two lines. Prickly heat travelled the length of Ella's body as she looked back down at the test. All these months of trying so hard, of arguing with Sam, of mood swings that were so un-Ella like. She hadn't felt like herself in so very long, and now tears flooded her eyes at the sight of those two little lines she'd waited nearly two years to see.

She swallowed, shaking her head and wiping the test off, placing it on the top of the bin beside the toilet. Dropping the tissue into the toilet, she stood, pulling her bag down off the door and taking another test out of that damn box.

That one had two lines too. And so did the next. Ella couldn't see for tears anymore, but had six beautiful lines that told her that after all this time and effort, she was pregnant.

"Ella?" Holly's voice came from outside the cubicle. Ella grabbed another piece of tissue, wiping her tears as she opened the door.

"Ella, you've been gone for ages. I wanted to make sure you're okay." Holly frowned, and she pursed her lips at sight of Ella wiping her eyes. "Oh, sweetheart."

"I'm pregnant, Holly," Ella whispered, barely able to believe the words herself, let alone tell anyone. But she couldn't keep it secret, couldn't pretend it was anything else but the thing she'd longed for more than any other in the world.

Holly's eyes widened, and she ran the short distance to cover the gap between them, flinging her arms around Ella's neck.

"I KNEW IT."

"Shhh." Ella laughed, shaking her head.

"Congratulations. Oh, honey, I am so pleased for you. After everything. Sam will be over the moon too."

A grin took over Ella's face, and she sighed contentedly, squeezing Holly back. "I know he will. Finally, maybe everything can fall into place and we can get back to normal. Whatever that is."

"Yeah, until you stop being able to get any sleep at night."

That would be different; having her baby in her arms would make up for any loss of sleep.

Sam was supposed to be home for dinner, at least. She could tell him before they ate and invite Matt over so he could hear the happy news from the two of them.

She let go of Holly. "I need to organise dinner."

"You should go home now."

Ella grinned. "I would, but Sam won't be home until at least five. I want to tell him to his face."

"Congratulations, lady. You deserve it."

With a warm glow in her heart, Ella made her way through the office and back to her desk, picking up the phone as she sat. She dialled Sam first, getting his voicemail, which wasn't unexpected. He'd be in the middle of class.

"Hey, babe. I wanted to make sure you were going to be home for dinner. Love you, bye."

Next, she dialled Matt.

"Hey, Ella." His warm, happy tone came down the phone. It was as if their last encounter hadn't happened.

"Matt. You need to come for dinner tonight." If anyone was going to celebrate with them, it'd have to be Matt.

"What's going on?" he asked.

"You'll find out when you get there." Ella tried to hide the excitement in her voice. It would be easy to spill the beans, scream the news to the world, but Sam had to be next.

"What time?"

"Six-thirty."

"Fine. I'll be there. You've got me curious, Mrs Mason."

Ella laughed. "See you then."

She took a deep breath as she hung up the phone. How on earth she would keep a lid on this until she went home was beyond her, but this was something she had to say to Sam's face, to see the joy in his eyes at their success. All the weight that had been sitting on Ella's shoulders lifted as she smiled to herself.

The hours ticked by until it was time to go home, and Ella bolted at the first opportunity, her insides twisting with excitement. After all this time, what would Sam say? He'd be over the moon, as she was, and maybe, just maybe he'd spend more time at home with her as they entered a new stage of their life together.

As she sat in the hideous Auckland traffic, she daydreamed about his expression and how now they would have everything they'd ever wanted. It didn't matter if they didn't have any more. Sam would adore the child he asked for, and Ella would love and nurture them both for the rest of her life.

This would fix all the bad in their relationship, and her misery at his frequent absences. They would be happy and stronger than ever before.

She grinned at the sight of Sam's car in the driveway, and clambered from the driver's seat, eager to get inside the house and scream her news from the rooftops.

Sam sat on the couch, leaning forward slightly, his head in his hands like he was tired.

Poor thing. He works so hard.

"Hey, babe," she said brightly.

He raised his head, his eyebrows knitted together as if he was worried about something.

"Sam, I have something to tell you."

He pulled at his tie, loosening it and nodding as he took a deep breath. "Ella, I have something to tell you. Can I go first?" He sounded so serious.

She frowned. What could it be? Tension rolled through her, and she stiffened at his serious tone. Had he lost his job as they were about to start their family? That could screw so many things up.

"Sure."

He took her hands in his and pulled her down to sit on the couch with him, never meeting her eyes, looking down at his fingers entwined with hers the whole time.

Oh, God, what's happened?

Sam swallowed hard, his Adam's apple bobbing as he finally raised his face to look at her, stress etched across his face. Whatever this was, it wasn't pleasant.

Please don't let him have lost his job. Not now.

"It's like this, Ell. I love you—I mean, I really love you. Have since that first day we were together. But this whole baby-making thing has driven me insane. It's been so hard to live like this, with you so stressed over not being able to conceive and not knowing why. I felt like we were having sex to make a baby, not having as much fun with one another anymore."

Tears formed, stinging her eyes. What was he trying to say?

"Sam, I need to tell you ..."

"I don't even know how to say this, but there's someone else."

Ella's world collapsed with the words, blood rushing in her ears as she struggled to keep looking at him for a sign that this was some kind of sick joke. That was what her heart wanted. Her head told her he was serious.

"What do you mean, someone else?" she whispered.

"Do you remember Petra?"

"That student that showed up here? Are you for real?"

"She's not a student anymore. Hasn't been for some time."

Ella pulled her hands away. Her palm stung as she slapped Sam across the face, and he grabbed her hand to stop her from doing it again. Matt might have kissed her twice, but she hadn't initiated it, nor would she ever have slept with him or anyone else behind Sam's back.

"Ella, it was bound to happen. Our relationship was under so much strain, and we tried so hard, baby. We really did."

She bit back the tears, fighting them as she shook her head. "No. I tried. You gave up."

"She's pregnant."

A sick feeling in her gut grew, and she wheezed as she took a deep breath, fighting the urge to start crying.

"You fucking bastard."

A small *V* formed between Sam's eyes as he stared at her. Ella never swore; this was something new for her. She'd never felt strongly about anything enough to say the word that usually made her cringe.

"Ella ..."

"What do you want me to say, Sam? I did everything you wanted. Always."

He nodded. "I know, and I'm so grateful to you for it all. There was something missing in our relationship."

She fought harder, determined not to cry. "The only thing missing in our relationship was you."

Shaking with anger, she pulled away, scooting to the other end of the couch. Anything to put distance between them.

"I'm sorry."

"I can't even process this."

"She was there for me, Ella, and she wanted me. You were so hard to live with, and I couldn't cope with it. We had amazing moments, but it's been so difficult going through this."

Ella bit down on her fist. "I was right here, and *I* wanted you." She let out a sob, and he reached for her other hand. Angrily, she snatched it away, glaring at him.

He nodded. "I'll get out of here."

Sam stood, making his way to the door where she now saw his suitcase. Right beside the doorway—he was packed and ready to go. She'd walked straight past it without noticing, so entangled in her thoughts, her dreams of making him happy. Of making them *both* happy.

"I'll be in touch. There'll be things we need to sort out. You can keep the house. It's more yours than mine."

Ella fixed him with a steely gaze. "That reflects the effort *I* put into our marriage." She refused to cry, clamping her lips together and breathing heavily.

"Yeah, it probably does." He shrugged. "Goodbye, Ella."

And like that he was gone, the door closing behind him. Ella let out a sob, her lungs letting go of the air that had been trapped inside for what felt like forever.

Sam.

CHAPTER 21

MATT

I pulled up outside the house, puzzled at the lack of light coming from it. And yet, Ella's car sat in the driveway. Maybe they'd gone out in Sam's car.

So much for my dinner invite.

I'd been to this house hundreds of times, and it wasn't like Ella to forget. We'd only spoken about dinner a few hours ago, and she'd been so excited about something. I'd spent the afternoon debating whether or not to call her back and ask her if she was pregnant, but if it wasn't that, all I'd do was upset her. That was how happy she'd sounded.

I stepped out of the car, walking around and onto the footpath. Something just didn't seem right. The hairs on the back of my neck stood to attention as I approached the house. Call it intuition, but I wasn't about to get back into my car.

The living room curtains weren't drawn, and I tried to peek in the window but couldn't see a thing in the darkness that surrounded me. I moved to my right, to the door, and knocked, just in case.

Uneasy about just leaving, I waited for a while, looking around to see if anything was strange or out of place. Nothing stood out, and I pulled my mobile out of my pocket and dialled Ella.

Her phone was inside. The *Thunderbirds* theme played in the house, somewhere in the living room. Now I was on high alert. She never went anywhere without that damn phone.

"Ella," I called. Damn it. Why hadn't I taken that spare key when they'd offered?

Because you didn't trust yourself to stay away from her.

I knocked on the door again. "Ella?"

My phone still in hand, I dialled Sam and it went straight to voicemail.

Damn it.

I redialled Ella. This time, the ring cut off and went to voicemail. The door clicked as it opened, and in the shadow I could just make out Ella standing inside.

"Hey. Are you okay?"

"I'm sorry, Matt. Dinner is off." Her voice was low and calm, not that of the usual bubbly, happy woman I knew.

"I don't care about dinner. I want to know what's going on."

"I can't talk to you right now," she whispered. "I'm sorry."

The door creaked as it closed, and I planted my foot to wedge it open.

"Matt, please." Her voice cracked as she pleaded with me. I wasn't about to leave. Not until I saw her face and found out what was going on.

"Where's Sam? Is he home?"

At that, she sniffed, letting out a sob, and she pushed harder at the door.

"I'm not letting you shut me out. You're worrying the crap out of me now. Let me in. Tell me what's happening."

She let go of the door, turning back inside, and I followed her in, flicking on the lamp just inside the living room.

Soft light flooded the room. She sat on the couch, her shoulders slumped, and she looked at the floor, avoiding my eyes.

Something was wrong, really wrong, and I knelt in front of her, listening to the sound of her gasping.

"Ella," I said softly.

Reluctantly she raised her head, and my heart pounded as I looked at her. This was even worse than the previous times I'd seen her upset. Her usually rosy cheeks were devoid of all colour. She looked empty, like she'd lost every part of herself and was just a hollow shell.

If Sam had done this to her, he was no longer any friend of mine.

I didn't know what to say. I took her chin in my hand and raised her face to meet mine while I took a closer look. She closed her eyes and I let go, wrapping my arms around her, wanting to protect her and shut out whatever horrible thing had upset her. Ella was truly broken.

She stiffened at first before relaxing into my embrace, crying on my shoulder. The warm tears ran down the back of my shirt, but it didn't matter. She needed me.

"I need to know what's wrong," I whispered.

She shook her head violently, pulling away from me and curling into a foetal position on the couch.

"How can I help fix what's wrong if you don't tell me?"

"You can't fix it. No one can." A hiccup came from her as she spoke, still talking through the tears. "I need you to leave."

"Like hell I will. I'm not leaving you in this state. Where's Sam?"

"Gone," she whispered.

"Gone where?" This was driving me insane. I had no intention of leaving the house yet.

She swallowed hard and took a deep breath. "He's gone, Matt. He's left me."

Lost for words, I stared for a moment. Sam had left her? That made no sense. Sure, he'd been cranky over this infertility thing, but he loved her. They loved one another.

"Are you sure?"

Ella sucked in her lower lip, and I gripped her arm in the hope that it would steady her, give her the strength to tell me the whole story.

"He's with someone else now."

I stood and moved to sit on the couch beside her. She shrugged, and I pulled her into my arms and just held her again, rocking her as she cried. This was unbelievable.

If I understood what she was saying, he'd given it all up for what? Ella adored him, would have done anything for him, and had driven herself crazy trying for a baby all because he thought it was the right time.

"I'm pregnant, Matt." Her eyes filled with tears. As they rolled down her cheeks, I raised my hand and wiped the drops with my thumb.

"Does he know?" I asked, even more incredulous that Sam had done this.

Ella shook her head. "I didn't get as far as telling him. He was too busy telling me that he was having a baby with some other woman."

"He *what*?" I continued to stare as she nodded. He'd complained about how obsessed Ella had been about conceiving, but I'd never thought for a moment that he'd screw around behind her back.

"I'm so sorry, Ella."

"You don't have to stay. He's your friend. You should see him, find out for yourself what he's up to."

I growled. "If I saw him now, I'd only do something I'd regret. I just can't believe it. Never in a million years did I think he'd do that to you. I had no idea."

"He hasn't said anything to you?"

I shook my head. "No. I know he was going a little nuts with the infertility stuff, but you both were. I really thought you'd come through it together." I kissed her forehead, and she snuggled into my chest, her breathing slowing as she calmed.

"I'm not going anywhere." I squeezed her gently.

"What am I going to do?"

"Let me make you something to eat; maybe you could have a shower or bath to relax, and then I'll tuck you in to bed. You look exhausted, and that can't be good for you or the baby."

Her head moved against my chest as she nodded. "What would I do without you?"

I stared out the window into the darkness outside. "You will never, ever need to find that out."

We sat for what felt like forever, Ella still and silent except for the occasional deep breath. At least I'd stopped her from weeping, and it seemed as if I'd calmed her.

Another time, other circumstances, and I would have been over the moon to hold her. But my anger bubbled away, and I had to fight it from coming to the surface. Not until I was face to face with Sam.

"I'll make us something to eat. Okay?"

She nodded, squeezing me tight before letting go, looking up at me with those big, sad eyes. "Thank you," she whispered. "Thank you for taking care of me."

"You don't need to thank me. How could I be anywhere else but here?"

She sighed. "I feel awful. Here you are, invited for what should have been a wonderful, happy evening, and you get this."

I reached for her face, tilting her chin up to look her in the eyes. "I'm where I need to be." *Where I always wanted to be.*

"I'll go and see what's in the kitchen and make us some dinner. Something with cheese?"

Her lips twitched as she seemed to fight a smile. "Sounds good."

I kissed her on the nose and stood. As much to get away as anything. Her being so close brought so much temptation despite knowing what she was going through. This wasn't the time to act badly and make any kind of move. But being close to her had also dissipated the anger, at least for the moment.

Sam Mason could go to hell.

It didn't matter that I'd known him since kindergarten. That we'd played sport together, got our first girlfriends at the same time, been joined at the hip. Like brothers. All this time, I'd felt like I'd betrayed that closeness with the feelings I'd had for Ella.

Now Sam had hurt us both.

Even in talking to me about the bad times, he'd never mentioned anyone else. There had been no hint that he was screwing around, nothing to indicate that he wanted anyone but Ella. Even if they were having a rough time of it.

He'd lied to me.

I found bread in the kitchen, bread and a block of cheese. Soon the kitchen filled with the smell of grilled cheese sandwiches. They were quick and easy, and when we were finished, I'd run a bath for Ella so she could soak and cry some more if she needed. Anything to help ease the pain.

I couldn't imagine what she was going through. Finally her dream came true, only for her world to come crashing down around her.

When I closed my eyes, I saw their wedding, saw the love on both of their faces, saw the flickers of lust in Sam's eyes. I'd envied him so much that day, but I had no feeling for him now.

I carried two plates out to the living room. Ella sat, leaning against the arm of the couch, all her energy drained. I'd never seen her so deflated.

"I made these. Hope you like them."

She peeked between the pieces of bread and smiled. "These are such great comfort food."

"And they'll help line your stomach if you're hungry. Which I'd imagine you are, given that it's dinnertime and you're eating for two now."

The smile grew a little. "I can't believe I'm pregnant. After all this time." Her eyes grew sad, and I knew she was thinking of Sam.

"I'm sorry, Ella."

"It's not your fault."

"I know, but I still feel guilty. Maybe if I'd been here, I could have seen what was happening, stopped Sam from doing this."

She took the tiniest bite of her sandwich, closing her eyes as she chewed. She was so full of pain and holding it together because I was here, holding her hand and supporting her through what was probably the best and worst day of her life. My chest ached at the thought of just how heartbroken she must be.

"He said I could keep the house. I don't think he's interested in anything we ever had."

He just told me how much he loved you. What is wrong with him?

"This house is you. It always has been. You moved in and it became so Ella-like; I doubt he wants to take that from you."

She nodded. "I don't know if I can stay here, though. Not like this."

I reached out, resting my hand on hers. "Give it some time. Don't make every decision today."

"What do I do?"

I smiled. "Eat your sandwich."

Again, the tiny smile crossed her lips. "Yes, boss."

She closed her eyes again as she ate and sighed. This wasn't the night either of us had planned, but this was what we'd been left to deal with.

When we'd both eaten, I took the plates away and slotted them in the dishwasher. Standing in the doorway, I smiled at her. "I'll go and sort out this bath for you."

"Thanks, Matt."

I left the kitchen and turned right for the bathroom, just off the hallway leading to the bedrooms. The bathtub was huge and would take a while to fill. I smiled at the memory of Ella telling me this was one of the things she loved about this house. The house she'd bought with the man she thought she'd spend her life with.

It didn't matter what I tried to fill my thoughts with—what Sam had done kept hitting me straight between the eyes.

In the vanity unit, I found a big bottle of bubble bath, and as I turned the taps, I poured in a good measure to make it soft and bubbly. The more I could do to relax Ella, the better. The last thing she needed was the stress.

The scent of honey rose from the bath, and I smiled, realising at least one of the reasons why Ella smelled the way she did. Soon the room was full of that scent. I'd done the right thing; surrounding her with the familiar might just help.

I sat beside the bath, running my fingers through the water, making sure it was the right temperature, and losing myself in thought over what had just happened.

I'd gone into automatic pilot, taking care of her, but at the base of it all, what the hell was Sam doing? We'd talked, and he was going to make things up with her. I couldn't get my head around it all.

How could you do this?

It was weird. We were so similar and yet so different, but we'd always been honest with one another. At least, until Ella came on the scene. Then I'd covered up my feelings for his sake. What a joke. Maybe I should have put it all out there, told her how I felt right at the start. If she'd chosen Sam, I'd have lived with it, and now I wouldn't be hurting so much.

But she would.

Here I was again, feeling torn, but in no doubt this time what the right thing was to do. Ella needed me, and maybe she only wanted my friendship, but at least I had her in my life and I could take care of her. The way she needed.

The bath was filled to halfway, and I twisted the taps to see if I could get any more out of them. Water sprayed from the cold tap, and I laughed out loud as it hit me, springing back and away as it settled.

"What on earth are you doing?" Ella's voice came from the door, her eyes growing wide as she took in the sight of me.

"I thought I'd have a wet T-shirt competition for one?" I shrugged, leaning over to twist the taps shut. "That cold tap of yours is possessed."

She laughed. "There's always been something not quite right about it. I guess you've only ever encountered my non-haunted shower."

"I'll get out of here. Your bath is ready."

As we passed in the doorway, she grabbed my hand. "If you want a fresh shirt, Sam's got plenty in the bedroom." Her expression dropped. "At least, he did. I'm not sure what's in there now."

"I'll be fine. I'll take it off and hang it over the heater. I'm sure you'll be okay if I burn a little electricity. It's a bit chilly anyway." I smiled.

"I hadn't noticed. Thanks for taking care of me." Her eyes spoke of her gratitude, and I nodded.

"Any time. I would hug you, but I'm a bit wet."

"As if it makes a difference; I'm about to get a lot wet." Her mouth fell open as she said the words, clearly realising the double meaning as I suppressed a smirk. "Get out of here. You're not supposed to make me laugh."

I placed my hand on my heart. "My life's not worth living if you're not smiling, Ella."

She rolled her eyes, pushing me out the door. "Go and dry off."

I swivelled my hips as she closed it. "What? You don't want me to dance it dry?"

Flicking the oil column heater on in the living room, I slipped off my T-shirt and draped it over the top. It wouldn't take long to dry once the heater warmed up.

Venturing back up the hallway and into their bedroom, I opened one of Sam's drawers. The emptiness of it was the same as the feeling through the house. This wasn't Sam's house anymore, even if a lot of his things were still scattered around.

I picked up one of their wedding photos sitting on the top of the chest. "Screw you," I muttered, closing the drawer and placing the photo back.

As I passed the bathroom, Ella's sobs echoed down the hall. I couldn't go in, that wouldn't be right, but I put my hand to the door. "Ella," I whispered.

It killed me to hear her, crying in the quiet.

"Ella," I said again, this time so she would hear me.

"I'm okay," she said in a voice that was clearly not okay.

I sank to the floor against the door, closing my eyes as she continued to sob. Resting my head against the door, it was all I could do to stop bursting through it, but she needed to get this out, and I needed to give her space.

Absorbed in the sound, I lost track of time, steadying myself on the floor a while later when she opened the door.

"Matt?" Her eyes were rimmed red, swollen, and any happiness I'd glimpsed before she got in the bath was long gone.

I pulled myself to my feet. "Hey," I said.

She had a faraway look, as her eyes glazed over. "The bath was a bit hot. I feel …" Her knees buckled, and I caught her before she hit the ground.

She was limp, like a ragdoll, and I scooped her up, carrying her into the bedroom and placing her on the bed. I'd fantasised of doing this, but in my dream we were in love and about to become one. All those soppy romantic thoughts I'd saved for her.

Instead, she whimpered as I pulled the blankets over her, making sure she was covered. I knelt beside the bed to stroke her temple.

"Don't go," she whispered.

"I'm not going anywhere. Not while you need me."

Tears streamed down her face again, and my heart broke at the sight of her so forlorn.

"Stay with me, at least until I go to sleep?" Her eyebrows dipped as she pleaded with her eyes. So afraid to be alone, but having lost the one person in her life who should be here with her.

"Ella, I …"

"Please, Matt."

I exhaled, slowly nodding, and climbed on the bed beside her, Ella under the covers, me on top. As chaste as I could make it.

Lowering my arm over her, careful not to touch her in any way that might scare the crap out of her, I felt like I could breathe again as she wriggled back against me.

"Thank you." Her voice was so small, so un-Ella like.

"Any time." That long curly hair was right in front of me, and in spite of myself, I buried my nose in it, breathing in that pomegranate shampoo smell, overindulging.

I love you.

Now was not the time to go anywhere near that. I could weep for what she must have been going through. What on earth was Sam thinking? Not only sleeping with another woman, when he had the perfect one at home, but leaving her? Ella worshipped the ground he walked on, and even if she was remotely attracted to me, it didn't detract from the love she bore him. She had committed to being with him for the rest of their lives.

I couldn't get my head around him sleeping with another woman, let alone having a child with her.

"Matt?" Her voice was so small and childlike, the simple act of her saying my name nearly broke my heart.

"Yes?"

She rolled over to face me. I'd never seen her looking so sad. Not Ella.

"I'm glad you're here."

I lifted my hand to her face, pushing back the lock of dark hair that fell over her temple.

"So am I. I've got something I need to take care of once you're asleep, but I'll come back afterward if you want me to."

She nodded. "Only if it's not a bother."

She was always thinking of other people's feelings, even at her worst. "You're never a bother. Do you still keep the spare key hanging in the kitchen?"

Ella nodded again. "The green key tag."

"I'll grab that so you don't have to get out of bed again. I'll crash in the spare room. If you're lucky I'll make you breakfast."

The tiniest of smiles crept across her face. "You? Make breakfast?"

"Get used to being pampered for a while. I'll be here to take care of you. If you want me to."

Her lower lip wobbled.

"Don't cry, Ella. It'll get better. I promise," I whispered. There wasn't much else I could say. How could it get any worse? "Close your eyes." I stroked her hair and she complied, taking deep breaths.

I watched as she fell asleep, the deep breaths giving in to longer, slower ones.

Now to find Sam.

CHAPTER 22

MATT

I plucked the key from inside the pantry, where it sat buried with glue and tape and other random junk. Picking up my phone, I dialled Sam, and it went straight through to voicemail.

Damn it.

My shirt was dry, and I pulled it on, reaching for the switch on the heater. *No. I'll leave it in case Ella gets out of bed.*

I didn't know where to go, but I walked out to my beat-up Mazda anyway, climbing into the driver's seat and starting it up.

I sat for a moment. What I needed was to clear my mind and drive around for a while to sort out my thoughts. My head was a mess of Sam and Ella and the baby, not to mention me.

Pulling into the street, I drove around the block at first, and then went a little farther. I put the window down to let the cool night air flow through the car, breathing deep to try to calm myself.

I pressed the call button again.

This time, it rang, and Sam answered the phone, and I swallowed down the urge to scream at him for what he'd done.

"Where are you?" I asked.

He mumbled a nearby address, his voice echoing through the

Bluetooth, and I turned the car around, the wheels squealing on the smooth asphalt.

Take a deep breath.

The longer I drove, the greater my anger. I gripped the steering wheel tight at the thought of the woman I'd left behind, sleeping in the bed she'd shared with her husband. My former best friend.

I drove around the streets. At times it seemed as if I was going in circles as I struggled to find the place. I was distracted by my building annoyance, with Ella's tears so fresh in my mind.

Finally finding the right road, I slowed as I drew closer, peering out the window at the letterboxes, looking for numbers to guide me.

I spotted it. The letterbox with the fading number, barely visible in the dark. The fence beside it was overgrown with vines. A little more growth and no one would ever work out what number this place was.

Pulling over, I opened the door and stepped out into the street.

I stood outside the rundown old house. If it weren't for his car parked in the driveway, I would have thought it deserted.

Knocking on the dirty old wooden door, I waited for a moment before Sam opened it, and I had to stop myself from punching that smug look off his face. The one I'd seen before.

"Hey, Matt."

"What do you think you're doing?" I hated him for leaving her as much as I loved her.

"I guess you've spoken to Ella. I was going to call you and let you know."

I shook my head in frustration, resisting the urge to smack him in the mouth. "She invited me to dinner."

His lips turned into a frown. "It's not what it seems."

"Tell me if I have any of this wrong. You ask your wife to have a baby. When it gets too hard and all she wants to do is make you happy, you screw around and leave her. Do I have it right?"

The silence was uncomfortable as we stared at one another. "I couldn't take it anymore."

That was all he said.

"I thought you were going to make things right. I thought that was what we talked about."

Sam swallowed hard. "It's not that I don't love her, Matt. Come on."

"But you're happy to leave her alone at home, devastated. At least I could be there for her, but I shouldn't have needed to be. You're her husband, Sam." I bit down the temptation to tell him about Ella's pregnancy. That was her news, not mine, no matter how much it might hurt him now he'd made his choice.

I scraped my palms with my fingernails, resisting the urge to fist my hands. "What do you think you're doing?"

He grabbed my arm, a look of desperation in his eye. "You know how I feel about Ella, but I needed more. I needed to feel wanted again. It was *once*, and then Petra tells me she's pregnant. What was I supposed to do?"

My breathing sped up as I looked at him.

"You weren't supposed to get involved with anyone else. Even once is one time too many. You were wanted. *Are* wanted. Ella loves you more than anything, man. How could you do this to her?"

A woman appeared behind him. This must be the one he'd left Ella for. She was young, maybe around the same age as Vanessa, and about the complete opposite of Ella. Tall and thin with blonde hair, she eyed me up at a distance.

"Matt, this is Petra."

"No disrespect, but I don't give a fuck who she is."

Sam's face distorted in agony, and Petra recoiled. "You can't treat her like that."

I'd had enough. "Really? You cheat on your wife, my friend, and you want me to accept this?"

"Dude, we've known one another all our lives. You can't let a woman come between us. And you can't blame Petra."

My blood boiled, the fists trying so hard to form. "She's not *just* a woman. It's Ella." I glared at him. "I don't blame Petra. I blame you."

I turned, walking away rather than making things worse. Screw him.

"Maybe you'll do a better job with her than I did."

I closed my eyes at his words. How long had he known I was in love with her? Had he walked away knowing I'd be there to pick up the pieces? Him knowing didn't matter anymore.

"Maybe I will."

I walked the short distance to my car. As I reached the door, I looked back. Sam stood in the doorway, Petra wrapped around him, but there was no joy in his eyes, only sadness.

What an idiot.

I started the car, sighing as I buckled my seatbelt. What the hell had happened? Whatever it was, I wanted nothing more to do with him.

My phone buzzed, and I picked it up before taking off. Ella had clearly woken up.

Thank you.

I smiled. At least she had me. I had no idea how she would have coped with no support. When she was at her most vulnerable, the man who was supposed to take care of her had walked.

You're welcome. I'm on my way back. Want me to pick up anything on the way?

Chocolate? I'll be okay. I wanted to say thanks.

Oh no, lady, you're not pushing me away that easily.

Chocolate it is. And I'm hungry again. Might stop off at KFC and be back soon.

Hahaha you're always hungry

At least she was laughing, even if it was only via text. I put the car into gear, indicating and moving out into the street, driving away from Sam, the man I'd known from childhood, the man I'd always shared everything with. *Never again.*

After all this upheaval, when she was on solid ground again, if Ella would have me, I'd be hers. I'd always felt bad about wanting my best friend's girl, but after the way he had treated her, I no longer cared.

Now I got to take my time, give her the romance she needed, and support her through her pregnancy. Nothing else mattered but her.

I drove to Westgate. It was between Ella's place and where Sam was, and I could get both chocolate and KFC there.

People milled around me as they did their evening shopping, but all I could think about was Ella. Ella, who made me laugh, Ella, who made me cry, Ella, who had me twisted around her little finger from the moment we met. It didn't matter who I was with or, where I was—everything always came back to her.

Now I was free to revel in it.

I grabbed a trolley at the supermarket, buying grapes, her favourite fruit. I swung past the deli to pick up some smoked salmon. We both shared a love of that. Sam had never been keen on fish, or any other seafood for that matter, and we had often grossed him out gorging on the stuff.

I found the chocolate she liked, Cadbury Dairy Milk. Throwing two big blocks of it in the trolley, I made my way toward the checkout.

Only one line was open, and I waited in the queue, tapping my foot impatiently. My phone buzzed in my pocket again, and I smiled. I'd bet anything it was Ella telling me to hurry up.

Instead, it was Vanessa. She had gone home for the holidays at the end of the semester.

I'm trying to get hold of Ella. She's not answering. Is she okay?

I guessed she either hadn't got an answer out of Sam either, or had assumed I would know. It sucked that she was back on the farm and not here; the more support we could give Ella the better.

After paying, I threw the shopping bags in the car, climbing into the driver's seat. The KFC drive-through was nearby, and I dialled Vanessa before starting the car and put the speaker on Bluetooth.

"Matt."

"Hey, Ness. I thought it was easier to call you instead of text."

"Is Ella okay? It's not like her to not answer. Her phone is never far from her."

I took a deep breath. "I need you to promise me that you'll keep this to yourself. No telling your parents until Ella's ready."

I had to pull the phone away from my ear; her squeal was so loud.

"She's pregnant, isn't she?"

Shit.

"There are a couple of things you need to know."

"Is she pregnant? Please tell me."

I closed my eyes, swallowing hard, knowing that her happy, excited tone was about to disappear. "It's not that simple."

"Are you two finally a thing? Did she dump Douchebag?"

Oh, Vanessa.

"No. I don't even know where to begin, but Sam dumped her."

"What?" she screamed down the phone.

Good one. Your parents will be curious if you made that much noise.

"Shhh. Sam left her. Which is why you can't get hold of her. She's shut up at home. I'm grabbing some junk food and going back to her."

She sniffed. Vanessa had as big a heart as Ella did. Even if she didn't like Sam, she'd take this hard.

"She's pregnant, and he doesn't know. And you have to keep all of this quiet and act like you don't know when she tells you."

"I'm glad you're with her," she whispered.

"I'll take care of her for as long as she needs it. You know that."

On the other end of the line, she took a deep breath. "I know she's in good hands. I was calling to let her know I'd be back in town next week."

"I'll let her know. Maybe she'll call you."

"Thanks, Matt. You know, it's weird. You went away not long after we met, but you feel more like part of my family than *he* ever did."

My heart caught in my throat. I'd felt that, denied it, and thought I was imagining it. "I love you guys, that's why. Don't worry about Ella; she's in good hands."

Vanessa laughed. "Those hands I always wanted on me?"

I rolled my eyes. "Some things never change."

"That's why you love me. Call me if Ella needs *anything*."

"Will do. Bye."

I started the car, pulling out of the car park and onto the road. A quick trip to pick up the chicken, and I'd be on my way home to Ella.

Home.

I couldn't start thinking of it that way. Hell, I'd never been more certain of my feelings, but who was to say how she would ever feel about me.

That all had to go on the backburner, to be resolved another day. Right now, I had a friend in pain. One who needed me.

It took half an hour to get through the damn queue, and my stomach grumbled, as if reminding me to feed it. By the time I pulled up outside Ella's place, it wouldn't stop.

She was wrapped in her bathrobe, sitting on the couch when I walked in the door, and she gave me a small smile as I placed the food on the coffee table.

"Chicken?" I walked toward the kitchen, and she grabbed my arm as I went past.

"Thank you for coming back."

"There's nowhere else I'd rather be."

Her smile grew a little as she let me go, and I brought back two plates and cutlery for us to eat. "Hungry?"

She nodded. The toasted sandwich wouldn't have gone very far as a dinner meal.

"Where did you go?" Her voice shook. She knew me well enough to know the answer.

"I went to see Sam."

She clutched my arm as I sat back down. "You didn't do anything stupid, did you?"

"If you're asking if I hit him, the answer's no. Not that I didn't want to. I wanted to talk to him, see what he had to say."

"And?"

"He's an idiot."

Ella leaned against me, resting her head on my shoulder. "I'm sorry for coming between you. I never wanted it to be like this."

I sighed, shaking my head. "It's not your fault—only his."

She lifted her head, her blue eyes boring through me. "I'm sorry that he let you down too. He loves you. He hated you being away."

I nodded. "I know. Hell, I tried to run away from my feelings for you because I love him. Sam's like a brother to me, and the last thing I wanted to do was to hurt him. But he wronged you, and I'll never forgive him for that."

"You're a good friend." Her lips had a smile on them, but her eyes were sad.

I love you.

"I don't like the way he treated you." I picked up a plate. "Let's eat before this goes cold."

All I wanted to do was to take her in my arms and kiss the pain away, but she had to move on from today for that to happen.

At least she had me.

CHAPTER 23

MATT

The first few days were the hardest. The following day was Friday, and Ella called work to tell them she was sick. The truth was, she couldn't face the world, and I couldn't blame her.

Almost immediately, her mobile rang, and she held it up to me. "It's Holly. Can you get it?"

"Who's Holly?"

"My friend from work. She knows I'm pregnant, doesn't know the rest. I don't know if I can talk to her." Tears built again, and I took the phone from Ella's hand, pressing the *accept* button before it went to voicemail.

"Hi Holly."

Stunned silence greeted me. "Hello?" I said.

"Uh hi. Is this Sam?"

"No, it's Matt. Sam's … Ella's friend."

"Oh. Is Ella there?"

I caught Ella's eye. Her chest heaved as she fought back the tears.

"She is, but she's not able to come to the phone."

"Is she okay?"

I touched Ella's arm. "She'll be fine. I'm staying here for a few days to take care of her."

"Why? Where's Sam?" Damn it. Why couldn't she leave things be? If I could have brushed her off, then Ella could have caught her up when she saw her next. When she was better prepared to deal with this.

I put my hand over the phone. "She's asking why I'm here and why Sam's not. Do you want to talk to her?"

Ella shook her head. "I don't know if I can say it."

"Want me to tell her what's going on?"

She nodded. "She'll only worry."

"Hey Holly, sorry, I had to check in with Ella. Um, Sam left her last night."

I held the phone away from my head as an ear-piercing shriek came from it.

"Shit. Sorry. I guess that's why I'm talking to you and not her."

"She's upset, but I'm here."

"Damn it." I didn't know Holly, but it was clear she cared about Ella. I squeezed Ella's bicep, winking at her.

"I'll look after her, Holly. Promise."

She sighed. "Well, tell her that I'm thinking about her, and to give me a call when she feels like it."

"I will."

When I hung up the phone, I pulled Ella into my arms, kissing the top of her head. She leaned into me, resting her cheek on my chest, and I rocked her. "She cares."

"I know," she said, her voice so small.

By Sunday, we needed milk and bread, and I went down the road to the supermarket. I returned to find Ella standing in the backyard, wisps of smoke floating up from the wheelie bin she used for rubbish.

"What the hell are you doing?" I picked up the garden hose as a flame flared out the top of the plastic bin. The top edge of the bin was a little saggy looking from the heat.

"I burned the bed sheets." She sounded flat, uninterested. I doused the small fire with the hose, shaking my head.

"You could have thrown them out. Would have been less mess." I grinned.

"I have to go and see a doctor."

"What? Are you feeling okay?"

Her gaze met mine, her eyes so sad. "I have to get tested for STIs. We were having unprotected sex trying to get pregnant. What if it wasn't only this other woman? What if there were more? What if that woman has some hideous disease?"

"Oh, sweetheart. Sam wouldn't ..." I stopped myself. Up until three days before, I would never have thought he would leave her.

I don't know what he's capable of.

I nodded. "Want me to take you?"

"I'll be fine. I'll go tomorrow." It seemed the simple act of burning the sheets had given her strength to draw on. "You don't have to stay either. I really appreciate you being here, but I need to work through all this."

"Ella, I ..."

"I need to do this for myself. Please don't think I've forgotten how you say you feel. That's always at the back of my mind." Her lips curled up into a little smile. "There's so much to process, so many things to think about."

"And I'll be here whenever you need me."

"I know." She placed her hand on my chest. "There's a big part of me that wants to say 'to hell with him' and move on with you if you want me. But it's been three days and the last thing I want to do is kill our friendship by rebounding. If I hurt you in all of this, it would kill me."

Tears rolled down her cheeks.

"Call me when you need me," I whispered.

She nodded, and I kissed her lips with more tenderness than I could bear.

And then I walked away from the woman I loved, trying to get her head around everything that had happened. All I wanted was to turn around, take her in my arms, and tell her I didn't care if she rebounded with me. I already knew I wanted to spend the rest of my life with her.

But she had to be ready to take that step.

PART IV

You are the only one I want

CHAPTER 24
MATT

She's broken, and there's nothing more that I can say or do to fix what my best friend has done to her.

I can't find any way to pick up the pieces. There's one thing left to do.

Let her go.

I ran. The heavy rain soaked me in minutes, but I kept running, trying to tire myself out. Trying not to think about her. I ran until I couldn't breathe, bending to cope with the pain in my chest, not from the exercise, but from the act of walking away.

My hands on my knees, I raised my face to the rain, letting it cool me, but nothing made me feel any better. I'd taken the biggest risk of my life, and now I had to wait it out and hope she'd come to me.

It had been three months since we stood in her back yard, and there had been no calls, no texts. She hadn't posted on Facebook, so it wasn't only me she hid from. Ella had gone to ground, and I couldn't blame her. She not only had herself to look after, but the baby. I could weep at what she must be going through.

Vanessa didn't let up. Without fail, at least once a day I'd get a text or a Facebook message from her, wanting to have coffee. Maybe it was selfish, but I couldn't face her. She'd held so much hope that I'd waltz in and pick up all the pieces, but the pieces had to be ready to be picked up.

Despite her maturing while I was gone, Vanessa didn't understand how everything she wanted didn't simply fall into place. Ella had to want it, and I had to be patient while she worked out everything at her own pace.

Staying away was hard, and even though I still stood in the pouring rain, looking at the sky with the overwhelming urge to run to her place, no matter how far away it was, I couldn't.

One thing had benefitted from me trying to find distraction: my career. To fill the gap that now existed in my life, I'd thrown myself into my work, taking on every little project I could find. My manager fretted that I'd burn myself out, but I thrived on the long hours.

I started running again, heading back to the office to shower and change. It was a little after one o'clock now. Around five I'd head home and spend the evening tapping out code while watching TV and drinking beer. Cooking for one was easy, but after running in the rain I figured a warm night in with pizza sounded good.

Returning to the building, I headed up in the elevator. As I walked through reception, Carrie, the new receptionist, eyed me.

"I hope you're not dripping water everywhere."

I shrugged. "The rain stopped on the way back; I dried enough, I think. If not, I'll bring the towel back out after my shower and clean up after me." I shot her that flirty grin, making the young blonde blush and look away.

"Is there anyone you don't flirt with?" A familiar voice made me turn to the right. Vanessa sat on a couch, her arms and legs crossed, with one eyebrow raised as if she was telling me off.

"What are you doing here?"

"You don't answer my calls, my texts, or my messages. What's a girl supposed to do?" She gave me that look, the one she shared with Ella, which immediately filled me with guilt. So sad and confused.

"I've been busy. Let me shower and warm up, and I'll make a coffee if you want one."

I'd never seen her look quite so smug. "Sounds good."

"Back in a few." I got to my desk and grabbed my bag. *Maybe I should get out of here, now. I'm sure I can slip out the back door.* No. Vanessa hadn't done anything wrong; I just didn't want to deal with her interrogation. No matter what happened, it'd be good for us to at least stay friends.

The shower at work was crap, and I'd be lucky to get more than a couple of minutes of hot water before it decided I wanted to freeze. I made the most of it, getting as much time as I could, washing down quickly before drying myself off and pulling on my shirt and pants.

Dropping my bag back behind the desk, I turned left and headed to the kitchen. Carrie stood at the fridge, a bottle of milk in her hand. It looked like she was after coffee, too.

"Can you leave that out, please?" I asked.

She smiled, opening the bottle and tipping some into her cup. "So, that girl out there. Is that your girlfriend?"

I shook my head, meeting her eye. "Oh. *Oh.* Oh, no, she … well … it's a long story."

"I'd like to hear it sometime." She stirred her coffee with the spoon before licking it clean, sucking the metal through her lips.

This was unexpected. That was what I get for flirting.

"I'm in love with her sister."

Carrie dropped the spoon, twisting her mouth and rolling her eyes. "So, she's your girlfriend's sister?"

I plucked two mugs from the cupboard and, taking a spoon from the drawer, added coffee and sugar to the cups. Picking up the milk bottle, I poured a little into each before adding the water.

"Not my girlfriend. That's the 'long story' bit."

"But you love her?"

I grinned, couldn't help it. The thought of Ella still did that to me. "More than anything."

Maybe that was a dramatic thing to say, but that was how I felt. She filled my heart with so much love and joy, even when she wasn't a part of my life.

"That's cool. Good for you." Carrie grinned. "If you ever want to talk, you know where to find me."

She turned, walking out as I picked up the cups and followed. I nodded at Vanessa, indicating for her to follow me, and we went out the back and into an office that had been claimed as an unofficial lunchroom.

It was empty. This place had a fairly casual way of doing business. A lot of the coders worked from home, coming into the office when we had project meetings. I preferred coming into the office most of the time. With those who occupied desks around me not there, it was quiet, and I found it easier to concentrate than I did being at home. Here, there were no distractions.

I put the drinks on the coffee table, sitting on a couch. Vanessa sat beside me, looking around the bare room.

"So this is your work?"

"It is."

"Why aren't you talking to me?" She fixed her hazel eyes on me, and she was hurting. I could see it.

"I'm sorry. I'm not ignoring you. Not in a mean way. I don't know what to say to you right now."

She frowned. "I want you and Ella to sort things out and be together. I know you both want to."

There it was. That glimmer of hope. The one I didn't need, the one I'd hidden from.

"Is that really what Ella wants?" There. I'd asked the question.

Vanessa licked her lips, as if she was thinking about what to say. "She has asked me if I've heard from you. She misses you. You should call her."

"I told her to call me when she was ready. She knows where I am. I'm not going anywhere."

Vanessa nodded. "She's so sad. I hate seeing her this way. I think she feels like she's lost both of you."

I picked up the coffee and took a sip. After being drenched in the cold rain, this was so good, warming me up, and I closed my eyes as I swallowed.

"You still love her, right?" Vanessa's voice was tiny, and I opened my eyes to see her clutching her coffee cup, pleading with her eyes.

"I can't stop thinking about her. I haven't stopped since the day we met."

Tears welled in her eyes, and I smiled, reaching over with my thumbs and wiping them away before they rolled down her face.

"I don't know what's going to happen, but you can believe this. I will always be there for Ella in whatever capacity she needs me. And I'll always be there for you. You're not too bad, squirt."

She grinned, rolling her eyes. "Are you ever going to stop calling me that?"

I put the coffee cup down, taking hers and placing it beside mine on the table. Wrapping my arms around her shoulders, I hugged her tight.

"Never."

I let go of her. Her eyes looked happier now we'd talked. "You interested in pizza for dinner? I'm going home at five and have some work to do this evening, but I was going to order pizza for dinner and sit in front of the television."

She nodded. "Sounds good."

"I'm not working on anything urgent. Maybe we can watch a movie or something."

Vanessa pulled me closer, hugging me again. "That sounds good, big bro."

She kissed me on the cheek, and damn it, I fought back tears as she walked away. She was always so warm and welcoming, just like her older sister. Vanessa deserved only the very best.

If I'd ever had a sister of my own, I would have wanted one like Ness.

CHAPTER 25

ELLA

Vanessa squeezed Ella's hand. "I can't wait to see this baby of yours. Do you think they'll be able to tell us what the sex is?"

Ella shrugged. "Hopefully."

Her sister leaned over, her face inches from Ella's bump. "You need to co-operate. Do you hear? Your auntie wants to know what you are."

She sat up, a satisfied grin on her face. "That should do it."

Ella laughed, rolling her eyes. "You are going to be one bossy aunt."

"He or she is going to love me." Vanessa poked her tongue out. "I don't care what it is, as long as it's healthy."

"I'm supposed to be the one who says that."

"Ella Mason?" A woman in a white coat stood at the entrance to the reception area. Ella smiled, standing, and pulled Vanessa to her feet.

"This way please." Ella followed down a corridor that led to a dark room. She took a deep breath as she saw the ultrasound machine. This was it.

"I'm Lisa," the woman said. "Shall we have a look at that baby of yours?"

Ella grinned, her stomach twisting with excitement.

"If you'd like to get up into the chair, we'll get started."

Ella lay back in the seat, Lisa covering her legs with a sheet. "If you could pull your clothing up so we can get a look? The sheet's just to cover you up."

Ella nodded, raising the sheet to cover her underwear as she pulled up her dress exposing her belly.

Vanessa sat beside her, grabbing Ella's hand in hers. Ella would be eternally grateful for the support of her sister through all of this, glad she was living in the same city now.

"This is going to be a bit cold." Lisa held the bottle of gel above Ella's stomach. She gasped as the cold gel hit her skin, laughing as Vanessa squeezed her hand.

The transducer spread the gel out as the technician slid it across Ella. She grinned, looking up at the screen, when the picture changed, and there was her baby. Breathing, kicking, its little heart beating visible on the screen.

"Hello," she whispered.

"Oh my God, Ella. Your baby looks huge. What is it?" Vanessa asked.

"Ness, let the lady do her job."

With a flurry of clicks and measurements, Lisa labelled pictures of the baby's organs while Ella watched, entranced. Another few months, and her baby would be there.

"Ella." Vanessa nudged her, and she turned to see Vanessa nodding toward Lisa.

"Did you what to know what you're having?" Lisa directed the question to Ella.

"Yes," Vanessa said.

Ella laughed. "Yes, I do."

In a blur the images changed, and a few screens later, Lisa paused the picture.

"To me, that looks like you're having a boy."

Ella swallowed, her heart racing. A little boy. She couldn't wait to hold her son in her arms and love him.

"He looks pretty good considering he's half douche."

Ella elbowed Vanessa in annoyance, even though her heart sang at the sight of her baby.

"Must be the cool Ella part shining through." Vanessa rested her head on Ella's arm.

"I'm glad you're here to see him," Ella said, blinking back tears.

"Me too."

IN THE EVENING, still excited about her earlier ultrasound, Ella had arranged to meet Sam at his place. Her lawyer had prepared all the paperwork for who would get what. Sam had barely anything but his car and his personal belongings. He'd left Ella with the house and everything else inside.

Ella bit down on her bottom lip. Now or never.

Gathering all her courage, she knocked on the door. When Sam opened, all those old feelings came flooding back.

"Ella. It's good to see you. You're looking good."

If he noticed she wasn't wearing her usual tighter-fitting clothing, he didn't say a word. Ella had deliberately worn a long, flowing dress in case her small eighteen-week bump showed.

She nodded. "Thank you. So are you."

Sam held the door, ushering her in.

The living room was tiny, and the other woman sat on the couch, clutching at her small belly, meeting Ella's eye as if meeting a challenge.

She looked so young that Ella's heart went out to her, but a pain began in her gut when she remembered this was the girl—no, the woman—who had slept with her husband, knowing he was married.

"This is Petra."

"I know." Ella nodded, her eyes narrowing as the young woman smiled.

Sam frowned. "Of course you do."

"There are some things we need to talk about," Ella said, turning back toward Sam.

"I agree. You have the papers for the asset splitting?"

She took a deep breath, pulling them from her bag. "I do. Sam, there's something else …"

He took the papers, moving toward the couch and sitting beside Petra. Petra snuggled up to him, wrapping her hands around his arms as if claiming him. As if Ella needed any reminder he wasn't hers.

Sam cast an eye down the paper. "It looks okay, but I'll have to sit down and go through it properly."

"We will," Petra said, with a smug smile.

God. I want to punch her.

"Sam, I …"

"I guess you're with Matt now. Good on you. He always did hang around you like a dog on heat."

Take a deep breath. Then give them a surprise.

"At least he knows what he's getting. I guess with Petra being pregnant, we know why we never stood a chance."

Ella's heart fell at the words he thought were painful. *Screw him.* Her bump would stay secret. Sam wasn't stupid. One day he'd find out and maybe even put the dates together, but Ella no longer wanted him as the father of her child.

When it came down to it, Ella was alone.

"Everything is in there; you just need to sign," Ella whispered.

He flicked through the papers, as Petra hovered. No doubt she wanted him to sign. She looked up at Ella. "Leave them with us."

What the hell does it have to do with you? Ella held it in, glaring at Petra. Sam was completely oblivious to the tension.

"Give them to your lawyer, *Sam.* I'm sure he'll know what to do."

She turned to face the door. The sooner she was out of this place, the better. It didn't even compare to the cosy little house her and Sam had together. Wallpaper peeled off the walls. It felt damp, and not looked after.

"I'll walk you out, Ell."

She looked back over her shoulder to see Petra staring daggers at her.

Sam escorted Ella out the door, down the path, and to her car door. "Hey. I'm sorry how things turned out."

"So am I," she said.

He looked back over his shoulder, toward Petra, standing in the doorway. "You know, maybe it doesn't have to be the end. We could still see one another from time to time. I mean, when we weren't trying to make a baby, the sex was pretty good."

Ella clamped her lips together, taking deep breaths. "You *still* want to have sex with me?" She said each word slowly, deliberately, loudly.

Sam cringed, backing away from the car. She watched as he scuttled back toward Petra, who stood there, her arms crossed. Smiling, Ella opened the door to her car, settled into the driver's seat, buckled her seatbelt and drove into the night.

Back to her empty, lonely house. The house that no longer reminded her of *him*.

I miss you, Matt.

The house was dark, and Ella flicked on the living room light as she entered. This was her house, through and through, from the dainty floral wallpaper, to the curtains. There was nothing about this place that reminded her of him, nothing physical. There were memories of happier times, but those were in the past now.

If this house was to be full of love and laughter again, Ella had to do something about it.

Maybe I should ask Vanessa to move in. Ella smiled at the thought of her sister coming to live with her. Not little miss independence. Vanessa had been itching to leave home since she was seven, when she put her backpack on and headed down the long gravel driveway leading out from the house to the road. Their father had given her a five-minute head start to let her think she was getting away before going after her.

At sixteen, Ella had rolled her eyes and laughed at her sister's attempt to attain freedom. Now she understood that need more than anything. She needed to get away.

She'd saved up her annual leave at work, and she had a little money tucked away her parents had given her. Maybe it was time for a break, time to finally clear her mind before coming back to wait for her baby's birth and start a new life.

Maybe Matt would start that life with her.

CHAPTER 26
MATT

I spotted Vanessa from across the food court. She was the one with the smile a mile wide, waving frantically at me.

"Hey, squirt," I said, bending over to kiss the top of her head before sitting beside her. I swiped a fry from her tray as I placed mine down on the table.

She looked out from under her eyelashes at me. "I thought we'd agreed you wouldn't call me that anymore."

I grinned. "I didn't agree to anything."

Vanessa rolled her eyes and picked her burger up, taking a big bite out of it. She closed her eyes, moaning, as I shook my head, laughing.

"So, how are you?" I asked.

"Good," she mumbled through a mouthful of food. She chewed and swallowed, taking a big gulp of Coke from the plastic cup in front of her and letting out a loud burp. "But I bet it's Ella you really want to ask about."

"Staying away is so hard, but being there is even harder. It's been four months," I said quietly, dipping my head to look at my burger.

"She asked me about you again."

I met her eyes. "What did you say?"

She shrugged. "Told her she was an idiot. That Sam was an idiot. That you are the best thing that could ever happen to her, but if she doesn't stop moping around after that douchebag that she'll lose you."

I swallowed hard. "What did she say?"

"Some waffle about how it was so soon, and how she has all these conflicting feelings. Matt, she loves you, and maybe she always did. But she has to work out the mess in her head. So, she's going away."

My mouth went dry. Going away? I never intended this break from being around her to be permanent. Not when I loved her and needed her so much.

"Where's she going?"

"She's taken a couple of weeks off work, and she flew out to the Cook Islands this morning. To go sit on the beach and do some more moping, I guess. She wants to take some time out before she gets too pregnant to fly."

I couldn't stop the smile creeping across my face. Vanessa always did call a spade a spade.

"Do you want to know what I think you should do?" she asked.

"I'm all ears."

She leaned in close, as if what she was about to tell me was a huge secret. "Go after her. Do the big romantic gesture. Tell her that you're there for her." Vanessa pursed her lips. "Ella's not good at being alone. She needs friends or family or the man she loves with her. She'll love being in the sun in the day, and hate being by herself at night. I've got all the details for her trip, she emailed them to me. Uni has been so crazy busy, I only found out last night." Tears gathered in Vanessa's eyes as she spoke. "Go and love my sister. She needs it. She needs *you*."

I reached out, rubbing her arm to give her some comfort. "Thank you."

"What for?" She sniffed, rubbing her nose on the paper napkin I offered her.

"For being my friend. For loving me and Ella."

"You two are so loveable. And you're good together. Dad would be over the moon."

I laughed. "How is your father?"

"Still pissed at Sam, but then, he always thought he was a bit off. I don't think he's hugely surprised."

I nodded. I well remembered Mr Brown's attitude as far as Sam was concerned. "What about the baby? Is he at least happy about that?"

"Happy he's going to be a grandfather, especially when the whole 'trying to get pregnant' thing was wearing Ella down. I think he wishes it was yours, though."

I chuckled and sunk my teeth into my burger, moaning at the taste, just as Vanessa had.

"Do you and your burger want some privacy?"

I waggled my eyebrows at her while I chewed, looking around the food court at the other tables.

"Did I tell you I have a boyfriend?"

I shook my head, taking a sip of my drink. "No. Who?"

"He and I are taking some classes together. He's sitting at that table over there." She waved her hand in the general direction of a whole bunch of tables with people sitting at them. *Real helpful.*

"Why is he sitting at another table?"

"Because I wanted to talk to you about Ella. And break the news that I found someone else."

I put my hand to my heart. "I don't know if I'll ever recover from this heartbreak, Ness."

She rolled her eyes. "As if you were ever interested in anyone but my sister. Anyway, I'll let him join us now."

She waved at the tables, and a lanky dark-haired guy walked over, placing his tray on the table and sitting on the other side of her.

"Matt, this is Connor."

Connor peered at me from below the fringe that flopped down over his forehead. "Hey."

"Connor, this is Matt." She beamed, lighting up as she looked between her boyfriend and I. It was so good to see her that happy.

He'd better take care of her.

Later that night, I made my way back to my apartment. It was cold and dark, and after my conversation with Vanessa, empty and lonely. Connor had been respectful, and was clearly as enamoured with Vanessa as she was with him, which made me pleased. I'd watch over her for the rest of my days, no matter how things went with Ella.

I sat on the couch and flicked on the television. Vanessa was right. Ella might enjoy the time alone for a little while, but she wasn't one to stay by herself for long. Not that I thought she'd look for other company, but being by herself would ultimately make her more miserable.

Maybe this was my chance to swoop in, tell her I love her, and have the time away from everything else to show her how much.

I picked up the phone and dialled my boss. Since this whole Sam thing had been going on, Dominic had been freaking out at how many hours I'd put in to work and had been harassing me to take a break. Now I was about to take him up on that. With a couple of hours work tonight, I could finish up what I was working on and I'd be free to go to Ella.

She might freak out if I showed up, but I no longer cared after my conversation with Vanessa. Worst-case scenario, she would tell me she needed more time, and I got a break on a tropical island.

I had to take the chance.

If she was ready, everything would be worth it.

CHAPTER 27

ELLA

Ella stood by the pool, bending to run her hand through the water and then wincing as she stood. The last couple of weeks, her bump had seemed to explode in size as the baby grew. Every part of her body ached, and she made her way to a lounger and spread her towel over it before sitting down. She ran her hands across her now five-month belly as the baby kicked, smiling at the contact.

"Let's get some sunshine," she whispered, leaning back.

She closed her eyes, the sun on her face warm and comforting and the gentle breeze cool. Perfect. This was a nice spot; she'd chosen the side of the resort restricted to adults. There were a few people around, but there would be plenty of peace and quiet while she took in some rays.

It would be so easy to fall asleep out here.

Another tiny kick made her smile again. They'd recently grown from little butterflies to full on feet against skin. At least, that was how they felt. Over the next few weeks the kicks would grow stronger. Everyone she knew who had been pregnant said she'd get sick of it sooner or later and just want it to end.

Not Ella. After everything, each kick was a welcome reminder that she'd conquered one of the biggest struggles of her life.

Her bag, lying on the ground beside her, vibrated, and the distinctive *Thunderbirds* theme had her sitting up in confusion. Matt had stayed away, as they had discussed. She missed him every day, but didn't have a clue how to let him know. It had taken so long to feel ready, and the longer she left it, the more she'd wondered if he still wanted her.

Ella reached for her bag, pulling out her phone and taking a deep breath before answering.

"Hello?"

"Hey, beautiful." A familiar voice came from her right, and she turned her head to see Matt a couple of loungers over.

"Matt." Her heart beat fast as she looked at him, his smile lighting up his whole face. She hung up the phone, slipping it into her bag.

"Who?" His grin grew wider, and she rolled her eyes with a smile.

"Oh, so it's like that, is it?"

"Do you come here often?"

She laughed loudly, ignoring people around them turning to see. "This is my first time, actually."

He cocked his head, raising his eyebrows. "I bet that's what they all say."

Ella bit down on her bottom lip, running it through her teeth as her cheeks flushed. Matt had given her the space she needed to work out what she wanted. Now he was here with her, and this was a deliberate move on his part—no way had this been a coincidence.

For the first time in forever, hope filled her being. All those glimpses of his heart, and now it was right in front of her.

"Matt, what are you doing here?"

He stood, moving toward her. And then he said the words she hadn't dared dream.

"I came for you."

She opened her mouth to speak, words sticking in her throat as emotion overwhelmed her. She'd cried so many tears for Sam, but the reality was that Matt was always the one who had cared for her, shown her understanding when she needed it, and been there when she'd called.

Now, as their eyes met, all she saw was the love he held for her. The love he'd always kept in.

He knelt beside the lounger. Matt gripped her arms, bending his head to kiss her, claiming her mouth with his. No backing away now.

His lips were soft and warm, and this time, there was no guilt for either of them. She was free to love him, and maybe that was the way it should have always been.

When he pulled away, he smiled, scanning her face and taking in her features as if seeing her was something new.

"I tried. I tried so hard to stay away, but I couldn't. This must be weird, me turning up here, but I couldn't think of any better way to start again."

She ached, *ached* to be in his arms, to feel them around her once more, all the while knowing that if that happened, she wouldn't want him to ever let go. This was their clean slate, the chance to start all over again. "Sorry. Who are you again?"

Matt laughed, winking. "That's my girl." He took her hand in his. "Want to go for a walk along the beach?"

Ella grinned, her heart warmed by his presence. "I'd love to."

Matt stood, helping her to his feet, bending to pick up her bag. She took it from him, unable to wipe the grin from her lips. As long as he was there with her, that would stay plastered all over her face.

Taking a deep breath, she linked her arm in his, taking her bag with her free hand and slinging it over her shoulder.

"How did you know I was here? Oh. Vanessa." Ella grinned, resting her head on his shoulder. This couldn't be more perfect, the soft beige-coloured sand between her toes, the clear blue water stretching for miles in front of them, and the cloudless sky, sun shining brightly.

"She told me what you were doing. I was on the verge of showing up at your place anyway; I got sick of waiting. Maybe it was impulsive, but I had to see you."

Ella lifted her head, smiling at him. His cheeks were pink, and he looked away as if suddenly shy. She took a deep breath and slid her hand across his chest. Matt turned his head. "I'm glad you're here," she said.

Those dark blue eyes scrutinised her for a moment, the corners of his mouth turning up into a smile.

"I thought we could hang out together, have dinner, and then ..."

"Then?"

Matt grinned. "Whatever the lady wants."

Ella's heart leapt to her throat at the warm, loving look he gave her. She'd seen so many sides of Matt, but this was the next level. Away from all the turmoil and stress of home, they were free to pursue whatever this was. Despite her being pregnant with Sam's child, Matt was here and ready to start something new.

"I'm sorry I didn't call you. I thought about it. So many times I thought about it. But it always felt too soon, and ..." She bit down on her bottom lip. "I thought you might have changed your mind and moved on?"

Matt shook his head. "As if there was ever any chance of that. I've waited for, what? Four years? Like a few more months were going to make any difference. You had to be ready."

"Is that why you're here uninvited?" The words slipped out before she could stop them. "Oh, Matt. I didn't mean it like that."

He stopped, taking a deep breath. The air was warm, but there was a cool breeze. It would be pleasant, but for the afternoon humidity. "I decided to take a chance. Vanessa said you missed me. I wanted to see your face. I've missed it."

"I've missed you." She licked her lips. "I felt guilty at first. But after what Sam did, there is no way I want him in my life again. So I can make myself happy now, or prolong staying miserable."

Matt twisted around, grasping her arms. "What's going to make you happy, Ella?"

She scanned his expression. He had hope written all over his face, and she was what he hoped for. "You."

The joy in his eyes was too much to bear, and her cheeks ached from the grin she now couldn't wipe from her lips. For a moment they stared, no sound, no gestures, just two people truly discovering one another for the first time.

It didn't matter that there were other people on the beach. All Ella saw was the man who had loved her for so very long with nothing to stop them from being together.

He bent his head, pressing his lips to hers in a kiss that bonded them, sealed whatever deal they'd made. There would be no parting them now, of that she was sure. The kiss also settled her heart, giving her the final sign that this was real and it was here.

"I swear to you right here and now that I will never take you for granted," he whispered when they broke contact.

Tears rolled down her face. "I know."

She closed her eyes as he wiped the tears away with his thumbs. "Do you want to know what I think?" he asked.

"What?"

"We see where things go. Take it as it comes. We have all the time in the world. I'm going nowhere."

Ella opened her eyes as he kissed her cheek.

"I like that idea." She slid her arms around his neck, resting her head on his chest.

ELLA YAWNED, dropping her fork to her plate. Even getting to midday without a nap had been hard. Lunch had helped brighten her up, but now she struggled.

"Am I keeping you awake?" Matt's lopsided smile betrayed his bemusement.

"I get tired in the afternoons. Especially here, where it's so much warmer than home. I've slept like a baby the past two nights."

He grinned, reaching for her hand. "If you think that's how babies sleep, you're going to be very disappointed."

Ella laughed. "You know what I mean. Walk me to my room?" She flicked a glance at him. Was he staying here too? The thought of him sharing her room made her heart flutter.

"Sure."

Matt took her hand as she stood, and they walked through the resort. All colours of hibiscus grew on either side of the path. The fragrant scent of the flowers filled the air as they drew close to her door.

"Where's your room?" she asked as she swiped the card.

"About five down from yours. Vanessa could tell me what type of room you had, but not which one. I guess I lucked out."

In a move brave for Ella, she put her hand on Matt's shoulder, pulling him down for a lingering kiss on the lips.

"Aren't I lucky?" He grinned.

"That'll have to hold you until later." She straightened the collar on his cotton shirt, patting it as she pushed at the door with her other hand.

"How about I swing by and pick you up for dinner about six? We can eat in the restaurant."

"Sounds good."

He bent again, pecking her on the cheek. "See you then. Have a good sleep."

Ella leaned against the door as she closed it, waving her hand to fan her face. Her holiday had become a million times better than it had been that morning.

Matt was here, and he wanted her. Her body was exhausted, but her mind was racing. How on earth could she sleep knowing that he was so close and ready to love her?

She looked down at her protruding belly, full of a life formed with the man she thought would love her forever. How was this supposed to work? Sam still didn't know; he was next to impossible to talk to without her feeling like she was to blame. That Matt would still want to start a new relationship with her at this stage in her life made her heart glow. He didn't seem to care.

Ella yawned again. So much to think of, and yet the child who grew inside her fought to make her sleep. At least, that was what it seemed like. It made up for the times when soon enough she'd suffer from lack of sleep.

She didn't bother stripping off, lying down on top of the bed and yawning again as she closed her eyes. Dinner with Matt. That was what she'd focus on. Not worry about what came next, or how quickly it might happen. Matt was there. That was all that mattered.

For the first time in so long, Ella drifted off to sleep with a smile on her face. She finally had something to be happy about.

REFRESHED, she'd woken and went into the shower. Although the room was cool, her skin still tingled from the heat of the sun, her hair sweaty from the outside humidity.

She stood under the water, closing her eyes as it washed the feeling away. Despite lathering on sunscreen, she had patches where her skin was red, but the water helped cool them.

Running her hand over her bump, the baby gave her some of those small kicks that made her smile. They'd slowed when she'd slept, and she smiled at the thought of her boy napping when she did. *He must get tired too.*

She dressed in a sarong as a skirt, and a light buttoned shirt. A romantic dinner with Matt. Whoever thought she'd end up in this place with him? To think that back when they'd met, she'd thought he didn't like her.

Every memory took on a new life as she remembered his reactions to things. The look on his face when he'd seen her in her wedding gown. And she had been worried that she looked okay.

That day must have been so hard on him.

A gentle tap on the door told her he was there, ready to take her to dinner. Excited, she pulled at the door handle and caught her breath.

Dark-brown board shorts, a white and grey striped button-up shirt, and that look in his eye that told her how he was feeling.

"Ready?"

She nodded. "I'll grab my bag."

"Did you have a good rest? I watched a movie and fell asleep, too."

Ella picked up her bag from beside the bed, her stomach flipping at what was to come for the evening. If she knew Matt at all, he'd be caring and patient. Despite the length of time he'd waited for her, he wouldn't rush.

"I feel a lot better. I think the little man got a sleep, too." She patted her stomach.

The corners of Matt's mouth crept up into a smile. "You're having a boy?"

Ella went through the door, pulling it closed behind her. "Found out not long before I left." She swallowed. "I tried to talk to Sam when I gave him the lawyer's papers, but he was with Petra and still blaming me for his bad choices. If I try calling him, I just get his voicemail. I don't know if things are going well for him."

Matt linked fingers with her, squeezing her hand. "He made his own bed."

"I know. It just makes it harder."

He leaned over, kissing her below the ear. "Then let's forget about him and get on with our night."

The words sent shivers down her spine, and he tugged at her hand, pulling her toward the restaurant. She followed willingly, her mind in turmoil about how the night might end. For now, she was content to be in his company, which she'd always enjoyed no matter what was going on in her life.

The restaurant was dark, the tables lit with candles, and she leaned against Matt as they stopped at the entrance.

"Table for Carver," Matt said, slipping his arm around her waist.

"When did you book that?"

"This morning," he murmured in her ear.

"Getting ahead of yourself?" She grinned as they weaved through tables, sitting at one near the window. Outside, the waves gently hit the sand, and Ella was filled with an urge to run out and get her toes wet.

"I planned ahead. If you'd told me to go away, I would have eaten dinner by myself."

She reached across the table, placing her hand on his. "I would never have told you to go away."

His eyes blazed with desire, not only the love she'd seen before. Her heart was in her throat as he ordered for both of them, steering clear of all those things she wasn't supposed to eat and ordering steak. It did seem crazy to be on an island in the Pacific and not be able to gorge on seafood.

In the candlelight, Matt kept glancing at her. "You keep blushing. Am I embarrassing you?"

She shrugged. "I loved the idea of coming here, but I'm sitting in a restaurant, wearing a sarong and feeling half-naked." She looked around. The tables were full of people dressed in a similar fashion.

"Here we go," the waiter said, smiling as he placed the plates on the table. Ella's mouth watered at the smell of the steak.

Matt had a grin a mile wide as he looked her over. "Nothing wrong from where I'm sitting."

"I feel so self-conscious. I've been ordering room service and hanging out in the air-conditioning instead of sitting in here."

Matt took a bite of his steak. "We can always go back to your room after we've eaten. You don't have to feel half-naked then."

Ella nodded, chewing a fry. "I like that idea. This place is amazing, but the humidity is really getting to me."

"Then you can be completely naked."

She took a deep breath, the food going down the wrong way. Matt leaped to stand behind her. She choked, and he patted her on the back as she held up her hand and reached for a glass of water.

"You shouldn't have said that." She laughed, trying to catch her breath.

"Why not? A guy can hope, can't he?"

He sat in the seat beside her, placing his hand on her arm. "I had hoped that we could move to the part where I get to tell you how I feel, and you fall into my arms."

"Matt," she whispered.

"I want you. And not only tonight. For always."

Ella licked her lips, taking another sip of her water. "I know."

"If you're not ready, we can go back to your room and we'll talk. About anything. All I know is that I need you in my life, and I have missed you like crazy. It's been so hard to stay away."

Tears welled in her eyes; he looked so earnestly at her. Here he was, laying open his heart, and it scared the hell out of her. "It's been hard to keep you away."

He placed his palm on her cheek, and she closed her eyes at his touch. This was who she wanted, who she'd thought about every single day since the time he'd left her standing in the back yard. So many times she'd picked up the phone to call him, only to put it back down because she didn't know if she was ready.

But how would she know if she didn't give him a chance?

Sam had been the one to burn her, not Matt. Never Matt.

"I think I've eaten enough," she whispered.

"There's no going back." He leaned in closer, and she could smell the beach on him, the salty air.

"I don't want to go back."

Ella closed her eyes as his lips brushed hers. This wasn't enough; she wanted more, she wanted everything. She wanted to be greedy and take all he could give her.

And she knew more than ever that Matt would give that to her willingly.

CHAPTER 28
MATT

My heart went from zero to a hundred in about three milliseconds when Ella said she didn't want to go back. Free to explore the attraction between us, she embraced it rather than running away. And her running had been my biggest fear.

I'd wanted her for so long, my mouth went dry, and it was like a part of my brain put its brakes on. All I could do was stare.

"Matt?" Uncertainty was in her voice, and she continued to look at me. Truth was, she still took my breath away with every action, every smile. I'd seen her at her best, and at her worst, and right now she looked more relaxed than she had in a long time.

And she wanted me.

"Let's walk along the beach to your room. Some more sea air might help us sleep." I winked, my heart leaping to my throat as she blushed. She wore no makeup for a change, the natural flush of her cheeks endearing in the candlelight.

"Am I going to get any sleep?" There was that grin, the one where her whole face lit up, and she dazzled me.

"Not if I have anything to do with it." This really was the point of no return. She was mine, and I would never let her go. No matter what.

Ella giggled, looking away as if shy all of a sudden. This seemed to be doing her head in as much as it did mine, and there was only one thing for it.

"Let's go." I rose, holding out my hand for her to take.

She hesitated. "What. No dessert?"

"Ella, get your butt out of that chair. You know what I have in mind for dessert."

She slipped her hand in mine, laughing softly as she stood, not taking her eyes from my own. Twisting her mouth, she pointed at her swollen belly. "I would offer to race you, but I think I might be a bit slow."

"I'd carry you if I had to."

She leaned on me, kissing my bicep. "Let's go, then."

I couldn't get out of there fast enough, charging the bill to my room and leading her down the beach to her room. This time I followed her in the door as she unlocked it, pulling her into my arms as soon as we got on the other side.

"Matt," she whispered.

I stroked her creamy skin, grazing my lips down her neck until I reached her collarbone. She moaned, running her hands down my back, clinging to me as if she meant to hold on just as fiercely.

"I love you, Ella."

The words came out before I could stop them, and she opened her eyes wide, her eyebrows twitching with uncertainty.

"Matt, I ..."

"You don't have to say it. Not yet. I'll be here, waiting."

Her mouth curled into a smile, and she pecked at my lips, holding me close.

"I want to be with you. I can't say that I don't love you; that would be a lie. It's so soon after ..."

She didn't need to finish the sentence. Moving on wasn't the problem, but it still seemed that Sam had left her a short time ago.

"You'll tell me when you're ready. I'm going nowhere."

Now I could kiss those bee-stung lips freely and without abandon. I could indulge in that scent, revelling in it, knowing she belonged with me.

My fingers fumbled with the buttons on her shirt, and I slipped it off her shoulders, revealing her soft, smooth skin, her shoulders a little tanned by the sun.

"Matt," she whispered.

I met her gaze, her eyes filled with longing and bewilderment, as if this was some feeling she'd just discovered. I'd never get enough of this woman.

"I'm the size of a house."

I chuckled, slipping my hands behind her back, unclipping her bra and pulling it forward.

"You're what? Five months pregnant? Hardly house size." I threw her bra to the floor, cupping her ample breasts in my hands, running my thumbs across her nipples as she sighed. "You're beautiful. That's what you are."

Sam had once told me Ella's body was a work of art, and though I'd caught a glimpse of it that first night, now I could run my eyes over her, taking that beauty in. Apart from her tanned shoulders and arms, her skin was the colour of cream.

This was every single fantasy I'd ever had and more.

Pregnancy had changed her body a little, but she was that same Ella that I'd laid eyes on that night, and there were no more barriers to us being in love.

Her breath quickened at my touch, and I bent my head to take one of those nipples in my mouth, rolling my tongue over it as she moaned.

I pulled her closer as I licked it, losing myself in her, running my hand down her back, claiming what was mine.

"Matt." This time she cried my name, gripping my shoulders, running one hand through my hair as she pulled me to her. That was the word I'd always longed to hear, and I switched to the other breast, kneading her back with my fingers, that honey scent making me harder as I indulged in the fantasies I'd been tortured by for all this time.

I raised my head and looked at her. Her nipples had swollen, hardened from my attentions. This was only the start.

"Tell me you're mine," I whispered. "I want all of you. Every last piece."

"I am." She cupped my face in her hands.

"Say the words." I wanted to hear them from her lips, know that she was as connected to *us* as I was.

"I'm yours." She leaned over, initiating a kiss that made me tingle, pushing her tongue into my mouth, and I met her with every stroke. I could never get enough of touching her, tasting her.

Now she reached for my buttons, each one separating from the buttonhole in her fingers, and as I stood up straight to make it easier for her to push off my shirt, she shoved it from my shoulders, planting kisses on my chest that left me gasping, left me wanting more.

"Ella."

"I want you to feel as good as I do."

"Baby, I feel good because I'm with you, because I dreamed of this moment."

She paused, raising her head and looking me straight in the eyes. "You dreamed of me?"

I raised my hand, running my fingers through her dark hair. "I dreamed of nothing else. All I've ever wanted is you."

Tears welled up in her eyes. She took a deep breath, as if to counter them. I tightened my grip, pulling her face to mine so I could kiss her again. She tasted so good I could kiss her the rest of my life.

Her hands were on my shorts, the waistband loosening as she unbuttoned them. I couldn't wait any longer as I tugged at the knot she'd tied in her sarong, letting it fall to the floor. Nearly naked, she was even more beautiful than I'd imagined. She couldn't be more perfect if Michelangelo had sculpted her.

I ran my hand over the curve of her belly, the tightness of her skin over the baby.

"You're so beautiful."

She blushed from her cheeks down to her throat, her skin turning a light shade of pink.

"Lie on the bed."

Ella's lips twitched as they curled into a smile, and she walked to the side of the bed, slipping under the covers and grinning at me, wearing nothing but a pair of panties, and that devilish smile. Every time I looked at her, I fell all over again.

"Come on." She beckoned me with her index finger and I walked to the other side of the bed, dropping my shorts the rest of the way, my underpants with them.

Ella pulled back the covers, and I laughed, snuggling in beside her, pulling her near naked body into my arms. This was real.

"No show for me?" She pouted, and I raised an eyebrow as her hand snaked down my chest, heading for my cock. It had been hard since I'd held her, smelled her, felt her in my arms.

"What type of show?"

She shrugged. "I don't know."

I laughed, reaching for her hand, guiding her to her target. "There's your show. That's what you do to me."

Her touch nearly set me off, I was so ready to be inside her, but I had to hold it, had to wait.

"Are you going to tell me what that tattoo is now?"

She'd remembered. I wasn't about to lie with her. Not with her hand gripping me like that.

"It's a bee."

"I know that."

"It represents you."

Her lips parted as her brows knitted in confusion. "What do you mean?"

"That bubble bath, and all the other things you use that make you smell like honey."

She locked her gaze with mine, her eyes searching my own. I hoped that all she found was love and sincerity. That was all I had for Ella.

"You really do love me," she whispered.

"Always have."

I wasn't going to wait any longer, and I pressed my lips to hers, gently at first, but growing in intensity as our tongues found each other and I stroked her body. She was everything I'd ever imagined, curvy and soft, and she pulled away, giggling as I placed my hand on her belly.

"That tickles." She did that cute suck-her-bottom-lip-through-her-teeth thing as she looked at me, her cheeks pinking up with blush.

I ran my hand over her stomach again and up her back, laughing.

"I guess, then, I have to find all that out about you. Where I need to touch to make you laugh, what I need to touch to make you cry out my name."

Pulling my arm out from underneath her, I spread her legs, moving between them. She watched me with big eyes.

"You're overdressed." I wagged my index finger at her while she giggled, and I slipped my fingers into the sides of her panties, pulling them down and throwing them onto the floor. "That's better." Planting kisses down her pregnant belly, I nuzzled the tiny patch of soft hair between her legs.

"I usually have a Brazilian, but waxing hurts so much now I'm pregnant." Ella rolled her eyes as she said the words, and I grinned, shaking my head.

"I love you the way you are." I pressed my face back between her legs, finding her clit with my tongue and licking her slowly. She bucked her hips, moaning as I breathed her in.

"I've wanted this for so long," I murmured.

"It feels like forever since I've been touched like this."

How long had it been? How long since she had been made love to and not screwed in the mechanical fashion Sam had described? However long, it would be all she got from this day forward.

I went back to work with my tongue, her breathing accelerating as she wriggled under me, pulling away, pushing forward. Ella was the one in control of all of this, though I doubted she had any idea.

She moaned, calling my name as I teased her with my tongue. Her fingers raked my hair as her body stiffened, and she groaned loudly. I had her.

"Matt?"

I knelt over her, and she smiled at me, her grin growing as her eyes scanned my face.

"Yes?"

"That was amazing."

I touched my lips to hers. "It's just the start." Frowning, I looked around. "Shit. Hang on a minute."

"What?"

"I've got a condom in my wallet. In my shorts. On the floor."

She laughed, wrapping her arms around my neck. "Are you worried about getting me pregnant?"

I grinned, shaking my head. "I don't think that's going to be a problem. I want you to feel safe."

"We don't have to, if you don't want to. I trust you."

"That's a big thing to do. How do you know I haven't been with half of Europe?"

She reached up, stroking my hair, smiling affectionately. "Because while I'm sure you weren't celibate when you were away, you would have been careful. Because you're that kind of responsible, considerate man. Besides, I want you inside me."

If it were possible to be any harder at the moment, I would have been. My dream girl was right under me, and I was all she wanted.

"I only ever want to be with you from now on," I whispered.

She smiled slyly. "Now you have to work out how to get inside me while dealing with this." She ran her hands over her baby bump, and I rolled my eyes.

"That's easy."

Ella's eyebrows crept up as I grabbed another pillow, lifting her off the bed and sliding it under her.

"Now you're at exactly the right angle. And I get to look at you."

She laughed, rolling her eyes and shaking her head.

I took her in. My beautiful woman lying in front of me, ready and waiting for me to complete what I'd started. Claiming her for all eternity.

In one move I slid inside her, and she gasped as I pushed slowly, not wanting to hurt her in any way. She felt even more amazing than I'd dreamed, hot and wet and tight around me as I moved back and forward, building up a rhythm that left her moaning. Her soft voice repeated my name as I sped up, needing my release, but wanting to give her as much pleasure as I could.

She reached for my arms, running her fingers down them, the touch of her hands making it harder to hold on. Everything I ever wanted was right here.

She sighed, and I closed my eyes. Nothing had ever felt this good, and I'd be damned if anything or anyone would ever get in the way of Ella and I being together again. With a groan, I let go, opening my eyes in time to see the look of utter joy in her gaze, and I knew she felt the same.

"Ella," I whispered.

As I collapsed beside her, she rolled over and was on me in an instant, covering my face with kisses, stroking my chest, showing me the depth of her emotion.

"I love you," she murmured.

Those were the three little words I'd ached to hear from her. Now they were mine.

"You know there's no take-back on that."

"I know." She smiled, planting a kiss on my chest and snuggling against me. "I love you, Matt."

"I love you too." I kissed the top of her head. "You'll never get rid of me now."

"I don't ever want to."

Tears rolled down her cheeks, and I wiped them away with my fingers, stroking her face. Her eyes were full of love and yet sad all at the same time.

"I wanted you from the first moment I laid eyes on you," I whispered. "Across the room, at that party. You wore that black dress, and drank vodka through a straw. I think I fell in love with you that night."

She took a deep breath, closing her eyes. Without a doubt she would be thinking of that night, of how it ended. I couldn't erase her memories, but I could give her some of my own, tell her of my love for her.

"I'm sorry."

"For what?" I pressed my nose to hers, and she opened her eyes again.

"For not seeing it earlier. I had no idea until you told me after the wedding." She licked her lips as I pulled away again. "A tiny part of me wanted to run away with you."

"I wish you had," I whispered.

She grinned, the beautiful big grin that lit the dimples at the corners of her mouth.

"I'm here now."

CHAPTER 29
ELLA

Matt was everything Ella ever dreamed he'd be. Warm, loving, attentive ... she thought she'd had the best sex of her life before him, but the connection between them was electric, as if they were always meant to be.

They lay in bed, drifting off to sleep to the gentle hum of the air conditioning. They were tired after the exploration of one another's bodies, each giving the other everything, but wanting to give more. Exchanging the magic words that sealed the deal. *I love you.*

Ella rolled over, shaking herself out of her sleepy stupor, and looked at Matt. He was magnificent. She smiled at his bare chest, visible above the sheet in the dim light of the room. She'd felt the strength of those pectoral muscles, the ones she'd snuggled against more than once. Below them were those beautifully defined abs, leading down to his *V* that went ... well, now she'd seen where that went.

And right above that *V* was the bee. All those months he'd carried it around, etched into his skin for her. Despite the time and distance, his love for her hadn't wavered. The tattoo might be subtle, but it was a sign of his commitment.

Her heart warmed as she gazed at him, seeing him in a different light. He was still the same amazing man she'd known for all this time, but he was also someone new she had to get to know. There was so much the pair of them had to discover about one another.

She ran her hand down his chest, tracing his abs, needing to touch him, needing to make him feel good. Sleep could wait. She grinned as he opened his eyes, snapping awake as she gently ran her fingers over his cock.

"What are you after?" He gave her a sleepy smile.

"You."

Matt kissed her, softly at first, but growing in intensity as her grip tightened and her movements grew more frequent.

"Get on your stomach," he growled, sending shivers down her spine.

She did as she was told to the best of her ability, rolling over to be on her hands and knees. He pulled her up and backwards, impaling her as she sat back up.

"Is that what you wanted?" he whispered in her ear, rocking her as he stroked her breasts.

"Yes." She whimpered, closing her eyes. He gripped her hair, pulling it away from her neck as he clamped his mouth to her shoulder, moving up toward her ear, nipping her skin with his lips.

"Ella."

Her name was an aphrodisiac on his lips, aided by his fingers finding her clit.

"I saw you from behind once, and noticed the mole on your neck. I love that there's a trail of freckles from your shoulder leading to it," he murmured in her ear, biting gently on the lobe. "It makes me want to see what else I can find."

She laughed, rocking her hips against his hand, as he nuzzled the nape of her neck.

"Don't do anything, baby. Relax and I'll do it all."

He was perfect. She threw her head back on his shoulder as he grazed his lips down the other side of her neck. She was lost as she came, calling out his name as he nipped at her skin, moving so slowly the action left her wanting more.

"Matt." She turned her head, finding his lips as he groaned, coming deep inside her. He held her to him for a moment, then let her go to lie down and grin back up at him.

"Say it again," he said.

"What?"

He raised his eyebrows, and she grinned. There was only one thing he wanted to hear.

"I love you."

Matt flopped on the bed beside her, finding her lips with his for a long, deep kiss that took her breath away. He scanned her features as they lay next to one another, her gaze fixed firmly on his eyes.

"I've loved you for so long; I never thought I'd hear those words from you. I'll never give this up, Ella, I swear. You and me—this is it."

She nodded as he put his palm to her cheek, his fingers playing in her hair.

"I know," she whispered. It had been a long time since Ella had been so happy, so fulfilled, finding the joy in the smallest of things again. Life hadn't been this good since her marriage to Sam.

She found it hard not to compare the two men. They were so similar, and yet so different. Sam had a great body, but the sight of Matt even half-naked set her heart fluttering. He'd told her that he'd worked out his frustration, and it showed, his definition a million miles away from what she thought her own body looked like.

But he loved her body. The bits she saw as imperfect, he caressed as gently as any other part of her. His heart was in every touch, his fingers lightly stroking the flesh that she'd sometimes felt so self-conscious about.

Matt didn't care. He loved her.

And Ella loved him right back.

CHAPTER 30

ELLA

Ella stared at her phone as Sam's name came up on her mobile screen, part of her wanting to just let it go to voicemail. Ella had always been a softy.

"Sam?"

"Can we talk?"

Ella's heart raced. Did he know about the baby? She closed her eyes, picturing that day standing in his house with Petra watching their every move. He'd been happy enough to throw Petra's pregnancy in her face.

Now her back ached, and her ankles were swollen. *I hope Petra's suffering as much.*

Holly looked across the desk at her with her eyebrows raised, that 'what the hell are you doing talking to him?' look on her face.

"What did you want to talk about?"

He let out a breath, like he'd been holding it.

"It's Petra. I don't know if the baby's mine. I'm going out of my head, Ell. This whole thing just screwed up my life so bad, and I think it's all for nothing."

"What do you mean you don't know?" She tapped the desk with

her fingernails, torn between hearing the rest of the story and hanging up the phone.

"It wasn't just me. She slept with at least two other guys in the same period of time. Everything's wrecked. I've done such a stupid thing." He was clearly distraught from his tone. Reaching out to her had to be difficult.

"Yeah, you did."

"Can you come and see me? I just want to talk."

Ella teared up, closing her eyes. "Sam, I'm with Matt now."

"I know."

She licked her lips. "I'll clear it with him first. I doubt he'll be over the moon at me seeing you."

For a moment, there was an uncomfortable silence. "Thanks, Ella."

"Where are you?"

"Same place as you saw me last. Petra's moved out. Gone to her parents until she's worked out what's going on."

Ella opened her eyes to Holly, inches from her nose. "I'll call Matt and let you know."

She hung up the phone, rolling her eyes at the other woman. "What are you doing?"

"You sounded and looked like you had some kind of crisis going on. What does the dickwad want?"

"Sam wants to see me. Apparently he might not be the father of that woman's child after all."

Holly moved back around to her desk, leaning back in her chair. "That's karma. Are you going to see him?"

"Only if Matt's okay with it."

"Do you need to ask permission?"

Ella laughed. "No. Matt and the baby are the most important people to me right now. I need to tell him what I'm doing at least. I don't want to hurt him just to help Sam."

Holly rolled her eyes. "But you're still going to see him."

"He sounded hurt, and he was still mine and Matt's friend. I know who I want to be with, Holly. Sam's not going to come between us."

Holly grimaced. "I should hope not. Who knows what diseases he's picked up from her."

Ella laughed. "I'd like to say I don't care, but that's not true. I loved him a lot, but he's as much to blame for their situation as she is. He didn't have to go near her."

Ella dialled Matt. His light, happy tone was a world away from Sam's sad one. Matt was eternally cheerful since they'd gotten together.

"Ella." That was all he said and she sighed, prompting a smirk from Holly.

"Sam just called me. He wants me to go and see him."

"What for?" The tone changed to serious.

"Well, apparently, Petra's baby might not be his. She was sleeping with at least two other men. Wonder if they were married too."

There was silence, and Ella could imagine the look on his face. He'd have that intense gaze going on, the one that gave her the tingles.

"Do you want to see him?" he asked after a few moments.

"He sounded miserable."

"Go see him if you have to. He did the most stupid thing he could have ever done and he's turning to the one person who he knows has a big enough heart to still care."

She cradled the phone, rocking back and forward. Matt was so good for her. He trusted her. "I'll go and see him after work for a little while. It might be a good opportunity to tell him about the baby."

The silence again. Matt and Ella had spoken about this, and he'd understood that in her agony over Sam's infidelity, she'd held back from telling Sam about her pregnancy. Sam would have to know one day—that was inevitable one way or another.

"Okay. I'll see you at home for dinner." He paused. "Love you, Ella."

"I love you too."

She gazed at the phone for a few moments after hanging up. Matt was her everything now. He'd helped heal the deep wounds she'd been left with, and made her see a future. It didn't matter what Sam did or said—it was her and Matt forever. He would never have any cause to worry about her love for him.

"So ..." Holly's voice broke into her daydream, and Ella looked up to see her friend's curious stare.

"Yes. I know what it's like to be hurt. He needs someone."

"Does it have to be you?"

Ella shrugged. "Matt and I were his best friends. Who else does he have?"

ELLA PULLED up outside the house Sam lived in. The sight of the dilapidated building made her frown. They'd lived in a beautiful home, ready to bring a child into their lives, and he had given it all up for this.

Taking a deep breath, she opened the car door, stepping out onto the path. She locked the car and took tentative steps toward the place, her stomach tied in knots.

Ella knocked on the door before she chickened out and ran away. Sam needed a friend.

She gasped as she opened the door. He had, at a guess, about three-day-old stubble. His eyes were bloodshot and exhausted, like he hadn't slept for a week. *How long had he been like this before calling?*

"Sam," she said, not making any effort to hide the pain she felt. No matter what he'd done, she hated seeing him like this. So lost.

"I'm glad you could make it. Matt give you permission?" His tone wasn't bitter, as she had expected. More like resigned.

"Matt trusts me."

"Huh." He scraped his fingernails over his chin. "He's a good man."

"Yeah, he is."

"Do you want to come in?" Sam took a step back, and Ella walked through the door, straight into the living room.

Nothing had changed inside either. It was still cold, damp and miserable.

"Thanks for coming." Sam indicated she should sit on the couch. She sank into the soft fabric, looking around at the papers littering the desk in the corner, the carpet that badly needed vacuuming, the used dishes on the coffee table.

"I needed to make sure you were okay. You sounded terrible."

He nodded, sitting beside her. "I just keep going over and over in my head what happened between us. I did such a stupid, hurtful thing, and I'm so sorry, Ella."

Despite the months apart, she blinked back the tears. "You hurt me so much. How could you sleep with someone else?"

"Can I ask you something?"

Ella paused. What did he want? Answering a question with a question showed he wasn't listening, or didn't care about giving her the answer. "Sure."

"How long have you been sleeping with Matt?"

Her mouth went dry. What kind of question was that? She might have been drawn to Matt, but it would never have gone as far as Sam and Petra had taken it.

"We got together after you left."

"Are you sure?"

Ella licked her lips, remembering the day that Matt had said those three little words to her, the ones that had scared the hell out of her.

"I didn't have sex with Matt until after you dumped me." Her voice shook as she said the words. "He had feelings for me. He told me. But we didn't sleep together until I was alone."

Sam's head drooped, and he looked at his feet. "I always knew he had feelings for you. Right from the start. I knew him too well. I just never thought he'd swoop in and take my girl."

"I wasn't your girl for him to take." Ella took a deep breath in an attempt to summon up the courage to tell Sam the truth about the baby. "Sam, I ..."

"You were just so damn hard to live with. I couldn't deal with all the crap and stress around the baby thing. If you hadn't been like that, I wouldn't have been in that position, drowning my sorrows and having sex with someone else."

At that, Ella's resolve steeled. Sam could go to hell. "You are not blaming me for this. You're an adult. An adult who couldn't keep his penis to himself while I was waiting at home. I loved you."

Sam leaned back on the couch, his eyes on her belly.

"At least Matt gave you what you wanted. Your feet didn't even touch the ground, did they?"

The words hit Ella as if she'd been stabbed in the heart. The months she'd spent wallowing in self-pity, being miserable about losing the man who had walked away from her. This cold, damp house was suddenly suffocating, and Ella did the one thing she could do in self-preservation. She stood.

Sam looked at her in dismay. "Don't go. Everything's such a mess."

"Maybe for you." Without a backward glance, she set off for the front door, walking out into the sun and back to the car.

Her hand trembled as she slotted the key in to start it, the engine purr giving her comfort with the knowledge she'd soon be away from this place. Nothing about this was healthy. She could stay and listen to how much it was her fault he'd cheated while he sat there and took zero responsibility. No thanks.

Sam had to grow up.

She took a couple of deep breaths before indicating and pulling out into the street. *Chinese for dinner. Matt will like that.* She had to keep thinking of something else, anything else but the man she'd just walked away from.

At least this time, she wasn't alone.

CHAPTER 31
MATT

I let Ella go to Sam when he called her. Not that I ever would have been able to stop her. Not my big-hearted Ella. I knew she'd come back to me. But as the hours ticked away, I looked at the clock on the wall nervously. They'd had enough of a connection to have the relationship they had, and to get married. What did I have? I'd told her I'd love her forever; I'd be whatever she needed me to be. We were living together, but was it enough to keep us as one?

What if the love she had for Sam overrode everything she felt for me?

The last thought was the hardest one of all, the one that stabbed me in the chest over and over again. What if I was a stand-in after all?

And then my phone buzzed. The sight of it vibrating across the table brought a smile to my face and joy to my heart. It had to be Ella.

I hope you haven't started cooking dinner. I've grabbed some Chinese.

What were we doing? Celebrating? Commiserating? Times were pretty lean after we'd both spent so much money on our little overseas jaunt. She was either very happy or very sad to need takeout food.

I haven't started cooking. I need you home.

I pressed send, leaning back on the couch, putting my feet up on the coffee table. As long as I had her, the world could crumble around me and I wouldn't even notice.

Ten minutes later, the lock clicked as she turned the key and pushed open the door, carrying her handbag on one arm, and a plastic bag full of containers of food in the other. Her eyes were so tired, and she looked drained as if it was a huge effort to hold herself up, let alone the goods in her arms.

I sprang to my feet, taking her burdens and ushering her to the couch. I placed her bag by her side and the food on the table, smiling as she grabbed my hand and pulled me down to kiss her.

"You okay?" I asked, licking my lips to taste her on me. I'd never get enough of that.

"I am now." She smiled, but it was strained. Was it because she was tired, or was there something going on? I didn't want to pile on the stress. She'd tell me when she was ready.

"I'll get some plates and cutlery and we'll eat in here. Keep you off your feet."

Ella's smile widened, and she squeezed my hand tight. "I don't know what I did to deserve you."

I raised my hand to her face, dug my fingers into her hair and leaned in close. "You loved me. That was all I ever needed. I'll spend the rest of my life taking care of you. If you'll have me."

Those perfectly shaped eyebrows lifted. "Is that a proposal, Matt Carver?"

It hadn't been, but her thinking in that direction warmed my heart. It didn't matter to me if we ever married. We were together.

"It will be when you're free to marry me. Until then, it'll have to be a promise."

"I like your promises," she whispered. "You keep them."

I have never made her cry, and will never be the cause of her tears. And I did the one thing that Sam had seemed incapable of doing. I held her in my arms and kissed any melancholy away. Because I loved her.

When I let her go, she sat on the couch, leaning over toward the table to open the takeaway containers. I walked to the kitchen, returning with plates and forks and spoons, ready for our feast.

Ella seemed to be struggling to stay awake; everything tired her out these days. But I had news to help relieve her burden. Something that might put a real smile back on her face.

We sat in silence as we ate, her attentions on her plate, mine on her. As she filled her stomach, it became harder for her to fight her exhaustion. This pregnancy was hard work, but she juggled everything without complaint.

"I've got some good news," I said.

She gave me a tiny smile. "What's that?"

"I got a promotion."

Ella's mouth dropped open, the excitement in her eyes growing as she looked at me.

"Matt." Her voice was soft, caring, and full of pride. I'd been determined to get this job. It was a big leap from what I'd been doing, but it came with a lot more money.

"Yep. I'm a lead software designer now."

Tears welled in her eyes, and she moved her plate from her lap to the table, the edges of her mouth curling into a grin. "I thought you said that was at least a year away."

"Well, turns out they were really impressed with me. I have the qualifications, and although I haven't been in the other role long, I've shown that I know what I'm doing. I get to lead a team, and it means a lot more money." I forked a piece a broccoli from my plate, taking a bite out of it.

"I'm so excited for you. That's wonderful."

I chewed, smiling as I swallowed. "Good for you, too. Any time you want to finish up work, we'll be fine. It's a decent bump, enough that we can live on my salary."

Her shoulders slumped, as if the pressure hanging over her had been released, and she leaned forward to kiss me.

I put my fork on my plate, placing it on the table, and opened my arms, slipping them around her as our lips touched. I didn't know if she couldn't find the words, or if she simply wanted to kiss me, but I knew how good this was for her, for us.

"I know how tired you are, baby. This whole thing has been so stressful for you. Let me take care of you, even if it's only for a little while," I whispered.

She nodded, sighing. "I'll be okay; the baby will be here soon and I can ..."

"Get a lot of sleepless nights and become a zombie?" I teased, stroking her back.

"Are you bullying me to give up work, Mr Carver?" She leaned back, her eyebrows twitching.

Running my fingers through her hair, I chuckled. "Never. I want you to know you have options. That no matter what, I'm here for you —no other reason."

"I love you."

I never tired of hearing those words from her lips. "I love you too," I whispered, squeezing her tight. She squealed, and I let go as she laughed, rubbing her belly.

"Let's get dinner out of the way, and I'll give you a back rub. We can have an early night if you like. Maybe you can tell me how your visit went with Sam."

"That sounds amazing." She sighed, picking up her plate.

You're amazing.

By the time we finished dinner and a back rub in front of her favourite evening soap opera, Ella was almost asleep. I cleared away the dishes, and came back into the living room to find her lying on the couch with her eyes closed.

"Come on, princess. Let's get you into your bed."

She yawned, taking my hand as I pulled her to her feet. She smiled a sleepy smile. "What would I do without you?"

"You'll never need to find out."

In the bedroom, I stripped off, and watched as Ella undressed, pulling on one of my old shirts. She'd been wearing them a bit lately; I think they made her feel closer to me, and none of her usual tighter-fitting clothes went near her now the baby had grown so much.

She pulled back the blankets, climbing into bed, wriggling around and turning over. No matter what position she slept in, she was uncomfortable. If I could have taken some of that away, I would have. Instead I slipped into bed, offering her my arms.

I stroked her hand, content to hold her. As much as I desired Ella, she was so tired. I wouldn't push the idea of sex.

I closed my eyes when her breathing grew slow and steady, preparing to join her in her sleep.

"You didn't ask me about today," she mumbled.

"I didn't want to pry. I'm not going to be a dick about who you see. You love me—that's all that matters."

She nuzzled my cheek. "I won't be seeing him again. All I wanted to do was tell him how sorry I was."

I tightened my grip around her. Reaching to stroke her face, I took in every feature from the eyes I adored to the lips I couldn't help but want to kiss. This was perfect. She was perfect.

"I still didn't tell him about the baby. I mean, that it's his."

That was still hanging over us. He had to be told, but it would come at a cost to us. How big that cost was, I couldn't be sure.

"Ella, I thought you were ..."

"I tried. I really did. But I got there, and he was full of remorse for what he'd done. For himself, not me. It was all about how he'd let himself down, being tempted by someone else, but it was still my fault for being so hard to live with ..." Her voice trailed off, and I pressed my lips against hers in a gentle kiss.

"Have to admit, you going to him scared me a little. I know you and your big heart. And I know how much you loved him."

She let out a long breath. "He slept with another woman. No matter what happened, there was no going back after that. Even if he wanted back in my life, I couldn't live with it. I wish he was easier to talk to." She sighed. "When you kissed me, before you went away and after, I admit I was conflicted because I loved you as a friend. I would never have done that to him. I couldn't."

I pushed her hair back off her forehead. "I know. One day he'll be easier to tell," I whispered.

She nodded. "I feel so awful. This was his battle too. Even if he had as many mood swings as I did."

"He was the one who walked away."

Ella buried her face in my chest, closing her eyes as I stroked her hair and kissed her temple.

I lay there for a while after she'd fallen asleep, staring at the wall. Sam deserved to know, but I understood her reasoning.

He still couldn't take responsibility for his actions.

CHAPTER 32

MATT

Ella groaned. Seeing her in so much pain pierced my heart. She'd been having contractions for hours, and they were taking their toll on her. Her eyes closed as she breathed through it, and when it passed, she opened those beautiful blue eyes and smiled at me as if nothing was wrong.

"This is Sam's fault," I said. "It's that big head of his."

She laughed, despite the pain, her face contorting in discomfort.

"The good news is that it's time to push." Lost in our little world, I'd nearly forgotten the midwife was there.

Ella nodded.

"Next contraction, push."

I leaned over, kissing her nose. "It'll be over soon."

"I can't wait to hold my baby," she whispered.

"I know. Then I get to take you home and wrap you both up in cotton wool for a while."

She leaned her head against my arm. "You're too good to me."

"Loving you is the easy bit."

Those manicured fingernails tore at my skin as the next contraction hit, and Ella gasped at the intensity. I stood my ground. She could rip my arm off if it gave her the support she needed, no matter how big that child's head was.

Time and time again she gripped my arm, until finally she exhaled loudly. The baby's cry pierced the quiet morning. Ella lay back, closing her eyes for a moment, her forehead drenched in sweat.

I picked up a cool cloth, wiping her face one last time as she looked at me with hazy eyes.

"You have a beautiful, very noisy baby boy." The midwife placed him on Ella's chest, covering him with warm towels. His dark eyes gazed at her, his tiny hands resting on her breast.

Tears ran down Ella's cheeks as she touched him for the first time, enclosing those tiny fingers in her hand. Her boy, so precious, after all that she'd been through. Seeing them brought a tear to my eye too, as I fell in love with him. The two most beloved people in my life.

"His head isn't that big after all," I whispered.

Ella's chest shook as she laughed, shaking her head. "He's beautiful, Matt. I can't believe he's here."

I kissed her cheek, leaning my head against hers. "Our lives are never going to be the same again, you know?"

"Our life hasn't been exactly normal." She chuckled.

"What's normal?" I sat by her side as she fed him for the first time, and then he was dressed and wrapped, so tiny in the small clothing that looked so massive.

"Can you call Sam?" Her voice wobbled as she said the words, emotion overwhelming her. He still didn't know, but I guess seeing her baby brought this all to the surface.

I smiled, rubbing her back. "Of course I can." I might not like him, but I would never stand in the way of him getting to know his child. I'd protect both Ella and her baby for the rest of my life, but for this little boy, his father wasn't the enemy.

"I should have told him, Matt. I know that. He made it so hard. I don't mean to dump all this on you, but I don't know if I can make that call right now."

Kissing her temple, I squeezed her shoulders. "It's okay. That's what I'm here for. I'll call him."

I pulled my phone out of my pocket as the midwife came back into the room. "We'll get you into the shower and cleaned up." She smiled at Ella as she walked past on her way to the bathroom.

"I'll go outside, leave you to it." I kissed her again, and stood, turning as I got to the door. Ella watched me with tired eyes, a small smile on her face. I'd do anything for her.

Fresh air filled my lungs as I took a deep breath outside the building. I'd been there all night, holding Ella's hand as she'd dealt with every contraction. I might have been tired, but seeing her give birth had to be the most amazing experience of my life.

Now I scrolled through my contacts until I got to Sam, pressing the screen and closing my eyes as I held the phone to my ear. It rang a handful of times.

Should I leave a message?

"Matt." His tone was clipped, like I was some kind of business associate and not someone he'd known his whole life.

"Hey, Sam."

"What do you want?"

I opened my eyes, looking back at the building I'd exited. The white walls of the hospital seemed to go up forever, interspersed with windows. My girl was in there somewhere, and I needed to hold her hand again.

"I'm calling because Ella had the baby—"

"I can't do this. I can't be around you two. I'm sorry."

"But, Sam—"

"What does she want? To play happy families with both of us? I don't think so. I can't watch her loving you."

The words made my blood boil. "Stop being so damn selfish. She wants to see you."

"She was living with you and pregnant before her feet even touched the ground."

That did it. "Sam, Ella and I were never together before you dumped her. You broke her heart, and I picked up the pieces. I'm calling you because—"

"Just take care of her."

The line went dead, and I stared at the phone for a moment, my fingers hovering over the text buttons. I should talk to Ella first.

I trudged back inside, back to a room being tidied by the midwife while the baby lay in his crib, staring into space. She smiled at me as I bent, scooping him out of the plastic cot, and rocked him in my arms.

"Guess it's you, me and Mum," I said.

He seemed to try so hard to focus his little eyes on my face, and one arm escaped his wrapping, waving in the air. I took his little hand in mine and kissed it, rubbing my nose against his fingers. So tiny and precious ... I would never let anything bad happen to him, not while I was around.

"Love you, buddy," I whispered. If Sam wouldn't talk to us or see sense, I was it for this little guy. And I'd take that role on gladly.

"Do you have a name for him yet?" Ella's midwife asked.

I grinned. "We have a few picked out. Whatever Ella decides. She wanted to see this little guy before she made up her mind."

She nodded, walking toward me. "He's a lovely baby. I'm sure you'll come up with the right name; sometimes it takes a while."

The bathroom door opened, and Ella appeared in the doorway. Her eyes were heavy, her cheeks a little flushed. I'd tried not to think it, but in that moment, I'd have given anything to be the father of the child in my arms. I would be in the sense that I'd raise him with Ella, love him, take care of his needs, and be there for him. But there would always be a part of me wanting Sam in the equation. It sucked to think about it that way; he could only be a part of this little boy's life if he let go long enough for us to tell him.

"I love seeing you with him," she said. "Is Sam coming?"

I frowned. "About that."

She sucked in her bottom lip, nodding. "It's okay."

"One day he'll actually stop and listen. Right now, he's having a one-person pity party and wouldn't get past the fact that we're together. I thought about texting him, but I didn't know if you wanted him to find out that way."

Ella shrugged, struggling to keep her eyes open.

She climbed back into bed, and I sat beside it in a chair, cradling the precious bundle in my arms.

"He's beautiful, Ell," I said. "I think he's going to look like you."

"I think it's too early to tell." She rolled onto her side and smiled at me.

He yawned, and I rocked him back and forward, entranced by his little face as he wrinkled his nose.

"You'll make a good father," Ella said softly.

"I'm not …" I looked up at her to see her gaze locked on the baby.

"You'll raise him with me. He'll know you as the father figure in his life, and maybe one day he'll meet Sam and get to know him too."

I nodded. "He's pissed he threw away the best thing he ever had and wanted to lash out."

"We'll wait a while and try again. No matter how difficult he might be to deal with, he needs to know." She sounded so tired, and rolled onto her back, closing her eyes.

"Let's talk about this later. Right now, you need to get some rest. I'll stay here, holding this little one."

"Finn."

That was all she said.

"Is that what you want to call him? I seem to remember that being a name I was favouring, not you." We'd spent hours discussing names to the point where we both had our own lists. Now it seemed she was stealing from mine.

"Sue me. The more I thought about it, the more I liked it."

"Finn." I looked down at him in my arms. His eyes were closed, his small lips pursed. "Sweet dreams, little man," I whispered.

My whole world was in this room, and I'd do whatever it took to keep it safe.

Our family.

CHAPTER 33
MATT

Fifteen months later ...

I was running late. Of all the stupid things to happen, I'd managed to end up in a meeting at four-thirty p.m. on a Friday. One of the sales team had sold what we referred to as vapourware. Meaning, they'd pulled the product out of their arse. It didn't exist. And now they expected my team to pull them out of the crap.

After sending him scuttling away with his tail between his legs, I checked the time. Five-thirty p.m. Holly would have picked up Ella by now, her party starting at six with a barbecue before drinking. She was across town in East Auckland; it'd take me a good hour to get there.

I picked up my phone, swiping to unlock it, and keying in the text. *I've finished. On my way now.*

Grabbing my laptop bag, I waited for the lift to get to the basement car park. There were days when waiting for the elevator took ten minutes alone, and this was clearly one of them. My phone vibrated in my pocket. On the screen was a picture of Ella, Finn, and our daughter, Georgia. With all the trouble Ella had getting pregnant with Finn, we'd been lax about contraception the first few weeks of our renewed sex life. Georgia had been born almost exactly a year after Finn.

Be careful in the rain. The traffic will be crazy out there. xxx

We'd spent nearly two years together, and seeing messages on my phone from her still gave me tingles. They always would.

I'm still waiting for the lift. Don't let one of Holly's friends chat you up before I get there.

I selected the big wink emoticon, picturing her rolling her eyes and laughing as she read it. My Ella wouldn't look at anyone else, even if they did try hitting on her. She knew the same was true about me. I loved that she could have complete and utter trust and faith in me. I'd never let her down. Not in that way.

Finally, the lift bell dinged, and I stepped in, pressing the button for the basement. It was empty; I must have caught it at the right time, and I adjusted my tie in one of the side-wall mirrors. At least I'd look presentable coming straight from work.

Ella and I hadn't had a night out in what felt like forever. From our first evening together 'til now, the only time we'd been apart were the two nights she'd had in hospital with Finn and Georgia. And most nights since then had been spent with our family, Finn having started walking, Georgia trying so hard to roll over. These were the best days, the days when our children grew right before our eyes, the days when we were just all together.

But tonight was for us. Vanessa had offered to babysit when Ella told her Holly's birthday party was coming up. It would be a boozy night, and not somewhere we could take the babies. We leapt at the chance to have a night out.

Traffic was hell, the rain falling heavy in some parts of the drive, and as I sat on the motorway with the cars at a standstill. It turned to hail, tiny little stones falling everywhere, and for the shortest time giving the road the appearance of being covered in snow.

It was beautiful in its own way, despite my frustration at not being able to move more than a metre at a time. It was six-thirty by the time I saw the motorway exit.

Cheering in my head, I turned off, navigating through the streets until I came to Holly's place. I'd been here a couple of times before, but tonight I had to park a little farther down the road. She must have had half of Auckland there.

The music hit me before anything else. She must surely have invited her neighbours, or she'd be in for a visit from noise control before it was over. It brought back memories of all those parties Sam and I'd had, the house sometimes overflowing with students. I didn't think about those days much anymore.

People were everywhere, and the night was still early. I didn't want to be around if anything went bad, and I especially didn't want Ella here.

I smiled as I realised my current favourite song was playing, the one that always made me think of Ella.

And then I saw her.

You stopped the world. I couldn't breathe.

She sat in the corner, wearing that same dress she wore all those years ago when I first spotted her. It was a little tighter after the kids, and her breasts looked amazing, squeezed into the top. I'd have to get her out of it so she could breathe again. She was beautiful, her hair hanging in curls, framing that gorgeous face. Her makeup was immaculate with vibrant red lipstick, her nails painted to match.

In her hands was a lemonade bottle, and she drank the beverage through a straw, the image causing a stirring in my loins similar to the one I'd had back then.

This time though, she was mine.

A guy I assumed was one of Holly's friends sat off to the side, with his eyes on Ella. It might have upset me had I not known that she had done this for me.

I made a beeline for her, cutting through groups of people to get to my girlfriend. When she saw me, she raised her eyebrows, a cheeky smile in her eyes, and she sucked on that straw for all that it was worth.

Out of the corner of my eye, right on the edge of my peripheral vision, I saw the guy who had been looking at her stand.

No. There was no chance of anyone else stealing my girl this time.

Slowly, she rose as I came toward her, still sucking at that drink. With eyes only for one another, we closed the gap, and she grinned without taking the straw from her lips.

"Ella," I murmured, taking the bottle from her hands and placing it on a nearby table.

"Matt." She breathed my name, so sexy from her lips. We weren't going to last a whole evening in this place, that was for sure.

She reached up, clasping her hands behind my neck as I wrapped my arms around her waist. "You look incredible."

"I opened the wardrobe to find something to wear tonight and saw this. I know it's what I wore the night you first saw me."

"The night I lost you," I whispered.

"No chance of that happening again. You're stuck with me now." She grinned, and I leaned in to kiss her, tasting her lips, smearing that lipstick so perfectly applied.

"I love you, Ella," I whispered, pressing my forehead to hers.

"I love you, too. And our family."

I grinned, kissing her on the nose.

Ella's grip tightened. "Oooh I like this song."

I buried my face in her neck, and we moved, my nose pressing in to her skin, inhaling the honey fragrance that had driven me nuts for years. Words couldn't express how I felt about this woman. She was a part of me, and I relaxed my arms, reaching for her hands.

She looked up at me with those big blue eyes, smiling as I squeezed her hands.

"This song makes me think of you."

"In what way?" She tilted her head.

You are the only one I want. You are the only one I lost. She smiled as she listened to the words, shaking her head.

Ella let go, cupping my face in her hands. "Never losing me again."

"Do we have to stay?" I murmured.

"I don't know if Holly will notice us leaving. She's got a full house. What did you have in mind?"

I smacked my lips together. "Well, Vanessa is with the kids all evening. It's still early. I thought that we could go and get something to eat, find somewhere quiet to park, and make out in the car."

Ella laughed. We'd never really dated. As soon as we'd come home from the Cook Islands, I'd moved in with her. When Georgia was born so soon after Finn, we'd been so busy that we'd got on with our lives with the children. Any time I got alone with Ella was precious.

"That sounds wonderful." She snuggled in against my chest, wrapping her arms around me.

"I have plans for after we get home and Vanessa leaves, too," I said.

"You do?"

"I promise I'll help with the children tomorrow, but I don't know if either of us are going to get much sleep tonight."

Her body shook as she laughed. "I'm a human milk machine. I don't get much sleep any time."

"I know, and I swear you'll have a good time. Besides, you need to know you're so much more than a human milk machine."

Ella smiled up at me, pursing her lips in invitation to kiss her. Of course I took advantage, kissing her so hard she gasped. But then, I could kiss this woman for days and not come up for air.

"Want to get out of here?"

She nodded.

"Fish and chips by the beach?"

She squeezed me, breaking away from our embrace. "I'll get my bag, and we'll get going."

I watched as she walked toward Holly to tell her we were going. Those hips swaying as she walked made me sigh. It didn't matter how many times I saw her, each time was like the first.

Holly glared at me as Ella whispered in her ear, and I grinned like a crazy person, wiggling my fingers at her. Ella didn't notice, disappearing for a moment before returning with her bag and jacket, then skipping back toward me and grabbing hold of my hand.

"Let's get out of here."

She giggled as we made our way out and away from the house,

through the dwindling raindrops, the sound fading as we drew closer to the car. It wasn't far to a beach and a fish and chip shop, and then I could snuggle with her. Exactly what the doctor ordered.

Ella leaned back in her seat as I drove, and I glanced at her, smiling at how relaxed she looked. This was what she needed—what we both needed.

I drive to Mission Bay, pulling up outside a fish and chip shop, and got out of the car. Walking around, I opened Ella's door, taking her hand. She smiled lovingly at me.

"Date night, then?" she asked.

"Date night. I'm kind of hoping I'll score."

She laughed. "I'm pretty sure you will."

I grinned, wrapping one arm around her waist as we walked into the shop together. I stood behind her, holding her tight against me as she ordered for both of us. It wasn't the food I was interested in.

We sat in the corner of the little waiting area as they cooked our food, entangled in one another's arms, content to be together. She leaned her head on my shoulder.

"Happy?" I asked.

"Always." She snuggled in tighter, and I kissed the top of her head, barely noticing when they called our order number.

"That's us," Ella murmured, untangling herself from me, and taking hold of the paper-wrapped parcel. We walked back out to the car, and I opened her door before climbing in and setting off around the corner to the beachfront.

It was a still night. The earlier rain had completely disappeared, and the air smelled fresh, cleaned by the water.

"Want to sit in the back seat with me?" I asked as we pulled into the deserted car park.

She grinned. "I thought we were eating dinner."

"We are. I thought we could put the food in the middle and sit and watch the water. The benches will still be too wet to sit outside. And then we can fool around."

"I like the sound of that."

As I parked, Ella placed her hand on my thigh, squeezing gently.

"Be careful, young lady. I might change the order of what we're doing around if you carry on like that."

"Promise?" She looked at me wide-eyed, tempting me to do just that.

"You're trouble, Ella," I said, pecking her lips.

"I try my best." She grinned, picking up the food and opening her door.

We met in the back seat, sharing a loving kiss before she unwrapped the package. She picked up a chip, sliding it slowly into her mouth and winking at me. Laughing, I shook my head, taking a chip for myself. This was the life. Two people in love and enjoying being together.

The way we always should have been.

Moonlight lit the water. The rain had stopped falling, and it was beautiful and peaceful. We ate in silence, eager to finish our dinner and move on to other things.

"I think Finn asked where you were today," Ella said, breaking a piece of fish into bits and scooping one into her mouth.

"Really?"

"He said 'da da?' like it was a question, and not him just calling you that."

I grinned. He was such a daddy's boy at times, especially since Georgia had arrived. We were the best of mates.

"That's so cool. Makes me sad I won't see him until the morning."

She smiled until her dimples appeared. "He'll be mega excited to see you. Maybe we can take the kids out somewhere tomorrow, let Finn have a good run around with you. He'd like that."

The last chip lay on the paper, and I raised an eyebrow at her. "Do you want that?"

"Maybe, but do you want it?"

"Split it in half?"

She nodded, laughing as I broke the chip that maybe measured two inches in half, popping her piece into her mouth.

"I like sharing with you," I said, as I rolled the paper up into a ball, tucking it under the driver's seat.

"I like doing everything with you." She smiled, and I wriggled closer to her. She met me in the middle of the seat, and I wrapped my arms around her, kissing her softly.

The salty taste from the fish and chips was on her lips. "I love you, Ella."

"I love you too." I kissed her again, longer and deeper, her mouth opening to mine as my tongue sought hers. The stress of the busy week lifted when we kissed, our bodies pressed together as much as the car seat allowed. It was easy to get carried away with her, and I lost myself, kissing my way down her neck as I stroked one of her breasts, her nipple hardening under the fabric.

"Matt," she whispered, the urgency in her voice obvious as I hit that spot that made her gasp. From our conversation in bed that first time 'til now, I'd explored her, gotten to know every inch of her body. I knew what to do to make her sing.

Her hand ran down my back to my waist, then around my belt until it landed on my groin. The smell of her had already ignited action down there. Her touch hardened me beyond belief, and she pulled at my belt buckle, opening my pants and releasing my cock.

I looked around. There were people out and about, but none near the car. Making a mental note to get the car windows tinted, I returned to kissing her lips as she ran her hand up and down my length, each stroke bringing me closer to my end.

Ella backed down the seat, bending over, my entire body shaking as she took me in her mouth. What that woman could do with her lips and tongue, I marvelled at, although she often said the same about me going down on her.

We both took so much pleasure in pleasuring one another, and on this night she went to town, her lips tightening around me, her tongue flicking over me. I moaned, leaning back on the seat as she took control. Anything in the world she wanted, I'd give her.

"Ella," I cried out as I came, and she stayed there, not raising her head until she'd taken everything. But then, she'd given me everything—her heart, our children, our life. I would never take any of that for granted, not while I had breath in my body.

I zipped up as she sat back, a smug smile on her face.

"I like it when you say my name," she said.

Reaching for her, I pulled her into my arms, burying my face in her hair. "I'll only ever call your name."

She shook in my arms, and I kissed her tenderly, pressing my nose to hers. Ella sighed, snuggling into me, and we watched as the moon moved up higher into the sky.

By now there were more people in the car park, eating food, walking down toward the beach. Our solitude broken.

"We should go home." She linked her fingers with mine, squeezing gently.

"Vanessa won't hear the car. We could keep making out in the privacy of our own driveway."

Ella laughed, burying her face in my chest. "Can't we go home and go to bed?"

"Isn't this more fun? It's still date night."

She edged up, planting a kiss on my neck. "You've got a point. We'd be close to home, but still have a little privacy."

"Let's go. The sooner I can get you in this back seat again, the better."

Laughing, she let go, opening the door and moving to the front seat. "Hurry up then."

She didn't need to say it twice. I joined her in the front, starting the car and backing out of the park. It would take about thirty minutes to drive home, but with her by my side, the time passed quickly and comfortably.

With the lights of the city behind us, we drove the quiet streets to our home. I'd recently upgraded my car to something new and quiet. And a sedan. A 'family car', as Ella's dad had called it. I didn't mind. We needed all the space we could get with our recently expanded family. Georgia was only a few months old, but she had cemented her place in our lives as Finn had.

All that time Ella had waited, and she was in her element now with the pair of them. I didn't know a more loving and devoted mother. And she was all mine.

"Where's Vanessa's car?" I asked, as I pulled into the driveway.

"Oh, I meant to tell you. It's got a problem with the transmission. She came over in a taxi. You might need to give her a lift home."

I shook my head, grinning. "Now you tell me. You mean I'm gonna get hot and heavy with you and then have to wait to get laid?"

Ella reached for my arm. "Just think about what'll be waiting for you at home."

"I never think about anything else."

Her face lit up, dimples on show as she smiled, pulling away from me and quietly opening the door. I put my fingers to my lips as I followed suit, and we climbed back into the back seat, laughing quietly.

"You don't think she heard us?" she asked, looking toward the house.

I shrugged. "She'll have the TV going. Now, where were we?"

Ella leaned back against the car door, her eyes so animated, truly happy.

"Ella," I whispered, leaning over to kiss the curve of her breasts, pale in the gentle illumination coming from the street. I had to taste the creamy white skin, and I got lost again in that familiar smell. All mine.

Ella's breath hitched as my lips touched her flesh, so sweet and tender. My entire body was on fire, driven by my desire for her. At some point she'd go inside with the children, and I'd be left hanging while I drove across town, but I couldn't keep my hands to myself right now as I stroked her shoulders.

That throaty laugh as I took mouthfuls of her skin drove me insane, and I fiddled with the top button on the front of her dress.

Tap-tap-tap.

I sat up, Ella looking at me wide-eyed. All that heavy breathing had fogged up the windows. I couldn't for the life of me see who it was, but I had a fair idea.

Ella buttoned the top of her dress, laughing softly as she shook her head. Here we were, acting like teenagers, getting caught out in our own driveway.

I placed my hand on the window, wiping a little until I could see out. Vanessa stood outside, waving at us with a silly grin on her face.

She tapped on the glass again, and I opened the door a little. "What *are* you doing?" I asked.

"I heard the car." She wrinkled her nose, peering in. "Are you two having sex in the back seat?"

"No," Ella said.

"That's what it looks like." Vanessa grinned, raising her eyebrows.

"We hadn't got that far. You interrupted us."

I laughed at Ella's words. That much was true. I'd never understand their love/hate relationship, but Ella and Vanessa were always honest with one another.

"Well, your babies are tucked up in bed asleep. Georgia grumped at the bottle, but I explained to her that it came from Mummy's boobs, and she drank fine after that. I think she was just hungry, but I'm claiming that one."

Ella laughed, rubbing her forehead and shaking her head. "You can have it."

"So get inside and get into that big, soft bed of yours. Much more comfortable than the back seat of a car." Vanessa crossed her arms and winked.

"How do you know what our bed is like?" Ella asked, bemused.

Vanessa tapped the side of her nose. "Anyway, I want to get going. Connor is meeting me at my place. His car's in almost as bad shape as mine is. I don't know if it'll survive the drive out here."

"Want a lift home?" I stepped out of the car, holding a hand for Ella to grab.

"I'm fine, I'll call a taxi. What are you going to do? Drive me home in your sex car?"

"Nessa," Ella said, emerging from the back seat.

Vanessa shrugged. "Okay. Nearly sex car."

"Get in the front, and I'll take you home," I said. Ella held onto my hand, and I turned to her, pecking her on the lips. "And you, get inside, check on our babies, and we'll pick up where we left off when I get back."

She grinned, kissing me, lingering on my lips. "You betcha."

"I'll grab my bag," Vanessa said.

I leaned against the driver's door, and Ella wrapped her arms around my waist, giving me a quick hug before letting go. "Don't be long," she whispered.

"As long as it takes to make sure Vanessa's safe inside, and I'll be straight back to you."

"Thank you for tonight."

I ran my fingers through those long, dark curls. "We need to do this more often. I love being at home, all four of us. But, sometimes, it's nice to get Matt and Ella time."

She nodded.

"Get inside where it's warm." I bent my head, kissing her tenderly, and watched as she walked to the front door, crossing paths with Vanessa on the way out. The two women hugged briefly before Ella went inside and shut the door, leaving me to take Vanessa home.

Vanessa walked around the car, climbing into the passenger seat as I opened my door.

"So when are you two getting married?" she asked.

"Shouldn't that be up to us to decide?" I teased, flicking the key in the ignition, the car rumbling as it started. I backed down the driveway and onto the street.

"Well, yeah, but I want to be a bridesmaid." Vanessa poked her tongue out at me. All I could do was roll my eyes

"We have to wait for Ella's divorce to be final. When the final papers are through, I'll ask her."

"You could ask her now."

"I just want her to be free, Ness." I glanced at her. For once she didn't have that cheeky grin on her face, and was looking down at her hands in her lap. "It's okay. I'm impatient, too. But this whole thing was so messy. We're together, that's all that matters," The light ahead was red, and I slowed to a crawl before stopping.

"I know I give you crap, but you always were the right one for her."

Maybe it was time, regardless of Ella's marital status. I'd found the perfect engagement ring for her months before, stashing it away for the right moment.

I met Vanessa's gaze, nodding at the honesty in her face. "You know, I never did find out why your dad didn't like Sam so much. He talks, but he doesn't like opening up."

The light went green, and we moved on.

"He never respected her. Dad hated that. You know, my mum does everything for Dad. At least it seems that way. But they're real partners. They never do anything big without talking to one another, and they pick each other up if the other one is down."

She shrugged. "Sam never did that with Ella. He might not have been mean at the start, and he seemed to really love her. But he was happy for her to get wound up running around after him. He wasn't there for her."

I frowned. "They always seemed happy. Before I went away, anyway."

"That day you helped Dad on the farm? I think that was one of the best days of his life. He had me and Ella. I think, deep down, he wanted a boy to help him out, learn the ropes. I know that either of us could work on the farm, and we did when we were growing up, but you were everything Sam wasn't. And you took better care of Ella at times than Sam did."

"I tried so hard to hide the way I felt." I had no reason to keep that secret now. How I felt about Ella was out there.

"That was why I gave you such a hard time. I kind of hoped that you would push her to make a choice, make her realise more than Douchebag was out there. Maybe she would have denied it at the time, I never asked, but I think she loved you both."

I smiled. Vanessa had always supported me, had been there even when all it seemed was that she was giving me a hard time. I loved her like a sister, and would always be there to protect her if she needed me.

"I always feel safe with you."

That confused me. "Did you not feel safe with Sam?"

She shook her head. "I don't think he meant anything, but he creeped me out from time to time. The odd thing he'd say made me uncomfortable. You don't do that."

"What did he say, Vanessa?"

My blood boiled at the thought of her feeling that way. Sam had always seemed to be such a good guy; now it seemed he'd gone off the rails in more ways than one. How could we be two years past his betrayal of Ella and there to be still more bad?

"He'd make comments about my body. You, I could walk around half-naked and you'd be worried about me being cold. Him, I covered up because he was having a look."

"I'm sorry to hear that."

Connor waited outside her building, and I pulled over to the side of the road.

"Thanks, Matt." Vanessa opened the door before I could respond, stepping out of the car, and made her way toward him.

"Vanessa, wait." I pushed my door open and ran around the car, grabbing her into a bear hug.

"What gives, Bro-in-law?" She laughed.

"I'm sorry. I'm sorry that Sam made you feel that way, and I'm sorry I wasn't here to stop it. I hope you know I'll never be that creepy man."

"Let go of me and I might believe you."

I dropped my hands to my side. "Good night, Ness. Night, Connor."

She pushed herself up onto her toes, kissing me on the cheek. "Good night. Now go have some wild monkey sex with my sister. You know that's what you really want to do."

I laughed.

She was right.

CHAPTER 34

MATT

I pulled into the garage at home, letting out a big breath as I turned off the car and pulled the key from the ignition. Tonight had been perfect; now to go in and be with the woman I adored.

Inside, the gentle light of the lamp in the hall lit the way inside, our bedroom dark with no sign of Ella. Confused, I turned, walking back down the hall and into the children's room.

There she was, snuggled up with Finn, fast asleep with him in her arms. His head nestled into her shoulder, and her arm looped under his neck. They looked so peaceful and so content, I couldn't bear to wake her.

I turned back to the bedroom, stripping off my shirt and throwing it in the laundry basket. Closing my eyes, I reached up, rubbing my neck. Today had been tiring, and now deprived of my partner, I'd just settle in and catch some sleep.

Ella's palms landed on my pecs, and I opened my eyes to her running her hands up to my shoulders.

"You're awake," I said.

She smiled. "Finn woke up not long after you left. I climbed into bed and sang to him until he went to sleep. Guess I must have dozed off, too."

"You both looked very comfortable. I wasn't about to disturb you." I kissed her on the nose.

"Thank you for taking Vanessa home."

"It's never a problem." I swallowed. "She asked me when we were getting married."

Ella laughed. "What did you say?"

"I said I just wanted you to be free."

Her eyebrows dipped, her eyes sad at the words. She wanted that, too. We'd talked around marriage a lot, given that she was still married to someone else, and would be until we got that little piece of paper saying it was over.

"It got me thinking, though. I've got something for you."

One of those eyebrows crept up as I pulled away from her, fishing for a small box in my bedside table. We'd been through so much, and I'd waited long enough to do this.

She gasped as I went down on one knee, opening the box. Inside was a sapphire ring, the sapphire surrounded by diamonds. It was the same colour as her eyes, changing shade as it moved in the light.

"Matt?" she whispered.

"I don't want anyone else, Ella. Only you. I knew the moment I saw you—you were the one for me. And I would have waited however long it took for you to see it too. Will you please marry me?"

I took the ring out of the box, and she held out her hand so I could slide it onto her finger. I'd been sneaky and taken a ring from her jewellery box for the size. Now the new one fit perfectly.

"Yes," she whispered. "I want so much to be your wife."

"I know we have to wait a while longer, but let's do this soon." I stood, taking her in my arms. "I want to be your husband. I want to grow old with you."

I bent my head and kissed her, tasting those lips I loved, deepening the kiss until it left her panting.

When I pulled back, Ella looked at me with so much love.

"Get undressed and get on the bed." Ella grinned, reaching for the buttons on the front of her dress.

Laughing, I kicked my shoes off, dropping my pants to the floor and doing as I was told. "Now what?"

Naked, she climbed on the bed, straddling my hips, rubbing her body against me. "I'm in control now."

I reached up, running my fingers through her hair, pulling out the clips that stopped it from falling down around her shoulders.

"You were so beautiful, that first night I saw you. I had that image of you in my head for so long afterward." I ran my hands down her shoulders, cupping her breasts as I ran my thumbs over her nipples. "And now, you're all mine."

"For always," she whispered.

"For always." I pulled her down to kiss her, her tongue pushing into my mouth as I stroked her back, gripping her arse as she rocked against me. Feeling her wetness, I grew harder as she rocked faster, getting herself off pressed against me.

"That feels so good, baby," I said.

"I like making you feel good." She leaned over to kiss me again, and I was lost in the scent of her arousal, the feel of her skin against mine. I wanted this for the rest of my life. Nothing and no one else. Just Ella and I until the end of our days.

She sat up and I slipped my thumb in, stroking her clit and finishing her off as she threw her head back, calling my name. Pushing her back, I slid into her, groaning as her warmth enveloped me. I closed my eyes while she rocked again, taking control of the situation. Her palms pressed hard against my chest, and she moaned with every stroke.

"You're my dream come true," I whispered, taking in the overwhelmed expression on her face. Her eyes flickered open, and she smiled. "I love you."

Her face was so open, every emotion she had written all over it, and she scanned my features as if taking in every detail. She didn't need to say it back at that moment for me to know she felt the same.

She overwhelmed me, and I came, deep inside her, where I

belonged. Ella leaned over, kissing me again with all her tenderness. What we had was on a whole other level than anything I'd ever enjoyed with a woman. We were bonded in every way possible.

She was mine.

Ella flopped down on the bed beside me, and I pulled the blanket up to stop the cool air that flowed over me with the loss of her body warmth. She grinned as I rolled over to face her, and for a moment we gazed at one another, our eyes meeting in mutual adoration.

I lifted a hand, pushing back stray locks that had fallen over her face, and in silence we took in one another's features. It didn't matter what happened in the world around us—I could look at her face for hours.

Georgia's cry pierced the stillness, and I grinned, Ella shrugging.

"I'll get her," I said.

"No. You stay here. I'll bring her back to bed." Ella kissed me on the nose and leapt out of bed, grabbing her bathrobe as she went. I rolled onto my back, closing my eyes and smiling at what had just happened. Every time was like the first time for us, the thrill of being together.

Minutes later, Ella returned, Georgia in her arms and that content smile on her face. At that moment, I knew more than ever that this would be our life—making one another happy forever.

I couldn't wait to marry her.

CHAPTER 35
MATT

We were married on the farm. Ella's dream had always been to have her wedding at that little church down the road, but she'd had that. We wanted only good luck for our special day.

I held Finn in my arms, and Ella held Georgia as we promised to love one another forever. Vanessa and Connor stepped in so we could exchange rings, and I shared a little smile with the young woman who was about to become my sister-in-law. I was as proud of Vanessa as I was of my children.

And then I held hands with my beautiful blue-eyed girl, slipped a ring on her finger, and I swore to be hers forever. In return, she placed a matching gold band on my finger and vowed to love me all the rest of her life. The best part of it all was holding my wife in my arms and kissing her, as if nothing had existed before us.

Afterward, I held Finn on my hip as I slipped my arm around Ella's waist, Georgia cradled in her arms. We greeted our friends and family as husband and wife.

Finally.

Connor slapped me on the back. "Congratulations, man." He was part of our family too now, having slotted into our little group quite nicely. Connor was still besotted with Vanessa, and I was confident they'd have their dream day at some point. Knowing Vanessa, her wedding wouldn't be held in the country.

While the small wedding reception was in full swing in the house, I took Finn for a drive to see the sheep before the sun went down. He loved it when we came here. He was eighteen months old, but so clever. He had quite a few real words in his repertoire, and he knew how to make animal noises.

"Baa," he said as we drew close.

"That's it, buddy. We're going to see the sheep. Not that long ago I came down here with your grandfather to see if there were any lambs. We're too late for the first one, but I bet there are a few in the paddock now."

Finn grinned, showing all the tiny teeth that he had, and the odd gap. I loved this kid so much it hurt. He was so like his mother, but every so often I'd see a glimpse of Sam in him. The way he used to be.

I stopped the four-wheel drive, jumping out and going around to let Finn out of his car seat. We'd put his gumboots on in the house, and his legs were so small they nearly reached his knees. But he was happy, out with Dad on the farm.

We were in luck. Right near the fence was a lamb. Mostly white, but with black patches, it had found a good little spot of thick grass to nibble on. Finn's eyes widened. "Baa, baa." He waved excitedly as we drew near. The lamb stopped chewing, raising its head to look at him. It was smart enough to realise that the fence was between us and there was no way this little human was getting near.

"What do you think? Do you like that one?"

Finn stuck his index finger in his mouth, sucking on it as he nodded.

"Maybe we should ask Grandpa if we can keep him. We'll make a little pen for it."

Finn reached up, and I scooped him into my arms so he could be high enough to look at the rest of the animals. "This is going to be our life one day soon. You, me, Mum and Georgia. We're going to be so happy here. I love you all so much."

I pressed my lips to his forehead, kissing him softly. He giggled, pushing away and wriggling so that I'd drop him on the ground to take one last look at the lamb.

"Come on, let's go see your mother. We can tell her all about what you've found."

My heart swelled as I helped Finn back in the car and buckled him in. Whether or not Sam ever cooled down enough to be in his life, it didn't matter anymore.

Our little trip down to the farm had tired him out, and Finn was nearly asleep in my arms as I made my way back into the house.

"Here, let me." Mum took him from my arms, kissing her first grandchild. "Let's get you into your pyjamas and into bed." He wrapped his arms around her neck, and I bent to kiss his face one more time before my mother disappeared with him. All the grandparents would be helping watch over him and his sister tonight.

I loosened my tie, sitting down and surveying the room. Ella stood with Vanessa, the two of them animated as they talked. My heart swelled watching Ella; the shine in her eyes that had disappeared when I'd returned from overseas had been back since we'd been together. Today, she was positively glowing.

My phone vibrated in my pocket, and I plucked it out. Who on earth could be calling me? Everyone I loved was right here in this room.

"Hello?"

"Don't hang up."

I froze. I'd know that voice anywhere.

"Sam?"

"I heard today was your wedding day. I had a look on Facebook and Ella changed her profile pic. You look happy."

I swallowed hard. "I am. We are."

"I really screwed up, Matt. I kept blaming Ella, but it was all my fault. The better man got her in the end. Congratulations. You don't have to tell her I called."

I'm well aware of that.

"The kids are gorgeous, too." He paused, and there was a moment of uncomfortable silence until he continued. "Take good care of my boy."

He knew.

"Sam, I ..."

"I did the math. Ella had something to tell me that day. I didn't want to listen. You'll be a better dad than I ever would have been. I couldn't even be faithful to my wife. Promise me you'll be good to her, or you'll have me to answer to."

My chest ached. Despite not having seen Sam since the day he left Ella, he'd been my best friend. I thought all the pain had passed; now it all floated to the surface.

"I will," I whispered.

I raised my eyes and locked gazes with Ella. Her brows were furrowed in concern and she started moving, making her way toward me.

"I should let you go. Take care. All of you."

I dropped the phone from my ear, staring at the screen as he hung up. Ella's hand touched my shoulder as she sat down, and she wrapped one arm around me, leaning her head on my shoulder.

"You okay?"

I cleared my throat. "Uh, yeah. That was Sam."

I turned my head to look at her, and she studied my face, clearly not liking what she saw.

"What did he want?"

"To congratulate us. He knows, Ella. He knows about Finn. He worked it out, but he told me to take good care of him."

Her lips parted as she drew in a deep breath. "I never meant to keep anything from him. He made it so hard."

"I think he realises that. I think that call was him letting go."

She leaned forward, nuzzling my cheek, soothing the ache in my chest. Nothing could get between us now. This was it for both of us.

"He let go a long time ago," she whispered. "How about we get out of here and on with our wedding night?"

We weren't going far; this was a trial for the start of our new life. Ella missed her mother, especially with juggling the two young ones, and her parents had spent the past few months building a new house on their farm. One for us.

Turning our backs on the city wouldn't be hard. I'd finish up the project I was working on and then we would start again, with Ella and I learning how to run the farm, preparing for the day her parents retired.

Everything was perfect. Vanessa would rent the house in Auckland, giving her somewhere more comfortable to live and a place to start a life with Connor, and I would still contract myself out if I needed to. All I needed was a computer and an internet connection.

Tonight was the first night my wife and I would sleep in our new bed.

"Sounds good."

Finn and Georgia had two sets of grandparents fussing over them for the evening. It was just Ella and I, on an adventure together.

I took her hand in mine, and we walked up the hallway. The children were sharing a room, Finn having recently moved into a bed, and I sat beside him, watching him sleep.

Maybe he wasn't my blood, but he was mine. He was a big chunk of my heart, along with his sister and his mother. So precious after the struggle to conceive him.

I bent, kissing his forehead. "Love you, champ," I whispered.

He sighed, rolling over in his sleep.

Ella patted down the blanket over Georgia. This would be hard. Even though we were only a couple of hundred metres away, they'd never been apart a whole night.

"She'll be fine. If she wakes, you know she'll have half the household making sure she's okay." I laughed, kissing Ella on the shoulder.

Ella nodded. "I know."

"Come on, sweetheart. Let's go."

She tucked Finn in again and kissed him before joining me in the doorway. "Whoever thought our lives would end up like this?"

Our mothers talked in the kitchen as we went through to get to the back door.

"Don't you worry about a thing," Mum said. "We've got this covered."

Ella hugged Mum while I hugged Ella's mother. "We know," Ella said. "Thank you so much."

"Enjoy yourselves." Mum winked. I rolled my eyes.

"Can we get out of here before they start talking about our sex life?" I asked.

Ella laughed, grabbing my hand.

Out the door, we walked the path to our new home.

Together.

CHAPTER 36
ELLA

Ella woke, rolling over to look at the sleeping man beside her. *My husband*. Every day she counted herself lucky that he came back for her.

When Sam had left, it nearly destroyed her. She'd pushed Matt away, but he wouldn't have any of that, and he'd returned to her life and swore never to leave it again. Despite her hurt at Sam's betrayal, she knew she could believe Matt. He'd never lied to her.

Georgia looked so much like Matt; there was no mistaking that she was his daughter. That smooth brown hair, the deep blue eyes ... Ella's heart caught in her throat every time she looked at her.

Finn looked more like Ella than Sam. She'd always planned to tell her ex about his child. But when she was with him, she felt the way she had for months before he'd left—like she wasn't good enough, like it was all her fault.

Matt never made her feel that way. He'd given her his heart, and she would always wonder how things would have gone if she'd had gotten together with him first.

But hindsight was what it was, and if she hadn't been with Sam, she wouldn't have Finn.

Now, her life was in balance, and Matt would keep it that way. She knew she could trust him.

This was the man who loved her, who brought her breakfast in bed most mornings before tangling in the sheets with her. Now she was the pampered one, but they shared everything.

He stirred, rolling from his back to his side, opening those beautiful dark blue eyes of his and smiling that crooked smile. The one that told her he was happy, and probably up to no good.

"Morning," he mumbled. His warm hand brushed up her side, resting just below her breast.

"Morning, husband." She replied.

His hand moved, cupping her breast, stroking the nipple with his thumb.

"I'll never get tired of you calling me that." He raised his head from the pillow, leaning over to kiss her deeply. His kisses made her melt, every single one, from the one before he'd left to go to the United Kingdom to this one. She'd always be glad he'd come home.

"I love you," she whispered.

He raised his hand to her hair, running his fingers through her curls. His passion was always right there for Ella to see in his eyes, in his gestures. He was the kindest, most gentle man she'd ever met, but engulfed her with his passion, gave her something to believe in. *Us*.

"I love you too, Mrs Carver."

This beautiful man was about to give up everything because she missed her family. She'd always appreciate that. In him she'd found her true soul mate, the man who shared her love of home and family, the man who wanted to live the same life she did.

"We need to go and see our children. Georgia will need feeding."

"Give us five more minutes. I want to fool around with my wife for a bit longer."

She didn't need a mirror to know how big her grin was. That was what Matt did for her.

"Yes, please," she whispered.

Ella had never been thin, and after two babies, she had more bumps and lumps than ever before, but every time Matt looked at her it was like he was a starving man, hungry for a meal of her. She knew it didn't matter to him.

He kissed her again, his tongue tracing over her lips before joining them. Her heart raced at his loving touch, the one that was all for her.

His fingers blazed a trail on her skin, stroking their way down her stomach to between her legs.

"Ella," he murmured.

She loved the sound of her name on his lips when he was aroused, and her body responded to his touch, that warm buzz covering her from head to toe at the attention of his fingers.

"Matt." Ella crying his name was muffled by another kiss, and she shuddered under him. Back before everything went bad, she'd wondered from time to time what it would be like to be kissed by Matt, to be touched by him. Now his kisses and caresses were hers alone, and she never wanted any other. Only him.

He moved, the air cooling around her, and she moaned at the heat of his breath between her legs. His warm tongue teased her before he slid into her, enveloping her with his body, with his love.

Together they moved, joined now as they would be for the rest of our lives. She would grow old with this man, and only ever know his touch from now on. She hadn't known what safety and security was until Matt.

Ella pulled the blanket over them to stop the cold morning creeping in. The farm could get very cold, especially in winter, but the house would be cosy and warm once they had everything moved in. *I'd happily wake up every morning like this.*

Matt kissed her, his lips lingering on hers as they always did. He groaned as he came, rolling over to her side as he pulled out of her, kissing her hard before chuckling. "You know, this is the longest since we've been together that you haven't been pregnant."

She burst out laughing. "Let's keep it that way. At least for a while."

After getting caught out with Georgia, she'd gone on the pill as soon as she could. Another child might be nice further down the track, but the two they had were so close in age, and a handful. If they ever did try again, it would be nice if it happened, but she'd vowed not to become obsessed with it.

"I like the idea of enjoying the children we have before expanding our family." He kissed her again. "Come on, let's get dressed and go see them. You must be bursting to see Georgia."

"Literally." She laughed.

"I love you." He kissed her one last time before pulling away and slipping out of bed. "I'm hungry too. Wonder what's for breakfast?"

"If I know my mother, she's making bacon and eggs for you. I hope you know moving here we'll end up gaining weight." She sat up, dropping her feet to the side of the bed and standing. "Race you to the bathroom."

Ella had the head start, her side of the bed being closer, and Matt grabbed her as she made it in the door, holding her by the waist as he kissed her neck.

"I'll turn the shower on," he said.

"Are we going to make it in the house for breakfast?" she laughed, knowing what that man was capable of in the shower.

"Unfortunately, we have to. Otherwise my stomach might eat itself." He flicked the water mixer on, pulling her under the shower with him as it hit the right temperature. In his arms, she snuggled against him. It seemed a shame to have to move on with their day, but the children were still so close, and the thought of seeing them again gave her butterflies. A night away was too long from Ella's babies.

Life was as sweet as it could get.

They had dressed and walked back down to the path toward the farm house, holding hands, leaning against one another. Matt and Ella were truly happy, and she wanted this feeling to last forever.

She pushed open the back door, entering the kitchen.

"Dad, Dad." Finn ran, nearly tripping over his own two feet, and threw himself at Matt's legs.

The big glowing warmth in her chest grew watching them together as Matt scooped him up, swinging him onto his hip. Finn giggled, the most glorious sound she could ever hope to hear.

"Have you been a good boy?" Matt asked. Finn nodded, wrapping his little arms around Matt's neck, hugging him tight.

"I bet you're itching to see this one." Ella's mother came toward her, with Georgia in her arms. Georgia grizzled, settling as Ella took hold of her, rocking her back and forward.

"I gave her the milk, but I think she really wanted her mother."

"I'll go in the living room and feed her."

She nodded. "I'll bring you in a hot chocolate, and then we can all have some breakfast."

"I smell bacon." Vanessa entered the kitchen, yawning and scratching her head, wearing one of those so short tops that left her flat stomach bare. Ella used to envy her that figure, but now she rolled her eyes at the sight of Vanessa's barely covered breasts.

"Aren't you cold?" she asked.

Vanessa grinned. "A little. I'm waiting for Matt to tell me to cover up. I know it winds him up."

Ella turned back to look at Matt who was still completely enthralled with Finn, pulling at Matt's face, laughing like crazy.

Matt moved his head a little to look back at her, spotting Vanessa. "Holy cow, Ness. You must be freezing. Go put a jumper on or something."

Ella grinned, shaking her head as Vanessa smiled triumphantly. "See? That's why I love your husband. He's like our missing brother."

"Nothing like a brother to me." She shot Vanessa a smug smile. Vanessa put her finger in her mouth.

"That's puke inducing. I'll go and put something warm on."

Georgia gave another grumpy grizzle. "Okay, okay, let's go find somewhere comfortable to sit."

Ella made her way past Matt's parents, smiling at them as she reached the living room. Her father sat in his recliner, his feet up, a coffee cup in hand.

"Morning, Dad," she said, nestling into the couch.

"Morning, love. Hope you were warm and comfortable over there."

Georgia kicked her legs, excited as Ella unclipped her nursing bra. Ella sighed as Georgia drank. After a night away from her, this felt so normal.

"It was a bit weird. It's so empty still. But that'll change soon."

He grinned. "I'm looking forward to you two moving in."

"I can't wait."

Eric took a sip of his coffee. "You've got a good man there, Ella."

"The best."

He smiled at her words, knowing the deeper meaning.

"She happy now?" Matt stood in the doorway, Finn still in his arms, and walked to the couch, sitting beside Ella.

"Take a look for yourself. "

Georgia's eyes fluttered as he bent to kiss her head and Ella winked at Finn, who clambered up Matt's legs and leaned over to hug her arm.

"Hey, baby." She turned my head to kiss his cheek, and he snuggled up.

This. This was all she'd ever needed. Her babies, the right man, their family.

Mine.

Perfect.

Forever.

in an instant

CHAPTER 1

MATT

Beep-beep-beep.

I groaned, rolling over to hit the 'off' button on the alarm clock. Four a.m.

Ella stirred beside me, and I slid my arm over her.

"Sam," she whispered.

I froze. What the hell was this about? "Ella?"

"Don't." She rolled onto her back, her eyes still closed, and I scanned her features as best I could in the moonlit room. She shook her head. Years ago I read that you shouldn't wake someone in the middle of a dream, so I held her tight instead.

She stilled. "Matt?" Her eyes flickered open.

"Hey. You were dreaming."

"Sam took Finn away." She gasped between words. The sound of her struggling not to cry broke my heart.

"Baby, Sam will never take Finn away. You know that."

"I know, but it was so real." Tears rolled down her cheeks, and I wiped them away with my fingers, kissing her temple.

"Is this the first dream you've had like this?"

She shook her head. "No. I've had a few."

"Why didn't you tell me?"

Ella shrugged, and I stroked her cheek with my thumb.

"I thought we weren't going to keep anything from one another."

She rolled to her side, facing me, and I bent my head, brushing her lips with mine. "I need to know what's going on in your head," I whispered.

"I'm sorry. I didn't want to worry you. It's nothing."

I rested my hand on her hair, pushing wayward locks back off her face. "Ella, I'll always worry. You're my one."

Her lips curled into a smile, and she snuggled up to me. "I know. You're my one, too."

I loved this woman with all my heart and soul. Having her next to me each and every night warmed me to the depths of my being.

She'd taken to sleeping in one of my shirts when she was pregnant with Finn, and never stopped. As much as I loved her naked, it drove me crazy seeing her in it, and the soft fabric pressed against my bare chest stirred the rest of my body awake.

"I want you to promise me that you won't worry about it. Sam knows where we are to talk to us, and one day maybe he'll want to be part of Finn's life. But you and me are it for Finn, and Sam knows that. If he wants to be part of Finn's life, it'll be on our terms." I planted a kiss on her nose, reaching over her to flick on the bedside lamp.

Ella squinted as the soft light filled the room, but now I could see her properly, make sure she really was okay.

"You're right." She sighed.

"I'm always right."

Her throaty laugh filled the room, her voice still a little husky from sleep. I loved her so much like this.

I licked my lips. "So ... uh ... there's still about fifteen minutes or so before I have to go out for milking."

"And?" One of her eyebrows crept up, but the smile in her eyes told me she knew exactly what I was meaning. "You are terrible, Matt Carver. So early in the morning."

"With you, it's all times of the day. Not just in the morning."

I wriggled out of her grasp, moving down to kiss her thigh. "You're overdressed."

"I'm only wearing a shirt."

I slid my hand up her leg, pausing at the apex where her thighs met. "If I'd known you weren't wearing underwear, I would never have let you sleep."

Our life together was perfection, and there was no better start to the day than being buried between the thighs of the woman I loved more than life itself.

My soul mate.

Up until the point I met Ella, I wouldn't have believed in any of that crap, but the connection I had with this woman was magical. We were meant to be together.

Her father usually took care of the cows, and I got longer in bed, but he and Ella's mother had recently gone on their first real holiday in years. They were currently on a cruise ship somewhere around Australia. For the next week, I'd have to leave the soft, warm bed I shared with my wife and shiver down the path to the cowshed every morning.

I slipped back into my underwear and grabbed a shirt from the drawer near the bed. I'd have a shower when I returned. There was no point doing so now when I was only going out to get dirty.

Ella's father, Eric, had employed a part-time farm hand who helped in the mornings with the cows. I was grateful for his assistance. It wasn't exactly my favourite thing to do, but needed to be done.

The herd wasn't huge; Eric had about fifty cows at the most. He provided milk to a small cheese factory nearby, and sometimes we were given the end result of his hard work. Despite my best efforts, I'd gained a few kilograms since moving.

"I'll be glad when Dad's back and I get to snuggle with you for a bit longer." Ella smiled. All I wanted to do was to climb back into bed with her, but if I did that, I'd never get back out of it. I pulled on my jeans instead.

"I'll get going. See you when I'm finished." I kissed her once more. She cupped my face, pressing her lips back to mine.

I left the house with a song in my heart, the recent memory of our bodies pressed together bringing a smile to my lips.

Oh yes, life was good.

The morning turned out to be a mess. Instead of crawling back early to my warm bed with my wife, I ended up repairing some fencing as some unexpected woolly guests ended up in the wrong paddock. It wasn't a big gap, but enough that I spent the next four hours fixing the problem and rounding up the escapees. In the distance I saw Ella, hanging out the laundry on the clothesline, the kids running in circles around her.

I knew she loved every minute of it.

Later, when they were in bed, she would tell me the stories of how they drove her crazy, alternating between playing and fighting. Every day was an adventure for the three of them, and I loved seeing them all so happy. The best feeling in the world was coming in from a hard day's work to a chorus of "Daddy" and holding my precious children in my arms.

Ella turned, laughing as she caught Georgia in her arms, spinning her. The sound carried on the breeze toward me, music to my ears.

She spotted me, waving and holding Georgia's hand in the air. At the sight of me, my little girl waved, and soon all three of them were calling out, their arms gesturing wildly. Ella reached for Finn, and he slid his hand into hers.

It must be close to eleven o'clock. Both the children had naps around now.

"Matt, the sheep are all sorted. Want me to do anything else?" Liam, the part-timer and Vanessa's ex boyfriend, stood behind me.

"I think we're good. Thanks for helping with those damn things. They'll be the death of me."

He grinned. "Mr Brown will be back soon enough to take care of them. You know how much he loves it."

I shook my head, laughing. "I'll always remember the first time I came here. The sheep were the first thing he showed me."

"I bet. I'll catch you tomorrow, then."

"Bye."

He stalked toward his car. Most mornings, he'd ask if I'd heard from Vanessa lately. They'd broken up before she moved to Auckland for university. While she'd moved on and was living with her boyfriend, Connor, Liam was obviously still a little hung up on her.

That rusty old bucket of bolts he drove started with a shudder, and I shook my head again as he drove away, the dust kicking up from under the car tyres.

Home.

I turned back to the house. The kids would be asleep by now if they had followed their usual routine, and Ella and I would have an hour or two uninterrupted before we all had lunch together.

I'd almost made it back when the sound of gravel crunching under tyres made me turn. Who on earth was that?

An unfamiliar silver sedan drew closer, pulling up in the grass about twenty metres away. The driver's door opened, and a tall, dark-haired man climbed out and walked toward me.

Sam.

I narrowed my eyes at the sight of him. Not only had I missed out on climbing back into bed with my wife this morning, the last person I wanted to see had arrived.

"Hey, Matt." Sam smiled, like nothing had ever happened. The last time we'd spoken was my wedding day, when he'd admitted to working out Finn was his and told me to take care of him.

There was only one thing he could want.

"Sam." It was hard to be polite to the man who had broken Ella's heart. But then, if he hadn't, would we be here at all?

"I'm sorry for just dropping in. I thought if I called, you'd tell me where to go. Hell, you still could."

I nodded. This shouldn't hurt as much as it did, but it was difficult to see him without remembering all the time we'd spent together. From two young boys starting school through to two grown men graduating university together, we'd been inseparable.

"You shouldn't be here."

"I had to see him."

I didn't have to ask who he was talking about. If it wasn't me, there was only one 'he' Sam could mean. *Finn*.

"You can't just turn up like this. How do you think Ella's going to take it?"

He took a step closer. "I've thought of nothing else. If she doesn't want me to see him, I'll get in my car and drive away. I promise."

That just made things even harder. I couldn't be angry at him being unreasonable when he wasn't.

"Sam, I can't even begin to know how Ella is going to take you being here."

He licked his lips, the corners of his mouth turning up into a smile. "I understand. I thought it was time I took a chance. I'm not surprised to find you living here, either. You liked this place so much."

I swallowed. *Hard*. I'd turned my back on him when he'd hurt Ella so badly, but there had always been a part of me that missed Sam. He'd been like my brother.

"We love being here. It's a good place to raise the children."

He grinned. "I bet it is. I was never a fan of the country, but I can see it's doing you the world of good. You're looking pretty well taken care of."

"If you're trying to say I'm out of shape, that's far from the case." I laughed, before the realisation that I'd just slipped back into that friendly banter I'd always shared with him slapped me in the face.

"I bet, Mr Fitness. No, I mean you're looking well. Ella does a great job of looking after the people she loves." His voice cracked. He'd thrown all that away, and it was something I would never take for granted.

"Look, I'll go and talk to Ella. If she tells me she doesn't want anything to do with you ..."

"I'll leave it for a while and try again another day. I don't want to hurt either of you. I just want to see him."

I let out a loud breath, torn about all of this. We'd always known Sam would come looking for Finn one day. Finn had been with me since the day he was born, and I couldn't imagine my life without him as my son. I was the one he called Dad, the one he came to when he skinned his knees, the one who read to him as he drifted off to sleep.

Finn was mine as much as Ella's and Sam's.

"I don't want to disrupt your relationship with him. You know of all the people on this planet, there's no one else I'd want raising him. It's my own fault I wasn't there."

My mouth was so dry, and I found myself unable to form any other words in that moment. We'd been so close in the past; no matter how far apart we'd been, we just knew one another so well.

"I'll be back shortly. Wait here and one or both of us will be out." I turned toward the house.

"I'm not just here for Finn, Matt. I miss *us*."

I stopped, closing my eyes. Until that moment, I'd thought nothing could break down my dislike of him. Before Ella, before all the bad things, I'd loved him. Now, his words raked across the edges of my nerves, pressing on that tiny bit of feeling I still had. Deep down, I missed us, too.

Sam had been by my side through all the good times and the bad. Right up until the moment when he'd crossed the line and hurt the woman we both loved.

"I know you, and I know how much you feel all that emotional shit. You've missed me too. Admit it."

Fighting the urge to just walk away, I looked back over my shoulder. "I'm not admitting anything. I'll go and talk to *my* wife, and maybe you can say your piece to her. That's all you're getting from me."

As I reached the door, I closed my eyes. Ella and her dreams. Of all the days for him to turn up, it had to be the same day she'd dreamed of this moment.

How the hell was she going to react?

CHAPTER 2
ELLA

I stroked Finn's hair as his eyelids gave that final flutter before sleep. He'd been playing all morning with his little sister in the yard, the pair of them wearing themselves out running around in the fresh country air.

Even now, the thought of us being here made me smile. I'd given up my job as a business analyst when I'd given birth to Finn and never gone back to it. Two years ago, Matt had left his role as a computer programmer to bring me home to my parents' farm.

He still took contract jobs, keeping his skills up while taking care of the sheep and cows with my father. We had each other and the children. That was all we needed to be content.

Mum and Dad had the opportunity to get some away time now we were here. The children and I had been out there, checking on the chickens, bringing in fresh eggs, and enjoying the beautiful summer morning.

Now my son was asleep, following his sister who had ended up on the living room floor, snoring. I'd picked her up, and snuggled her into her bed. They had their routine; I had mine. Matt was due in any minute.

I tucked the blanket in and pulled away from the bed. As much as

I loved them, it was good to get a break from the noise and chaos two young children brought to your life.

Matt stood in the doorway between the kitchen and living room with that intense look in his eye I knew so well. Two years from our wedding, and the flame just burned brighter and brighter between us with no sign of letting up. What he could do to me with just a look …

Two steps to get to me, and he placed his hands on each side of my head, digging his fingers into my hair and hooking them in to pull my face toward his. As his lips touched mine, he growled, sending a tingle from my head to my toes.

"The kids have just gone down for their naps. Want a nap with me?" I asked, when he pulled back.

He sighed. "Any other day I would leap at the chance. Today, we have a visitor."

"Who?"

Matt licked his lips, those deep blue eyes of his seeming to scrutinise my reaction. "Sam."

Blood rushed in my ears, and my stomach flinched, the memory of my dream still vivid. I had once loved Sam so much, but since he'd left me for someone else and then treated me as if the whole thing was my fault, my feelings had all but evaporated.

"What does he want?"

Matt wrapped his arms around me, and my body stirred. Any other day of the week I would have wrinkled my nose and protested that he needed a shower, wanting to get naked with him. Today, I buried my face in his chest, his T-shirt smelling of sweat and Matt. Familiar.

"He says he wants to talk. It's time, babe."

I nodded, gripping his shirt and taking a deep breath. "I know. We knew this day would come."

Matt just held me for a moment, knowing how scared I was that Sam might try to take Finn from me. We'd built this wonderful life on the farm, the four of us, but the fear that Sam might swoop in one day and push for custody had always weighed on me, no matter how likely or unlikely it was that he'd get it.

Call me selfish, but he'd treated me so badly when he left that there was always a part of me that felt he didn't deserve anything. But he was Finn's father, as I had tried so many times to tell him. He'd always been too busy pointing the blame for our failed relationship at me to listen.

"I need to shower. I've told Sam he has to wait outside until we're ready." He ran his hand down my face until he reached my chin, tilting my head to look up at him. "It's up to you if you want to go and talk to him while I'm in the shower. Your call."

I swallowed, nodding. "I should."

Matt grazed his lips against my forehead, squeezing me tight as if marking me with his scent. He didn't have a thing to worry about. My relationship with Sam had been mostly good until the night he'd told me he was leaving, but Matt was like a missing piece of me.

"I'll be as quick as I can."

I watched as he walked up the hallway toward the bathroom, smiling as he paused at the door of Finn's room and then Georgia's. Even the simple act of him checking on the children made my heart race. He was such a good father, doting on both of them equally, even though he wasn't Finn's biological dad.

Pursing my lips, I let a slow breath out. The last time I'd seen Sam was the day I'd gone to see him, in part to comfort him when he'd discovered the woman he'd left me for didn't know who the father of her unborn child was. That was three and a half years ago. What could he want now?

I walked through the kitchen and out the back door. My heart leapt to my throat as I came face to face with the man who had once promised to love me for the rest of his life.

He was clean shaven for a change, his skin tanned more than I'd ever seen when we were together. If I were any other woman, I'd be happy to see his eyes light up the way they did when he saw me. But this was the man who'd left me with my heart shattered in a million pieces when he'd turned his back on what we'd had.

"Ella. You're looking good."

I trembled as I nodded. I'd be stupid to pretend his presence didn't unnerve me. In an instant he could turn our lives on their heads if he had demands.

"Thanks. You look good, too. Relaxed."

The corners of his mouth crept into a smile. "I have so much to tell you."

He took a step toward me, and his Adam's apple bobbed as he swallowed.

"Let's sit down." There was a circular table on the deck with four chairs around it. In the summer, Matt and I would sit out here, looking out over the farm. My favourite place on earth.

Sam sat across the table from me, barely taking his eyes from my face. I must look weird. In the city I'd lived in makeup; now, I rarely wore it. There wasn't any need.

"I can't get over how different you look. You always said coming here was good for your soul. It shows," he said.

"I love it. Matt does, too. I think this is just where we needed to be. It's good for us and for the kids."

He nodded. "I can tell."

"What brings you here?" I had to ask; I couldn't hold back any longer.

He crossed his arms, leaning on the table. "I've been travelling. I tried Matt's trick of going away to work out who I was. Petra's baby wasn't mine."

"I heard. Matt's parents told him."

He shrugged. "I gave you up for what? I was so selfish. So, I went away to work out what the hell it was I wanted, picking up teaching jobs along the way. I worked with kids who had literally nothing. You should have seen them, Ella; they were amazing. It was the most incredible thing I could have ever done. Made me appreciate what was back here so much more. And they got to me. All I could think about was my little boy with you ..."

His words brought tears to my eyes. He was here to lay claim to Finn. I knew this day could come, but I couldn't bear the thought of Finn's world being turned upside down by a man he didn't know. I shook as I fought back the onslaught of tears, giving up when they streamed down my cheeks and I couldn't hold them in any longer.

"Ella?"

"Finn's just a little boy, Sam. I can't give him up, and I won't have him shipped between us like a piece of furniture. He has stability here, and he loves Matt. I know you're his father, but ..."

I didn't finish my sentence as Sam slipped around the table and knelt on the ground before me. He took my hands in his, squeezing as I tried to pull away.

"I have no intention of trying to take him away from you. This is his life. All I want is to be a part of it. To spend time with him."

I closed my eyes at the sound of heavy footsteps behind me.

"What the hell is going on?" At the sound of Matt's voice, I pulled my hands from Sam's and stood. Matt's brows were furrowed, his eyes angrier than I had ever seen them. His focus was entirely on Sam, and a sense of relief swept over me that it wasn't me causing his anger.

"I was reassuring Ella I'm not here to take Finn from her. That's all. I swear, Matt. All I want is to get to know my son and maybe somehow get my friend back."

Matt nodded, moving closer to me and grasping my shoulders. "We can't ever have what we had before. Not after everything you did."

Sam stood, holding his hands up in surrender. "I know. I can never make up for it."

At that, Matt relaxed a little. "We're agreed on that, then."

"I thought maybe I could meet Finn. I've got a little something for him in the car, and his sister, too. I didn't want her to feel left out. And then maybe I could come up here from time to time and visit. I'm back in Auckland teaching, and it's only a three-hour drive."

I stood and snuggled into Matt, meeting his gaze before looking back at Sam. "Finn and Georgia are having their naps right now. Georgia will be awake in about an hour, and Finn a half hour to an hour after that. He likes his sleep," I said.

"Takes after me, then." Sam grinned, and my heart ached for what was to come.

"No. He is far more energetic than you ever were. He sleeps to make up for it," Matt said.

Sam laughed. "So he sleeps a lot. Then, he's a lot like me?"

Matt squeezed me, his chest shaking as he laughed. "Maybe he's a bit like you."

"Ella, I'm not going to push anything. He's a kid. I'm not going to throw who I am at him; we'll get there, but right now I'm not about to throw his world into disarray. I swear."

The tightness in my chest eased as I nodded. As long as he kept his word I had nothing to fear, and I shouldn't. He cared enough to be here. Despite our differences, I couldn't fault him on that.

"Are you driving back tonight?" I asked.

"I've got a room at a motel in town. I thought I could stay the night and drive back tomorrow. Take my time."

I nodded. "Want to stay for dinner?"

Matt took hold of my hand, steadying the shaking, giving me the reassurance I needed without saying a word.

"That'd be great, if it's not too much trouble. I've missed your cooking."

Matt squeezed my hand. "You'll be in for a treat then. Ella's had a leg of lamb slow-cooking all day. The smell's through the house already."

Sam caught my gaze. I don't think I'd seen him so happy, not since the first few months after our wedding. Maybe he really had found peace with himself.

He still made me uneasy.

CHAPTER 3

ELLA

Georgia, as usual, made her presence known with a roar as she stampeded down the hallway and straight into her father's arms.

She rubbed her eyes as Matt pulled her up onto his lap, slamming her head against his shoulder as soon as she spotted Sam.

"This is Georgia, my Princess of Mayhem," Matt said, kissing the top of her head. Georgia snuggled in tight against Matt's side.

"Well, Princess of Mayhem, I've got a present for you." Sam picked up one of the two large packages he'd brought in from his car.

Her eyes widened, but she clung to Matt, chewing on her bottom lip as she decided whether to grab it or not.

Matt hugged her tight. "It's okay. I'll get it."

She nodded, smiling shyly as her father took the parcel from Sam's hands. Once Dad had her present, she grabbed hold of it with glee, ripping at the paper.

"I didn't know what they liked, so I tried to get something popular for both of them."

"Up until recently, she would have been happy with the wrapping paper." I knelt beside her, picking up the tiny pieces of paper Georgia dropped all over the place.

Inside was a huge teddy bear, and she hugged it tight to her chest, giggling as she planted kisses on it.

"I guess that's a hit, then?" Sam grinned.

"I guess so." Matt kissed Georgia again, rubbing his nose in the bear's fur. "He's beautiful, isn't he? Are you going to say thank you?"

"Tank you," she whispered, giggling again as she hid behind the bear.

"Thanks, Sam. She loves it," I said.

"I can see. I'm glad you like your present, Miss Georgia." He had this look on his face that I'd never seen as my daughter entranced him with her shy smiles, loving the hell out of her teddy bear. What would he be like when Finn joined us?

Overwhelmed by the emotions this had brought up, I caught a tear escaping down my cheek, and wiped it with the palm of my hand.

"You okay, Ella?" Sam asked.

I leaned against Matt's leg. Matt slipped Georgia onto his other knee so he could see me. His strong hand gripped my shoulder, squeezing gently as I looked up at him.

"I'm fine. This is just weird."

Sam nodded. "It will be for a while. I'll try not to intrude."

Georgia slipped off Matt's lap, joining me on the floor and holding the bear that was nearly as big as her up for me to see. "Bear," she said.

"Do you like him?" I grinned.

She nodded, squeezing him tight. "He's lovely, isn't he?" I said.

Georgia let go of the bear, flinging herself at me and wrapping her arms around my neck, no doubt unsure of herself because of Sam's presence. I held her tight, rocking her as she hugged me.

"She looks so much like you, Ella." Sam smiled as he watched us.

"I don't know about that. I always thought she looked like Matt. She's got his colouring. Daddy's girl." I kissed her cheek as she snuggled in tight against me.

Sam watched us as I held Georgia, his eyes full of sadness. Whatever he'd done, this must hurt. This was what he'd wanted with me once upon a time. Now I was here with his childhood friend who I'd built a family with.

I caught my breath as Finn appeared in the doorway. Not so far behind Georgia for a change.

"Dad," he yelled, running and launching himself at Matt as Sam looked on. He sat there, tearing up as he watched his son hug another man. In that moment I knew that however he'd wronged me, however much he broke my heart, his relationship with Finn was as important to establish as Matt's had been.

"Finn. Do you want to know who this is?" Matt asked, redirecting Finn toward Sam.

Finn nodded. He had the self-confidence that Georgia lacked so far, and he smiled at Sam immediately.

"This is Sam. He's come a long way to see you."

"I've got something for you, buddy." Sam choked up as he said the words, and I could only imagine how hard this was to be so close and have to hold back.

"Go on." Matt let Finn drop to the floor and Finn walked straight up to Sam, sitting down in front of him with the box he'd been presented with.

The paper lasted seconds, Finn aided by his sister who had dropped her bear by me and was now more interested in the wrapping and what her brother had been given.

"Oh, Sam." I spotted the Lego logo on the box. Finn and Georgia had some Duplo to play with, but this was the mother lode. Nice big blocks neither of them could eat.

"I figured boys *and* girls love Lego. Matt and I did when we were kids, but then it wasn't as fancy as this. We just built a lot of houses." Sam laughed.

"Look." Finn tugged on Sam's trousers, pointing at the picture on the side of the box. There was a tree, complete with treehouse and Duplo people, and a car. Plenty of things to build.

"Like it?" Sam asked.

Finn nodded. He turned back to Matt. "Can we build it?"

"How about you and Georgia build it with Sam. I've had so much to do today, I just want to have a rest," Matt said.

"Okay." Finn said turning back to Sam. "Can we open it?"

The joy in Sam's face brought tears to my eyes. Finn had given him a chance, and however small an opportunity it was, Sam grabbed it with both hands. Within seconds he was on the floor, tearing into the box and pulling out the pieces to start building.

As the three of them were in deep conversation about what went where, I stood.

"Where are you off to?" Matt asked.

"Going to check the food." I leaned over to press my lips to his.

"I'll come with you. I could do with a beer. Sam?"

Sam looked up. "Sure. Sounds good."

Matt linked fingers with my own as we walked to the kitchen, giving them a squeeze before letting go so I could open the oven and check on the meat.

I grabbed a cup from the bench, filling it with water from the tap and adding it to the roasting dish.

"You're handling this well." Matt nuzzled my neck, and I sighed at his warm lips against my skin.

"What else do I do? We knew this day would come, and Sam has been so good." I twisted in his arms, turning to face him. "I can't fault him."

Matt scanned my features, reaching up and stroking my hair. "I love you, Ella."

"I love you too. Shall we go and see what our children are doing?"

"In a minute. I just need to hold you right now."

I closed my eyes, resting my head on his shoulder, breathing in that sweet Matt scent. I loved this man so much, more than I'd ever thought was possible. He was the rest of my life.

"Nothing will stop Finn from loving you," I whispered. He must be scared too. He'd laid claim to that boy the moment he was born. I'd reassured him then that he would be Finn's father just as much as Sam was, and now he needed that reassurance again.

"I know." He pulled back, kissing me with so much tenderness I wanted to cry again.

Matt let me go, and grabbed the beers from the fridge. I followed behind him, pausing at the doorway. Georgia sat on Sam's lap, giving him instructions while Finn connected blocks beside them. I shook my head, smiling at how Sam had just slotted in with them.

I still didn't know how we would explain Sam to Finn, but this had to be a good start.

CHAPTER 4
ELLA

After an afternoon of building and knocking structures down, we ate dinner before it was time to put the children to bed. Georgia was asleep on her feet, Matt scooping her into his arms and carrying her to her room. Finn and I trailed behind, leaving Sam in the living room. She sat, flopping over as he pulled off her shirt and slipped her pyjama top on.

"You are so tired." He laughed, kissing her on the cheek and trading her leggings for her pyjama pants.

"It's been a big day." I leaned in, kissing her forehead as she fell backward with a tired smile on her face. Rubbing Matt's shoulders, I pressed my head against his. "You read her a story; I'll sort out Finn."

"Mummy?" Finn held my hand tight.

"Come on, baby. Let's get you to bed too."

I walked out of Georgia's room and into Finn's room next door. Flicking on his night light, I pulled his pyjamas out of his top drawer and changed him quickly, tucking him under the blankets.

"Ella." Sam stood in the doorway, watching.

"Do you want to say goodnight?"

"May I read him a story?"

His eyes were so full of hope; how could I say no? I smiled, nodding. Finn was so tired he'd be asleep about thirty seconds into the book, but I didn't want to tell Sam that.

I plucked out *Jack and the Beanstalk* from Finn's bookcase. Sam moved toward me as I stood, and I passed him the book. "This is his favourite."

"Thank you so much, Ella."

I nodded, swallowing hard. It was difficult letting him do this, especially after the dreams I'd had.

Sam reached for my hand, squeezing it. It was such an intimate gesture, but under the circumstances, not as uncomfortable as I might have expected. I guess we'd been best friends, lovers, and man and wife for a while.

"I'll go and see how Matt's doing."

I didn't need to see; I knew how it went. Matt would be nearing the end of *The Three Little Pigs*, and Georgia would already be fast asleep. This was our nightly routine; we swapped between the kids, taking turns to read to each one.

The truth was that I couldn't watch Sam reading to Finn. I'd end up in tears.

I teared up anyway, watching Matt from the doorway. With Finn, he'd go out and explore the farm, the two of them in their gumboots. His little buddy. Georgia was a different story. She was his princess.

Her eyes were closed, and from outside the room I could see she was asleep. But Matt continued his story in his soothing tones, the ones that always made me feel better when I was sad.

As he finished, he leaned over and kissed Georgia's temple, smiling as he turned to see me. When he reached my side, he wrapped those big, strong arms around me and held me tight, kissing my temple.

"You okay? Finn already asleep?"

"Sam's reading Finn his story."

Matt let go, gripping my chin in a firm grasp and tilting my head to look at him. "How do you feel about that?"

"It felt like the right thing to do," I whispered.

He smiled, bending his head to kiss me tenderly. "You've got such a big heart, Ella. For what it's worth, I think it's the right thing to do, too."

I snuggled into his chest as he wrapped his arms around me again, closing my eyes at the familiarity. The day had gone better than I could have imagined. My Finn hadn't had his world implode. Everything was as it had been for the past few years.

"He's asleep." I opened my eyes to see Sam standing beside us with a huge grin on his face.

"Thanks for reading to him." Matt kissed the top of my head, squeezing me tight.

"My pleasure. Thanks for letting me. I doubt he heard a word I said; he was asleep as soon as his head hit the pillow." He turned his focus to me. "Want a hand with the dishes?"

"I've got those," Matt said.

Sam nodded. "Fair enough. I'll get going, then."

"I'll walk you out." I could handle that. Right?

We got as far as the kitchen, and Sam stopped to shake hands with Matt. "I really want to thank you for everything today. You both could have reacted so differently to me turning up."

"It was always going to happen at some point. You couldn't spend the rest of your life being an irresponsible jerk."

I stared at Matt. His lips curled into a smug smile.

"I don't even have a comeback for that. It's pretty accurate." Sam laughed.

He pushed open the door leading out toward the car, and I followed, flicking on the outside light as I went through.

We walked in silence off the deck, covering the short distance to the car.

"So, you're going home in the morning?" I asked.

"I might just pop in and say goodbye. If that's okay?" Sam shuffled his feet in the gravel, looking at his shoes. "Thank you. Thanks for being so understanding."

I sucked in my top lip and let my breath out slowly. "You're welcome. Come by in the morning for breakfast. Maybe around eight? Thanks for not pushing Finn."

He shook his head. "You don't ever need to worry about that. The only person who would be hurt by that is Finn, and I'm not about to screw up my own son's life."

"You're a good man, Sam Mason." The words were out before I could stop them. I even almost meant them.

He shrugged. "Maybe now. If I was a truly good man, I would never have hurt you. I'm such an idiot, Ella. You were the best part of my life, and I wrecked everything. But out of all the people in the world you could have ended up with, I'm glad it's Matt. I know for a fact he'll go to his grave loving you."

I nodded, smiling through the gathering tears. I thought speaking to him again would be hard, but it was easy. For the first time in I didn't know how long, he was honest with me.

"I hope you can work something out with him. He misses you," I croaked.

"All I can do is try. Right?" His expression was pained as he watched me struggle, and he covered the three steps between us, wrapping me in his embrace until the tears stopped.

"I loved you so much. I'm so sorry for all the pain I caused you," he whispered.

"I'm just glad you've learned. Maybe the next woman you convince to marry you will be the right one." I laughed.

"You were the right one. Matt's a lucky man. If anyone knows that it's me."

My breath caught. Here I was in his arms, and he was full of kindness and caring. All I'd had was concern that he was going to throw our lives into disarray. Any romantic love I'd had for him had gone.

"Sam ..."

"It's okay, Ella. I'm not hitting on you. I know that ship has long since sailed, and it's my own fault." He let me go, holding onto my arms. "You found your happiness, and that makes me happy." Pecking me on the cheek, he dropped his arms to his sides. "See you tomorrow."

I nodded. "Sure thing."

Sam opened his car door, waving as he closed it behind him. I wiggled my fingers in a half-hearted wave, not sure how to feel about that conversation. He'd grown up since I'd seen him last, finally taking responsibility for his actions. It was something I didn't know I'd ever see.

He started the car, and giving me a final wave, drove back toward the road.

Lost in thought, I didn't see Matt at first, standing in the doorway and watching me with a sad expression on his face. He grinned when I ran, launching myself at him, and he spun me around in the entranceway to the house.

"I don't know what you talked to Sam about, but seeing you in his arms again ..."

I pressed my lips to his, leaning in hard against him. He tasted so good, like he always did. He was all mine.

"He told me he was glad that you were the one I ended up with. He knows you love me."

Matt's eyebrow quirked, and his mouth twisted.

"I told him just how much you miss him."

He slid his hands down my back, giving me the smallest smile. "Is that right?"

"You know you do. I'm not saying you should be best friends. The last person I want around here all the time is my ex, but I understand. He misses you, too. All I know is that I ended up with the right one."

At that he grinned, kissing me again, making me weak at the knees as he held me tight. There was only one way this night was heading.

The best way.

Later that night, I kissed Matt's chest, breathing in that clean, soapy smell. We'd showered before climbing into bed together, and he'd been as tender and loving as he always was. Sometimes the emotion overwhelmed me, bringing tears to my eyes, but I wouldn't have things any other way.

"So?" He planted a kiss on the top of my head, and I raised my gaze to meet his.

"What?"

"This. Sam. How are you feeling about it all?"

I shrugged. "He seems to have good intentions, and he did as he said. How are you feeling about it?"

He let out a sigh, and I dipped my head, his chest rising and falling as he took deep breaths.

"Matt," I whispered.

"Hmm?"

"It's okay if you miss him."

He raised his hand to my chin, tilting my face back up. "Is it?"

"He struck a nerve with you. If anyone can see that, it's me."

In the dimly lit room, he smiled with that so-in-love-with-me smile that made me all goopy inside. "I didn't realise it until today, but I do miss him," he said.

Pushing myself up to kiss him tenderly, I reached to stroke his cheek. "Well, like I said, you don't have to be best friends with him again, but if you want to spend some time with him, it's okay with me."

Matt's smile grew. "Have I told you lately just how incredible you are?"

I shrugged. "You can always tell me again."

He switched off the lamp, and I dropped my head to his chest again, closing my eyes. After the bad dream the night before, the day had turned out not so awful after all. I just hoped Sam would keep his word.

I yawned. It had been an exhausting day, reliving memories of times that hadn't been so pleasant. Sleep overtook me as I nestled in the arms of my husband.

In the night, I woke, snuggling up to Matt's pillow, the bed empty. The sheets were cool. He'd been gone for some time.

"Matt?" I sat up, flicking on the bedside lamp.

Grabbing my bathrobe from the chair beside the bed, I walked down the hallway, digging my toes into the plush grey carpet along the way.

I found Matt in Finn's bedroom. He lay on top of the quilt with Finn's head resting on his chest. Both were fast asleep. For a moment, I stood and watched them, the room glowing faintly from the night light on the wall.

It didn't matter what happened with Sam; Matt was Finn's father, as far as he was concerned. Had I done the right thing not telling Sam? I still didn't know the answer.

Finn was happy, and that was all that mattered to me.

I turned, opening the hall cupboard and taking out a woollen blanket. Matt would be frozen if he stayed there all night, and I tiptoed into the bedroom, gently placing the blanket over him.

Our bed might be cold without him, but he was clearly where he needed to be, taking care of our boy.

With a smile on my face, I sneaked back to our bedroom, slipping off my bathrobe and climbing back into bed.

Snuggling under the covers, I closed my eyes.

Everything was still perfect.

CHAPTER 5

ELLA

I woke shortly before four to Matt climbing in bed beside me. Without a word, he took me in his arms and kissed me deep.

"I guess you found me, then."

"The bed was cold." I nuzzled his cheek, prompting a deep rumble of a laugh.

"I promise I'll make it up to you. Finn came in here when he woke up; I wanted to get him back off to sleep without disturbing you." Matt dropped his head to my neck, planting kisses that left me gasping.

"I understand. I've been there." I shifted my head to meet his lips with mine.

"Ella." He gripped my hair in that possessive move of his I knew so well. If I hadn't already been panting for him, that would have done it. I was his, and he wanted to make sure I knew it.

I was lost in the love I held for Matt, the love that overrode everything else. As he unbuttoned my shirt, sliding it from my shoulder, planting kisses on the exposed skin, all I could think about was how this man was my life. There was no better start to the morning. I was still in the warm glow of *him* when he left to milk the cows.

A little after eight, Sam was as good as his word, the crackle of gravel under the wheels of his car signalling his arrival. Finn and Georgia were already up and dressed, and I stood at the stovetop, scrambling eggs for breakfast as he knocked on the door.

"I'll get it." Matt stood. There hadn't been any disasters this morning stopping him from coming straight back from milking, and he'd been sitting at the table keeping me company while the kids played in the living room. His hand brushed my back as he walked past, and I turned my head to see his reassuring smile.

"Smells like I arrived just in time." Sam grinned, stepping into the kitchen as Matt ushered him in the door.

"Ella makes enough to feed an army. You're welcome to join us." Matt stepped past him, wrapping his arms around my waist and nuzzling my neck.

"Thanks." Sam walked past us toward the table, grinning as he spotted Finn and Georgia in the living room.

"Sam!" Finn ran toward him, grabbing hold of his hand and tugging him toward the big *Lego* structure he'd been working on with his sister. As they disappeared from sight, my chest tightened.

"You okay?" Matt murmured in my ear.

I leaned my head against his. "I'll be fine."

"I can stir this. You go take a look." He placed his hand on mine, pulling at the wooden spoon until I surrendered it to him.

I slipped out from his embrace, turning and kissing him on the cheek. "Have I told you lately just how incredible you are?"

Matt grinned, shrugging. "You can always tell me again."

I took the few steps to the arch through to the living room, smiling at the sight of Georgia happily building a tower while her brother issued instructions. Sam sat to the side, just watching. His eyes met mine, and the conflict was so clear in them.

He dropped his gaze, and I looked back over my shoulder at Matt. While stirring the eggs, his eyes were on me, and he winked, my lips smiling before I knew what I was doing.

Love you. He mouthed the words, waggling his eyebrows.

Love you, too. I mouthed back.

"Eggs are nearly ready. I'll just pop some bread in the toaster and we'll get seated," Matt announced.

I looked back toward the living room, meeting Sam's eyes again. He forced a smile. This wasn't exactly the most comfortable situation.

"Want a hand serving up?" I asked, turning and taking a step toward Matt.

"I'll be fine. Get the kids seated and I'll take care of everything."

I blew him a kiss, grinning at the smile on his face, my heart swelling at the look of love he gave me. I'd always wondered how I'd never seen it before he'd admitted his feelings.

"Finn, Georgia, breakfast is ready," I said.

Georgia dropped the blocks on the floor, taking a running jump at me. I laughed, scooping her into my arms and twirling her around.

Finn grabbed Sam's hand, pulling him toward the table. My anxiety over him being here had lifted the more time he spent without rocking the boat.

"Hope everyone's hungry." Matt carried a plate in each hand, one with toast which he placed in the centre of the table, the other with eggs which he placed in front of me. He leaned over, kissing me on the lips. "You first."

"Do you need help with anything, Matt?" Sam's words nearly made me choke on my first bite. It wasn't until after we'd broken up that I'd realised just how much I'd run around after him. He'd helped from time to time, but most of the effort was mine.

"Nearly done. I'll just get the kids' plates and then ours." Matt placed the bowls in front of Georgia and Finn.

"Yummy," Georgia declared.

"It does look good, doesn't it? I bet it tastes good too." Sam grinned as Matt returned with Sam's plate and his own. "Thanks, mate."

Matt sat at the end of the table, between Sam and I. His foot hooked around my leg as he smiled at me. He made what could be such an uncomfortable situation so easy to get through.

"Maybe next time we can grab a beer. There's that little pub Ella and I used to go to up the road from here." Sam spoke between mouthfuls, glancing up at Matt.

That was weird, him talking about our former life like that. There'd be a bit of that to get used to. It wasn't like our past didn't exist anymore.

"We'll see," Matt said. I itched to ask him what he was thinking, but it would have to wait. He was so good at hiding how he was really feeling, which always surprised me, given what an open man he could be. There was nothing we hid from one another—nothing we needed to hide.

"You're going to make me work for this, aren't you?" From the tone of Sam's voice, he wasn't angry at Matt's brush-off. He sounded determined. I guess he just wanted his friend back.

Matt stopped eating, meeting Sam's gaze. "I just want to make all the right decisions for my family."

Sam swallowed hard, his grin vanishing as his expression grew serious.

"I don't want to hurt anyone in all of this. All I want is to earn your trust again."

Matt took another bite, shaking his head. He chewed for a few seconds before swallowing. "That's going to be a tough thing to get through. You lied to me. You lied to *us*."

I licked my lips, looking between them. Matt's focus was back on his plate. Sam's on Matt. Finn and Georgia were engrossed in their food. "I think we need to save this conversation for another time. I don't think the kids need to hear this."

Matt nodded, reaching for me, raking his fingers into my hair and pulling my face to his in the most possessive move he'd made since Sam had appeared. He brushed his lips against mine. "You're right. Sorry."

Drops of egg hit the back of my hand where it rested on the table, combined with the sound of Georgia giggling, it wasn't hard to work out that she was responsible.

"Georgia." I said.

She pointed across the table at Finn, whose face was distorted as he pushed his fingers down on his cheeks, pursing his lips, his lower eyelids drooping.

I shook my head. "You two are diabolical. Eat your breakfast."

Sam ruffled Finn's hair. "Dude. That is not a good look at the table. You need to poke your tongue out as well." At that he mimicked Finn's face-pulling, combining it with his tongue hanging out.

I tried so hard to keep a straight face, but as the two of them sat there, identical looks on their faces, I fought the urge to smile.

Matt lost it, laughing loudly at the pair of clowns sitting at the side of the table.

"Do you think we should stop?" Sam asked Finn.

Finn nodded, placing his hands at his sides, a big grin on his face. When Sam followed suit, for just a moment Finn resembled his father so much it brought tears to my eyes. It had never been so clear.

"Ell, you okay?" Sam asked.

In an instant, I had Matt's arm around me, rubbing my shoulder.

I nodded. "I'm fine. You two just ..."

"I saw it too," Matt murmured, kissing my ear.

"What are you two talking about?" Sam looked between us, obviously complete confused.

"Not now," I said, nodding toward Finn who was spooning the last of his breakfast into his mouth.

Sam frowned, looking back down at his plate.

"I need a coffee. Anyone else?" Matt stood.

"Sounds great. Sam?" I asked.

Sam raised his head, meeting my eyes. He nodded, uncertainty written all over his face.

"I'll grab some juice for the kids too." Mugs clattered together as Matt took them out of the cupboard, and I took a bite of my breakfast. It was almost cold; I'd been watching what was going on around the table for so long.

"Finished," Finn yelled, his sister erupting into giggles again.

"Good boy. Do you want a drink?"

He shook his head. "Can I play with the Lego?"

"Glad my present is proving to be popular." Sam laughed.

I rolled my eyes. "Go on then." I turned to Georgia. "Do you want to go too?"

Her mouth was stuffed with food, but she swallowed it all down, nodding.

Bending, I kissed her on the top of the head. "You can if you want."

Neither of them had to be told twice, wriggling off their chairs and running back to the tower they'd been building.

"Ella, if I did something before, I'm sorry."

I shifted my gaze from the departing children back to Sam. "It wasn't you. When you and Finn were pulling faces, I saw how much he does look like you. I never really saw it before."

"Do you think?" He sat up straight, looking toward the living room wistfully.

"It was very clear. Just shook me a little."

"I guess the last thing you ever wanted was a reminder of me."

Matt sat back down, placing a cup of coffee in front of me. The other two he carried in one hand, extricating Sam's from his fingers and giving it to him before taking a sip of his own.

"It's not that. I mean, the time we had together was good for a long time. It's just that with not having seen you in so long, I guess I couldn't see the resemblance."

"I saw it too, Sam. Ella wasn't seeing things." Matt grinned.

Sam nodded, a smile spreading on his face. "That's cool. I'm really glad I came. I made a couple of false starts coming to see you two. I was sure you'd tell me where to go."

"We always knew it would happen one day. You just had to grow up." Matt took another sip of his coffee, coughing as Sam pushed his arm.

"Shit. Are you okay?" Sam laughed.

"I'll be fine." Matt coughed, and laughed, and coughed again.

I shook my head, watching the two of them laughing as Matt kept coughing.

I rose, walking to the tap and filling a glass with water. Returning to the table, I handed it to Matt as I sat. Matt sipped between small coughs, and I patted him on the back.

"I'm sorry for laughing. These are the moments I've missed," Sam said.

I rubbed Matt's back, smiling as he slipped his arm around my waist. Sam seemed genuine.

~

"I'll get going now." Sam stood after we'd cleared the dishes away. He'd helped Matt stack the dishwasher and now stood near the door, smiling at us both.

What was I supposed to say? 'It's good to have seen you' sounded weird, so I nodded.

Matt and I followed him out, walking the short distance to his car.

"Thanks again." Sam looked between us.

"You're welcome." Matt squeezed my shoulder.

Sam let out a big breath. "I'll call you in a few weeks. Maybe arrange another visit if that's okay. Have your numbers changed?"

I shook my head. "Our mobile numbers are still the same. Just drop one of us a text."

"Just you keep looking after this one," Sam addressed Matt. "Letting her go was the biggest mistake of my life."

Matt grinned, and kissed the top of my head. "I don't plan on ever making the same error."

"Bye, Sam," Finn yelled from behind us, standing with his sister on the deck.

Sam lit up like a Christmas tree. "Bye, mate. See you again soon."

Finn ran, latching onto Matt's leg, Georgia doing the same to me. Sam leaned over, kissing me on the cheek. "Talk to you soon."

I nodded. Matt wrapped his arm around my waist and held me tight as we watched Sam climb into his car and start it up. Finn and Georgia waved as he reversed, turning, and with a final wave, drove down the long gravel driveway toward the road.

The kids detached, giggling as they ran back inside the house. "Let's build a house," Finn yelled.

Matt leaned in, kissing my hair. "You okay?"

I wrapped my arm around his waist, snuggling against him while I watched Sam's car disappear into the distance.

"Better than okay."

I tipped my face up to meet his gaze, and he kissed me softly, pressing his forehead to mine.

"Let's go and spend the rest of the day with our children," he said.

"I love you, Matt."

"I love you, too."

He linked his fingers in mine, licking his lips. "I've been thinking. How about we have another baby?"

My eyebrows shot up in response. "I thought we were waiting until Finn went to school."

He shrugged. "Give it a bit of time to happen, then nine more months—he'll be near that. Isn't that close enough?"

I grinned, pulling him down for another kiss.

"We'll see," I whispered.

He traced my lips with his tongue, waggling his brows. "Can we see when the kids have their nap later on?"

"Maybe."

Yes.

ALSO BY WENDY SMITH

Coming Home

Doctor's Orders

Baker's Dozen

Hunter's Mark

Teacher's Pet

A Very Campbell Christmas

Fall and Rise Duet

Falling

Rising

Fall and Rise - The Complete Duet

The Aeon Series

Game On

Build a Nerd

Bar None

Hollywood Kiwis Series

Common Ground

Even Ground

Under Ground

Rocky Ground

Coming soon Solid Ground

Stand alones

For the Love of Chloe

Only Ever You

The Friends Duet

Loving Rowan

Three Days

The Forever Series

Something Real

The Right One

Unexpected

Chances Series

Another Chance

Taking Chances

Lifetime Series

In a Lifetime

In an Instant

In a Heartbeat

In the End

At the Start

ABOUT THE AUTHOR

Wendy Smith is a multi-platform bestselling author, whose book In the End, written as Ariadne Wayne, was named one of Apple's best books of 2017. She lives with her two children and two cats in New Zealand where she bases her books because she loves living there. All her stories come with a quirky sense of humour, and she cries over everything.

Find me online
www.wendysmith.co.nz
wendy@wendysmith.co.nz

www.ingramcontent.com/pod-product-compliance
Lightning Source LLC
Chambersburg PA
CBHW061118310726
48974CB00002B/593